"Wiltz moves with compassion and underst[a] vent Street's armed mansions an tween the dreams and fears . . .

"A gripping, thought-provoking drama. . . . Wiltz's message is that fear—and guns—are the enemy, and the choice is not kill or be killed. A calm, quiet voice that deserves to be heard."

—*Kirkus Reviews* (starred review)

"A shattering, prophetic conclusion. . . . A well-paced political novel that never forsakes craft for ideology."

—*Seattle Times/Post-Intelligencer*

"Terrific. . . . A complex novel in which quiet emotions and persistent memories come together in a hair-trigger environment in which blacks and whites spend every day suspicious of one another. Wiltz writes sparely; her every sentence is stripped bare, and she leaves only the story itself to involve the reader. The moving result is a stark, cold portrait of a city that longs to be as warm as its weather, a city at odds with itself. No less than a mystery of the soul."

—*Oxford Review*

"Wiltz writes beautifully and compellingly, creating the unique aura of New Orleans and a phalanx of well-developed characters."

—*Library Journal*

D0556741

ALSO BY CHRISTINE WILTZ

FICTION
The Killing Circle
A Diamond Before You Die
The Emerald Lizard

NONFICTION
The Last Madam: A Life in the New Orleans Underworld

GLASS HOUSE

CHRISTINE WILTZ

LOUISIANA STATE UNIVERSITY PRESS

Baton Rouge

10 09 08 07 06 05 04 03 02 01
5 4 3 2 1

Designer: Amanda McDonald Key
Typeface: Sabon
Typesetter: G & S Typesetters, Inc.

Library of Congress Cataloging-in-Publication Data
Wiltz, Christine, 1948–
    Glass house : a novel / Christine Wiltz.
        p. cm.
    ISBN 0-8071-1864-8 (cloth); ISBN 0-8071-2683-7 (pbk.)
    Fiction. I. Title.

    PS3573.I4784G57 1994
    813'.54—dc20
                                                    93-34216
                                                    CIP

The paper in this book meets the guidelines for permanence and durability of
the Committee on Production Guidelines for Book Longevity of the Council on
Library Resources. ⊚

In memory of Noel Tsai

Acknowledgments

I would like to thank Joe Pecot and Marigny Pecot for their support while this novel was being written, and to gratefully acknowledge Rhoda Faust, who most generously gave me a place to work during many noisy months; Lorraine Jones, Keith Veizer, and Martha Ward, who took me on a never-to-be-forgotten tour of the Desire Project; Marigny Dupuy, Susan Larson, Victoria Weiner, Patrick Bishop, Nancy and David Sutherland, Fredrick Barton, and James Colbert for their dialogues and information; the director of LSU Press, Les Phillabaum; Michael Pinkston, associate marketing manager of the Press; my editor, Gerry Anders; my agent, Vicky Bijur. Many thanks to you all.

And a very special thanks to Mrs. Alice Reynolds for our provocative talks and for being an inspiration.

Author's Note

What follows is a work of fiction, sprung from my imagination and the experience of living most of my life in the city of New Orleans. While the characters and events in my story are fictitious and not meant to resemble any person alive or dead, or chronicle any real events, New Orleans is deliberately portrayed as I observe it, in its uniqueness, its contrasts and contradictions, and in the quirkiness of its people, some of whom I've heard describe the city as claustrophobic and provincial. I have, however, taken liberties with the geography of the city. There is no street named Convent Street and there is no housing development called the Convent Street Housing Project, though there are streets that resemble Convent Street and housing projects a lot like the Convent. I hit upon these names as a way to describe an inarticulable quality about life in New Orleans, a quality that slips beyond descriptions such as claustrophobic and provincial. This quality has to do with the desire by people who live here to set themselves apart and do things their own way, to be islanders, to let the outside world come to them if it must, to keep it at bay if it does; in other words, to be cloistered.

Whence shall we expect the approach of danger? Shall some transatlantic giant step the earth and crush us at a blow? Never. All the armies of Europe and Asia could not by force take a drink from the Ohio River or make a track on the Blue Ridge in the trial of a thousand years. If destruction be our lot we must ourselves be its author and finisher. As a nation of free men we will live forever or die by suicide.

—Abraham Lincoln, 1837

GLASS HOUSE

1

Delzora Monroe arrived at work one morning and found the woman she worked for dead. The mild, humid New Orleans morning played a pleasant trick on the senses before the sun rose higher in the hard blue sky and the heat descended. Delzora went through the iron gate and walked up the red-brick path to the large Victorian house. The immaculate lawn was still covered with dew. She slid her feet across it, trying to skim along the very top of the thick St. Augustine to keep her Chinese canvas shoes from getting too wet as she went after the newspaper. It was lying underneath the azalea bushes, inside the zigzagged border of bricks, in the damp dirt.

"Damn nuisance," Delzora said under her breath. She talked a lot in this manner, to herself, keeping a running commentary on life's little aggravations, details gone awry.

Althea Dumondville had died in her sleep, but Delzora didn't learn that for a while because she didn't go upstairs right away. She did what she'd done six days a week for nearly thirty years. She picked up the paper, used a key to let herself into the house, went across the foyer, down the hallway, through the dining room, past the kitchen, to a utility room where she removed her wig and put it on a shelf next to the laundry detergent. What little hair she had left on her head stuck up in sparse tufts, a result of bad nutrition and wearing corn rows for too many years when she was young. She took off the flowered shift she was wearing, hung it on a hook on the back of the door, and put on a white uniform. She went into the kitchen and put a teabag on to boil while she swept the kitchen floor. When the water in the pot was tobacco-brown, she put a piece of bread in the toaster oven and got out the strawberry preserves. Then she sat at the kitchen table and had breakfast while she read the newspaper.

By this time Althea was usually in the kitchen harping on some damn thing or another. Delzora's attention strayed from the newspaper. She listened for sounds of life from upstairs but she heard none. She finished her toast, swallowed the rest of the tea, which was strong enough to raise the roof of her mouth and brought her plate and cup to the sink. While she stacked the dishes from the night before on the counter over the dishwasher and sprinkled cleanser around the sink, she talked gruffly to herself, just above a whisper, to express her aggravation at having to break her routine while she went upstairs to see why Althea wasn't downstairs being her usual aggravating self. She let the cleanser sit in the sink. At least it could be doing its work while she went to check on Althea.

When Delzora saw that her employer was dead she didn't become hysterical and run screaming from the room, nor did she faint or begin talking in tongues. She stood over the body of Althea, which was on its back in bed, and examined its face. She thought about the different corpses she'd seen—there had been many—and the various expressions left on their faces as their spirits passed out of this world. Most of the bodies she'd seen had been ravaged by some dread disease or were victims of some act of violence. It didn't seem odd that someone who had suffered a long illness would leave behind a body with an expression of peace and serenity, finally, on its face. Nor that the face of a victim of sudden and terrible violence would show the pain and terror of a violent end. An old man in the housing project had died in his sleep and was found with his mouth wide open, one last gasp, one final effort to delay a journey into the unknown.

But Delzora had never seen such an expression as was on Althea Dumondville's face. There was no way to describe it except smug. It was all in the curve of her mouth, since her eyes were closed. "There!" it said. Here lay the body of a woman who had no friends to mourn her, who'd chased off her only living blood relative, a niece, a good ten years ago. A woman who had reduced her life to nothing but a desire to be dead, one way to assure herself of finally getting something she wanted.

What had Althea Dumondville wanted? It puzzled Delzora. It wasn't right for someone in perfectly good health to want to die. Someone who had so many material possessions she lost track of them all but who still couldn't get what she wanted, whatever that was. Both women were roughly the same age, their early sixties, and both had lost their husbands when they were much younger. Yet Althea considered herself old, miserable, and alone, and so she said she wanted to die, had been saying it for a couple of years. It wasn't right. Delzora meant it wasn't right in a moral sense.

Delzora was a religious person. She bowed her head over Althea's body and said a prayer of peace for her. When she opened her eyes a two-inch-long cockroach was making its way up the white eyelet bedspread toward Althea's head. It stopped and waved its antennae around and crawled another inch before making another probe. Delzora took off one of her Chinese shoes and flicked the roach across the room. It flew high up on a wall but swooped right back down to the bed, landing on Althea's middle. Delzora acted quickly. She swatted it with her shoe, picked up its remains with a tissue, its body crunching under her strong fingers, and muttered with annoyance at the spot it left on the spread. She covered Althea's face with the bedclothes.

She went downstairs and called Mr. Untermeyer, the lawyer. After that she rinsed the cleanser out of the sink without bothering to scrub first. Her routine was irrevocably broken, maybe forever in this house. She went to the utility room and put on her wig. Without tea or toast or the newspaper, she sat at the kitchen table and waited for what would happen next.

The two policemen arrived first. They came into the foyer, the shorter one hanging back as the taller one, who was carrying a clipboard, glanced at her then let his eyes roam around leisurely, taking in the stairway, the hallway that led to the back, the rooms off to both sides of the foyer, even the ceiling. The shorter one stared at her and continued to do so while the other one stepped through the open pocket doors into the left front parlor. Delzora watched him, uncomfortable under the short one's scrutiny. He went no farther than just inside the parlor, made another survey there, and returned to the foyer.

"Where's the body—the deceased, ma'am?" He was looking up the stairway.

"Up there," Delzora said.

She led them upstairs and stayed in the hall while they went into Althea's bedroom. When they came out, the tall one walked the length of the wide hall, his footsteps heavy on the hardwood floors, stopping at the doorway to each room. With his head inside

3

the door of what once had been Althea's niece's bedroom, left as it was when the niece moved out, he asked, "Did she live alone?"

Delzora nodded, then said, "Yes," since he wasn't looking at her.

He lingered for a moment at the bottom of the narrower stairway to the third floor but did not go up. Instead he led the way back downstairs. The short one followed Delzora and stayed behind her when they got to the foyer.

The tall one asked her to give her full name and spell it, writing on his clipboard as she did. He then asked for her address and her age. Next he wanted to know how long she'd been employed there.

"'Bout thirty years," she said.

He paused longer than it took to write, but he did not look up; he would not meet her eyes, and the other one remained behind her, out of her sight. "How'd you get into the house?"

"I got a key."

Another pause. "How long have you had the key?"

"'Bout thirty years."

He paused so long this time that Delzora wondered if he was waiting for her to revise her answer. She was beginning to feel accusation in his pauses.

"Who gave you the key?"

Who the hell did he think gave her the key? But she said quietly, "Miz Dum'ville."

When Mr. Untermeyer arrived, in his seersucker suit, blotting perspiration from his upper lip with a square of white handkerchief, the officer asked him some of the same questions, no trouble meeting his eyes: Did he know how long Mrs. Monroe had worked for Mrs. Dumondville? Was he aware that she had a key to the house? Mr. Untermeyer glanced quickly at Delzora before he told the officer that Mrs. Monroe was not just an employee of Mrs. Dumondville but a trusted friend of long standing.

Awkwardly, this mismatched group waited for the medical examiner. He looked at the body and said he was certain further examination would show Mrs. Dumondville had died from natural causes. The policemen thanked Mr. Untermeyer for his time. They told him they would keep him informed. They said nothing to Delzora.

After the body was taken away, Mr. Untermeyer and Delzora

sat in the front parlor, she on the edge of the red brocade sofa, he on a side chair. He was solicitous, telling Delzora he hoped she hadn't undergone too much of a shock; telling her he would call Mrs. Dumondville's niece, who now owned the house; asking her if she would get it ready for the niece.

"It's ready,' Delzora said, her hands folded in her lap. "I work here every day. I keep it ready."

Mr. Untermeyer cleared his throat. "I can't guarantee that Mrs. Dumondville's niece will keep you on," he told her in his genteel southern accent.

Did he think she was a fool? Why would he think she expected him to guarantee her anything? She said nothing to him, but she decided the policeman was more tolerable with his outright dislike than Mr. Untermeyer with his asinine concern.

At five o'clock, as was her habit, Delzora left work. She was picked up by the same young man who dropped her off every morning. He drove up in a gleaming white Cadillac with custom Continental kits built into the front fenders and spiked hubcaps that looked dangerous. He was wearing tight, bright-blue leather pants and a matching vest without a shirt on underneath it.

He opened the back door for Delzora as she came down the walkway in front of the house.

"Don't you never come pick me up again without no proper shirt on, Dexter, do you hear?" Delzora said to him.

"Yes, ma'am."

"You look like a pimp from the Quarters, all got up like that."

Dexter held the door for her silently while she settled herself like a queen on tomato-red crushed velour behind dark tinted windows. Then her carriage pulled out, traveling a stately ten miles an hour down Convent Street under a canopy of graceful oaks. Behind the oaks were the houses of the rich, set back from the clean street and surrounded by emerald-green lawns and artful landscaping. The white Cadillac was as out of place here as an Iowa prize pig on a stroll.

The canopy of graceful oaks was broken as the car reached the intersection of St. Charles Avenue. The avenue was the buffer zone between the very rich and the very poor. Across it the canopy resumed. A block farther the Convent Street Housing Project began.

Delzora didn't think about it because she'd been this way too many times before, but across St. Charles, Convent Street was darker. The houses on one side, the project units on the other, were set closer to the street and to each other; there were no green lawns for the sunlight to filter through oak leaves and sparkle upon. The oaks themselves were brooding and scary instead of graceful over here. They weren't so much a canopy as good cover—for crime, for poverty, for sadness, for the darker side of human nature. The droppings of the oaks fell to the street and were never swept away by the city or the residents. They stayed, messy, dank, and filling the air with the sweet odor of decay.

Delzora, her head resting against the velour, her eyes closed, knew when the car crossed St. Charles. From dense silence the Cadillac slid into the sounds of people on the street, kids shouting to each other over rap music blasting out of boom boxes, and across the street from the project, rhythm and blues coming in a wave from the open door of the Solar Club, a saxophone riff swinging out over the street and gone.

This continued for a while until there was another wide avenue, another buffer zone. The Cadillac could roll straight across New Orleans on Convent Street, through the inner city with its random and opposite elements that blend into a sort of symmetry, elements dispersed in a rhythmical flow of dark to light, sounds to silence, rich to poor, black to white. This is the rhythm of the city.

2

The taxi ride from the airport seemed overly long in the high-noon heat of August. At one point, traffic on the Interstate stopped altogether due, as it turned out, to an overheated car engine and two lanes blocked for resurfacing.

Even with the air conditioner full on, the backs of Thea's thighs were sticking to the black vinyl car seat. She pulled her short skirt down as best she could and rested her feet on the tips of her toes, her heels against the seat, to raise her bare skin off the hot plastic.

The cabdriver, a genial man with a large moon-round face, jowls beginning to sag, kept turning one ruddy cheek toward her as he talked. It had been a long time since she'd heard such a heavy New Orleans accent, nasal and lazy, not a hint of southern prettiness. He seemed to be complaining and apologizing all at once for the road conditions, speaking of potholes, politicians, payola, and tourists.

"Gotta keep the tourists comin, no argument there, but wit'out oil, everybody's a special-interest group these days, every pothole's got money-making potential, y'know?"

But Thea was too mesmerized by the city to be distracted by either the heat or the driver's patter. Her attention moved from one side of the expressway to the other, taking in hotels, office buildings, apartment complexes, restaurants, fundamentalist churches, lounges, stores, parking lots. Nothing looked particularly different, yet nothing looked quite the same either, still the helter-skelter trashiness of commercial suburbia, perhaps just more of it. She was eager to reach that rise not too far past the last Metairie exit, to come up over it and see the city dropped slightly below, the skyline of the old city, the real city, not the suburbs.

The driver cut into her anticipation. "Been to New Orleans before, miss?"

"I used to live here," Thea said. "Almost ten years ago." She didn't mention that she'd been to town since then, but only once, eight years ago, she and Michael together. She had wanted to make peace with Aunt Althea, but at dinner the first night Aunt Althea demanded to know if they were getting married.

Michael was arrogant. "Not this year. Probably not next year either."

Across the table Thea felt her aunt bristle. "Well, you're not sleeping together in my house," Aunt Althea said. "My house, my rules."

After that it was a contest of wills, Aunt Althea's and Michael's, with Thea's feelings trampled somewhere in between. They had gone back to Massachusetts after only three days.

"Long time," the driver said. "Lot's changed."

"I'm sure."

"Yeah, for one thing, since you been here the whole riverfront's different downtown, new aquarium, park, streetcar line right on the river. Casino's comin too."

"Oh, really?"

"Oh yeah, you can bet on it." He laughed heartily.

Thea smiled but she didn't join his laughter. They were coming up on the rise now. She leaned forward.

"For better or for worse, who can say. Won't hurt my business none, but it ain't gonna be any safer drivin a cab, that's for sure."

More of his face than one cheek was visible from this angle. His eyebrow was lifted and his eye darted from the road to her, waiting for her comment, but Thea fixed her gaze on the city that, as they got higher, was spreading out all around her. They rode above the trees and rooftops of uptown to the right; to the left were the high-rise buildings of downtown, and ahead, not just the one she remembered, but two bridges now stretching across the Mississippi. The taxi angled toward the St. Charles Avenue exit and approached her favorite landmark, the golden spire of St. John the Baptist, wet with sun. Thea's throat tightened and her vision blurred.

Her reaction startled her. She didn't like this city. There was too much squalor and chaos in it, decay and poverty were visible everywhere, neighborhoods jumbled, too much violence. She didn't like the people in New Orleans either. Their bonhomie was a smokescreen for their prurient curiosity, their politeness a wall of indifference to retreat behind. What they said was not what they meant; what they appeared to be was not what they were. Ultimately they were affected, narcissistic, dramatic. They used their nerves as their excuse. Michael called the people in New England tight-asses, but at least you knew where you stood with them, at least what you saw was what you got.

Thea had wanted to move away, and now that Althea's death had brought her back she had no intention of staying any longer than it took to sort through her aunt's personal things and put the house up for sale. Yet something was happening to her, something wholly unexpected. She realized that even though she didn't live here anymore, she'd come home.

The driver was saying something about getting a gun. "Don't make no sense not to protect yourself, y'know? Hard to believe things could get any worse, but that's what they say." He went on talking about casinos and crime.

They came down the off ramp and headed toward Convent Street. Thea's urge to cry was gone, her equilibrium restored, and she was anxious to see the house on Convent Street again, but as the driver was getting ready to turn she sprang forward and put her hand on his shoulder, interrupting his monologue. "Don't turn here."

He clicked his blinker off but said, "This's Convent Street, miss."

"I know, but I want you to take me somewhere else first." She gave him directions and the taxi cut across uptown New Orleans, traveling some avenues divided by medians, streets covered by oaks, then through tireless backstreets and into a quiet neighborhood. The houses looked as if they'd seen better days: torn screen hanging from one porch; the whole front of another house sinking, the steps separated from the rest of the structure; across the street, a badly rusted awning over a picture window. In contrast, there was a house with red geraniums growing in the front yard, another with its trim freshly painted a bold primary blue.

At a weatherbeaten white two-story building with large display windows to either side of doors set catty-corner to the street, she asked the driver to stop. He shifted in his seat to look at her, as if his big head couldn't turn on its thick neck any more than to show some cheek. Thea was noticing that the galvanized pole the grocery store's sign had hung from was still there, jutting out from the overhang above the doors. But there was no sign on it anymore, only the pole, and the windows as well as the glass on the upper part of the doors were blanked out by some white material, perhaps white paper on the doors, anonymous, no longer a store, impossible to tell if it was inhabited any longer. She edged closer to the car window to see the second floor. There were curtains upstairs.

She let out her breath, only now aware that she'd been holding it, and slid to her former position on the seat.

The driver, as if to answer the question evident in the arch of his eyebrows, said, "This used to be a grocery store."

"Yes, Nick Tamborella's Neighborhood Grocery," Thea said. "My father."

"Yeah? I use to live a coupla blocks over." He pointed back in the direction of Convent Street. Thea was holding her breath again, waiting for him to say something about the shooting, but he said, "I moved out to the Parish seventeen, eighteen years ago." He wouldn't remember; he'd been gone too long. She breathed. He said, "They broke in my house three times in a month, I said that's it. The only people would buy here anymore were the blacks. I said let em have it."

Thea remembered all the burglaries, she remembered people moving, times getting hard at the grocery, those times the only ones she could remember her parents ever arguing. Her mother wanted to leave; her father said there were no neighborhood groceries in Metairie. Her mother would suggest he work at one of the big supermarkets, he would be a manager in no time, and her father, in his hot-blooded Italian way, would strike his chest with his fist and shout, "Nick Tamborella works for no one!"

And then one afternoon the arguing was all over. Maybe the happy life she remembered living above this grocery store was over before that afternoon; it must have been over once all the fighting started. She didn't know, she couldn't remember that. What she did know was that one afternoon there were two gunshots. After that she had not returned to this neighborhood until today. She'd been—what was the word?—displaced; she'd been displaced ever since.

The cabdriver was shaking his head heavily. "Too bad," he said. "Used to be a good neighborhood."

He took Convent Street back across uptown, heading toward

the river. When they got to the Convent Street Housing Project, Thea did not notice that what she could see of the project looked better now than it had ten years ago or that most of the houses across from it looked worse. She was thinking that she hadn't seen this many black people all together in one place since her move to Amherst. They were sitting out on their porches or front steps to escape the heat inside their houses. Women in big blousy dresses fanned themselves with newspaper; the few pedestrians moved slowly. On the project side of the street, little kids in their underwear squealed as they ran in and out of the strong jet of water coming from an open fire hydrant. Just past this activity, across the street, the side the cab drove down, Thea saw the Solar Club. It was impossible not to notice: a midnight-blue stucco facade on a tall wood house, the old roofline visible toward the back, and over the arched doorway *Solar Club* written in neon script, hot-orange, flame-colored. She didn't remember it being there before.

Then the scenery changed, and moments later Thea was standing in the shade of the huge oak tree in front of Aunt Althea's house. Her house. She had always loved this house, the sheer size of it, its gabled roof, its wide, curving porch, the four long front windows, their moss-green shutters, and the front double doors with their tiny panes of leaded glass, gas lamps flanking them. It didn't seem to be as bright a white, its green trim not as crisp as it used to be, as Aunt Althea had always kept it, but that didn't matter right then. The sight of it, graceful and splendid, gave her joy.

She went up the brick walkway and rang the doorbell. Through the little leaded panes she saw several different Zoras running as fast as they could on their short legs.

Delzora was crying as she flung open the door. "Goodness, honey, is that you?"

The smell of the house reached out for her as Zora did. The smell was pure Aunt Althea, and until that moment she had not known how much she disliked it. It had a diminishing effect, diminishing her joy at the sight of the house, her happiness to see Zora.

"Look at you," Delzora said pulling back from their embrace, beaming up at her, though Thea herself was not a tall woman, "still a skinny ole thing, and you done cut off all your hair."

Thea's hair no longer hung past her prominent collarbones but was cut to her chin. She wasn't using it to cover herself anymore,

11

with too-long bangs to hide her thick black eyebrows and, she had hoped, de-emphasize her too-large Roman nose, features identical to her father's and not at all like the light, bright, petite features on the girls at school, the girls Aunt Althea had so admired, the blonds she would point out and say, "Isn't that the prettiest girl you ever saw?"

Thea brought her bags inside and put them at the bottom of the stairway. "This house, Zora, it still smells the same. Like her."

"Everything here still be the same," Delzora said, assuring her. She closed the front door. "Where is your husband? How come he not be here with you?"

"Michael and I divorced last year."

"Lawd, honey, I'm sorry to hear that. You never tole your aunt?"

"I couldn't bear to. I couldn't bear to hear her say, 'Didn't I tell you?'"

Delzora shook her head. "God rest her soul, she weren't never slow to say I done tole you so."

"No, and it was hard enough, Zora, it was very hard."

"Well, don't you worry none, honey," Delzora said, taking two of Thea's bags and starting up the stairs with them, "everything gon be all right. You home now."

3

Most of the time the police are slow to respond to calls from the Convent Street Project. Take an incident before Burgess moved back into the Convent, of an intruder breaking into the apartment of Sherree Morganza, an out-of-work stripper. The perpetrator used a simple screwdriver to get in through the front window. Luckily Sherree's boyfriend Dexter had spent the night, and he managed to wrestle the intruder to the ground out in front of the apartment. Sherree called the police, but it was an hour and a half before they arrived. While they waited, Sherree and Dexter saw two police cars drive past on Convent Street. Sherree yelled to them and danced around waving her arms but neither car stopped. Sherree had resisted letting her good-for-nothing, lazy bum of a boyfriend move in with her, but after that incident she gave in.

"Guy broke in was a crackhead," Sherree told her friends, "and he just as well could have been a rapist too. What I'm supposed to do when there ain't nothin between me and a rapist that a screwdriver can't get through? At least the bum is some protection," she said of Dexter.

The night a lone cop was killed in his car on a street at the edge of the Convent, the police were not slow to respond, but their reluctance and awareness of danger could be seen as they advanced crablike in the dark, their knees bent, stiff arms extended, guns leading. They scuttled along the sides of the red-brick buildings, then over the grounds, hardly noticing that they trampled a newly sodded yard or that they went right through a vegetable garden, squashing nearly ripe tomatoes, eggplants, and bell peppers into the wet earth.

Burgess was sleeping when the scream of sirens closed in and created a wall of noise around the housing project. At first the sirens seemed to be part of a dream. It was a recurring nightmare of being hunted, thrashing through the jungle, panting heavily, terrified of being overtaken. Suddenly the jungle ends and he is in a city, in the slums, running through the stench of poverty, his way impeded by crowds of brown, half-dressed children who look mournfully at him as he runs past them, his legs brushing against their round distended stomachs. The terror turns stale, more of a dread of hands clutching him from behind, a hope that it will be over with soon. The sirens get closer, they seem to be everywhere . . .

With a lurch of his heart Burgess woke full of fresh fear of being caught. Janine was already up, the gun from the night table dangling in her hand as she looked out between the curtains. She went to the closet and got the cereal box with the money hidden in it and hid the gun with the money. She brought the box into the kitchen and buried it in the garbage. Burgess, meanwhile, felt under the bed for the pair of pajamas he kept stashed there. Before putting them on, he popped first the top then the bottom out into the air to make sure no roaches were crawling around on them. From the drawer of the night table he took out a salt-and-pepper beard and secured it to his face. It was a full beard, grizzled, covering most of his cheeks. Janine came back with a box of cornstarch. He dipped his fingers into it and dusted a small amount into his tight black curls. The residue he rubbed around his eyes and on his forehead. Janine snuffed away too-white places. Under the yellowy overhead light Burgess looked gray and sick.

Janine returned the cornstarch to the kitchen, then Burgess could hear her rustling the covers of the single bed they kept in the living room of the small one-bedroom apartment for just a night such as this.

Loudly and methodically the police raided the Convent. Periodically a clamor would arise as men were pulled under protest from their apartments and herded into the yard. The clamor came closer. Burgess could feel the bedclothes getting damp from his sweat. The light blanket he was under was smothering him. The tension in his muscles was so great that it was almost a relief when the fists hit his door.

"Police! Open up!"

Janine opened the door to two cops shining flashlights in her face. She moved too slowly for them and one shoved her back roughly.

"You here alone?" he asked. The other one turned on lights, kicked the pillow that had fallen from the single bed out of his path, and poked his gun into the hallway.

Janine shook her head, her eyes showing white all around the brown. This part didn't take any play-acting; her throat was practically closed with fright.

"Who else?" the cop demanded impatiently.

She answered slowly, "Mah daddy."

A man on the premises made her insignificant to them. They went past her, leaving her in the front room, going down the hallway. She followed them.

The one who did the talking swung the beam of his flashlight around the room, then pointed it at the bed as he switched on the bedroom light. "Hey, old man." The other one held his gun inches from the back of Burgess' head.

Burgess made a feeble attempt to turn. Janine, in the doorway, said, "He sick," and from the bed Burgess took in the dull, slack-jawed look on her face. He coughed, a phlegmy sound, and lifted the soiled sleeve of his pajama top to his mouth.

This movement caused the cop holding the gun on Burgess to grab Burgess' arm and stick the gun in his face. Burgess went limp in his grip.

Janine said, "He got TB."

That knocked the cop holding Burgess back. "Shit!" he said and the two of them hurried out, Janine at their heels. She locked the door behind them.

She ran softly on her bare feet back into the bedroom and leaned over Burgess. She still wore that uncomprehending stupid look, totally convincing. She smiled and it was gone.

"Hey, old man," she said.

He pulled her down next to him and they stifled their nervous laughter up against each other, but then they heard cries coming from the yard. They got out of bed and went to the front window, where they saw men getting their faces shoved up against the red bricks, their heads and sides whacked with billy clubs. One of them was Dexter. The cops cuffed him and a few of the other men and took them to a police van.

Burgess stood at the window and knew something bad was happening, something that was going to change his new life in the Convent. It was a life that sometimes offered to eradicate the past and gave him the illusion of having a future. It was false, all false. The past could not be eradicated. The future was full of fear.

He and Janine went back to bed. He tried to lose his worry by making love to her. He took a long time. He held himself on rigid arms and moved over her, slowly at first, then more strenuously. She reached up and clung to him and he carried her weight too. He exhausted himself. But still he spent a fitful night having more dreams of being pursued.

4

Everyone was afraid of something. Delzora was afraid she wouldn't have a job much longer.

The morning after Althea Dumondville's death, Delzora went to work and followed her usual routine. But as she was reading the newspaper, she was overcome by a feeling she was unable to identify at first. It was nostalgia. For a woman who rarely thought about the future, Delzora had projected herself into a future in which there were no newspapers: she would miss reading the morning newspaper, a luxury she would not be able to afford if she lost her job. She could look for another job in another big house, but work cleaning houses was hard to find and getting harder even though the younger women scorned it as a way to make money. In Delzora's world, the world in and around the Convent, there were not very many opportunities. More people than opportunities existed. Maids stayed for years, as Delzora had, in the houses of their rich employers. They passed the jobs on to relatives when they left. It wasn't that Delzora liked being a maid, keeping house for a woman who had bossed her around and never said her work was good, hadn't commented on it at all unless something was wrong. But there were worse lives to live. As she sat at the kitchen table missing the morning newspaper of the future, she realized she might be forced to move back into the Convent. It hadn't occurred to her before simply because she wasn't used to thinking about the future.

Delzora had not thought about the future in terms of possibilities and life's potential for many years. When her son Burgess was barely a year old, her husband died. She had to give up the small house they rented and move into the Convent Street Housing Project. In one way this was a good move because there were other husbandless women with children in the Convent and these women helped one another and became family to one another. When Delzora got the job with the Dumondvilles she didn't have to worry about Burgess coming home from school to an empty house. Someone was always around. But in other ways the move was not good. As the Convent became filled with more and more jobless people whose hope of finding work dwindled as the jobs themselves did, it became a dangerous place to live.

One night a man broke into her apartment, and Delzora, in bed, watched with terror as he took all the money from her purse. He came to the foot of the bed and looked down at her. She pretended to be asleep, though she wondered how he couldn't hear her heart crashing around in her chest. He looked and he quietly left. She felt lucky on two counts: the man had not hurt her or Burgess, and Burgess had slept through the burglary. Delzora didn't want him to know someone had violated their home so easily and casually. She was afraid he wouldn't sleep anymore either.

Crime escalated along with the drugs. One evening she picked Burgess up at a neighbor's, but when she tried to go home, a man was shooting heroin on her stairway. Delzora left immediately and stayed away most of the night, but it was too late. Burgess had seen the needle poking out of the man's vein. He asked endless questions about it. His curiosity was alarming. Delzora told him how bad needles were, what drugs did to people. She told him never to use a needle, never to let anybody give him one. That much he heard and listened to, but awareness of drugs was part of his life after that.

There was no way she could have protected him from it forever. The future, though, became more limited than it had ever been for Delzora. It was reduced to one goal—to get her son out of the Convent.

Finally the future arrived. Delzora moved several blocks away into an old house that had many of the same problems her Convent apartment had—rusty, clogged, noisy plumbing, inadequate heating, walls that were cold and clammy in the winter, not even a fan for the hot summer months, years' worth of other people's dirt, a smaller apartment in a white clapboard house blackened by the mold that eventually overtook everything in this damp, humid city. But it was out of the confines of a place that had seemed like a prison for lifers, where she was confronted day after day by hostile, sad, tired, sick faces. Here was something that felt like freedom.

So what had Burgess gone and done? He'd moved right back into one of the red-brick square buildings like a cell, with its years of grime, the muddy yard, the dopers all around, the ragamuffin kids. So he could be Mr. Big Shot. No matter what else he said, that was the real reason. Mr. Big with all his money. Money he got from drugs. Money that was sure to bring him to a bad end.

It seemed no matter what, once you moved into the Convent, you never really came out.

5

The house, the parlor at any rate, reminded Thea of an aging whore. Worn brocade covered curvaceous Victorian sofas flanked by overwaxed, heavily scrolled and beaded tables. The maroon velvet curtains were faded to a dark pink luridness. Bunched on the floor, their extra length, once opulent, was now frumpy. The crystals on the chandelier at the center of the room had a milky coating of dirt, like eyes glazed over with cataracts. Patches of gold-flocked wallpaper were balding. Near the ceiling a piece had separated from the wall and curled limply under chipped and yellowed dentil molding. Thea could hardly believe she once had thought this was the most beautiful room in the world.

Looking at the falling wallpaper she remarked, "I'm surprised Aunt Althea let the house go like this."

"When she gave up, the house looked to give up with her," Delzora said.

"What do you mean, when she gave up?"

"She jus come downstairs one mornin and said, 'Delzora, I decided I'm goin to die now.'"

"She decided to die and she did, just like that?"

"No, it took her 'bout two years."

This was curious, Aunt Althea's decision to die. Zora spoke of it as if it were simply another of her aunt's whims: I want a sapphire-and-diamond dinner ring to wear with my blue chiffon dress; I want a pink gazebo in the backyard; I want to go to Miami for Christmas; I want to die now. Thea felt sorry for Zora, having to put up with this last grandiose desire of her aunt's. All of Aunt Althea's desires had been grandiose, all-consuming, demanding everyone's attention until gratification was secured. It was this way even if Aunt Althea wanted to give you a gift. You were required to become totally involved in her desire to give you something, something she had decided you should have, which you should be present to purchase and which did not necessarily have anything to do with what you wanted. She never presented you with a package, a surprise, and she took great offense if you suggested you didn't want or need what she had decided to give. You were turning down an expression of love, for this was the only way Aunt Althea knew how to express love. She did not know how to be affectionate or compassionate or interested in someone else's life. She was entirely too self-absorbed. Her gifts were for the gratification of her desire to give, the sole manifestation of her ability to give anything at all of herself. And she was always very generous; she dominated you with her generosity. She had controlled Thea's mother with it, giving her younger sister things she could not afford herself, buying clothes and shoes for Thea. Thea's mother had felt both grateful and obligated, and she had passed those feelings on to Thea.

"She weren't interested in the house no more," Delzora said, "she didn't want to go out, she weren't interested in nothin 'cept her will. She was always callin up Mr. Untermeyer, tellin him to rewrite it. He flat refused when she tole him she was leavin everything to Clarence."

"Clarence? Her old gardener? I thought he retired before I left."

Zora nodded. "But he use to come by and check on her once or twice a year, ask her if she needed anything."

"Wait a minute. Clarence came by once or twice a year and she was going to leave him this house?"

"She liked the attention, honey. Anyway, she fired Mr. Untermeyer on the spot for refusin to favor Clarence in her will. I tole her them boys of Clarence's would take all her money and spend it on fancy cars. She fired me too but I didn't pay her no mind. I jus kep comin to work and she didn't say nothing to me about it. Pretty soon she called up Mr. Untermeyer and tole him she decided she weren't goin to rewrite the will. He said that was fine by him but he considered himself fired forever, to talk to his nephew from then on."

From the grave, she was doing it from the grave, manipulating Thea's emotions, frustrating her with ambivalence. Thea was grateful to her dead aunt, plenty grateful enough to feel sorry for her that she had been rejected by Aldous Untermeyer, who she always said was in love with her (although he was quite happily married); grateful enough to pity her aunt's hopelessly skewed perception of reality, to suffer guilt for her own rejection of the old woman (Thea, her namesake, had changed her name legally to the shortened form the moment she left town), and to be angry, very angry, that Aunt Althea really hadn't wanted to leave her anything at all because of her audacity, leaving New Orleans, turning down an education at Sophie Newcomb College, moving to Massachusetts with a man.

"Why in the world Clarence, Zora? Why not you?"

"Well, you know, she always preferred mens."

It was true. Thea could have done whatever she'd wanted if she'd been male and Aunt Althea would have said, "Isn't that just like a man," and instantly forgiven her. Aunt Althea lit up when a man was around, becoming chatty and coquettish, though she liked to give orders—get me a drink, move this plant, reach something for me—so she could have a man doing her bidding, under her control. She acted that way with all men, her husband, her gardener, delivery men, Thea's boyfriends, except with Michael and, a long time ago, Nick Tamborella, her sister's husband.

Thea sighed. "I guess maybe we'd have gotten along better if I'd been a man." But her second thought, to herself, was Maybe not, not the son of my father, the lowly Italian grocer Althea despised because he once told her that she treated every man she met as either a lover, a potential lover, or an ex-lover.

Thea opened the curtains. In the sunlight the room was less oppressive, less tawdry too, just shabby. "If I'm going to sell the house, I'll have to do something about this awful wallpaper," she said.

The light from the long floor window glinted on Delzora's thick glasses, making them opaque, blocking from Thea's view the dread with which she heard those words. That they were what she had expected made them no less dreadful. But she said, "Burgess do that kind of work. I can have him come round tomorrow."

Delzora's saying that brought up another feeling Thea associated with her aunt, that of being railroaded, having decisions made for her before she had a chance to make them herself. But this was not Aunt Althea, this was Zora.

"Sure," she said, "I'll talk to him about it."

Through the window they saw the Cadillac drive up in front of the house.

"Here my ride," Delzora said.

And here must be Zora's experience with fancy cars. Dexter got out of the car dressed in the blue leather pants and vest.

"Is that Burgess?"

"No, that ain't Burgess, but that's his car. He sends it for me every day 'cause of all the crime on the streets."

"He must do very well," Thea said.

Zora blew air through her nose and made a sound of disgust deep down in her throat. Thea felt her cheeks burn with the inappropriateness of her remark. After all, didn't black men like to spend their money, whether they made a lot or not, on fancy cars? The Convent Street Project was full of fancy cars. She was going to have to learn all over, remember not to make such remarks.

Thea helped Delzora gather her bags and followed her out to the front walkway. Dexter, his back to them, shrugged out of his vest and put on a white shirt. He unzipped his leather pants to tuck in the shirt.

"Dexter," Delzora called, "next time you get dressed at home, do you hear?"

He zipped up his pants and turned toward her. Thea started at the sight of his face, badly beaten, beaten out of shape.

"Yes ma'am," he said.

6

Bobby Buchanan came to visit Thea carrying his trademark can of beer in one hand, the remainder of the six-pack in the other. The city of New Orleans seems to have a larger than normal share of men like Bobby. They are from good families, families with money, which they have inherited and which affords them the opportunity not to work if they don't want to, or not to work very hard. They are wastrels, good-natured, easygoing, mild-mannered, the life of the party. They are observers for the most part, though they enjoy engaging in repartee. They don't appear to be complex people, but sometimes they are. Bobby, for example, was more complex than he allowed even himself to know; what he did know was that he sometimes did not feel very well mentally, and when he felt bad he did not know how to make himself feel better, so he drank.

Bobby had been Thea's boyfriend during most of their high-school years, part of the in-group of socially prominent teenagers from the neighborhood where Aunt Althea lived, and even though his part in the group was the clown, the cheerful drunk, without him Thea wouldn't have been part of the group at all. She was the outsider, the girl from the Catholic school, the girl who had moved in the middle of the year because her parents had been murdered. Aunt Althea had insisted she transfer to the exclusive private school not far from her house. Most of the girls at the new school had known each other since first grade. Their cliques were formed in cast concrete. It might have been different if, when Aunt Althea had married Cecil Dumondville, she'd been accepted by the blue-blooded Dumondville family, but she was forever an outsider too, only she hadn't seemed to know it. Thea didn't know how she herself could be so acutely, uncomfortably aware of her group status and her aunt so aggressively oblivious, playing her part of one of the daughters-in-law of the illustrious Dumondvilles, apparently never seeing the difference between herself, a middlebrow who'd been Cecil's bookkeeper before he married her, and the other two brothers' wives, who were themselves part of uptown New Orleans cultured society and snubbed her.

Bobby had saved Thea from being nobody except the girl whose parents were murdered. He was fun to be with, he was always saying he loved her, but he made no demands upon her, only small forays that were easily discouraged, perhaps too easily. Thea would hear the other girls talking about their boyfriends' wanting them to go all the way, the constant pressure, the danger of it all, and it made them seem so worldly-wise and sophisticated. Mostly she and Bobby just made out until their lips hurt. Bobby was easy, someone to go to parties and school dances with, not someone to get heated up over, to take seriously. He didn't seem to want to be taken very seriously. In a way he was the story of her life—steady, lightweight, always on the edge of the action but never the cutting edge, part of the group but never a key player.

When Thea opened the door she was struck by the possibility that Bobby had spent the past ten years in a time warp. He looked exactly the same, from his short curly blond hair to the boat shoes on his feet, no socks, and everything in between too: a white button-down Oxford cloth shirt with the sleeves rolled up to his elbows, khaki pants, the can of beer. And he still dispensed with polite social greetings and cut straight to irreverent one-liners.

"So now you're an uptown rich-bitch," he said, and she was surprised at how glad she was to see him, hugging him to her, his arms around her, what was left of the cold six-pack dangling at her back.

It was dusk, a time of day Thea liked during the warmer months in New Orleans, coming more as a cool drink borne by the breeze than as a fading of light. Thea took Bobby out to the screened porch at the back of the house to sit and drink it in along with some beer. Overhead the ceiling fan circled slowly and hummed, and outside the foliage swayed and swished gently, backup harmonies to the soft singing of the cicadas. In the midst of all that nature was the pink gazebo, looking every bit like the crown of a wedding cake clumsily dropped at a nuptial of the gods. To Thea it was a fatuous symbol of her aunt's yearning for some romance in her life, another of those consuming desires—months spent refining the design, adding froufrou, latticework and tiny turrets all around the roof, trying pink after pink until she found exactly the right shade.

"I wonder," Thea said, "if Aunt Althea pictured herself waiting in the gazebo for some polite southern gentleman caller to come woo her, Aldous Untermeyer maybe."

"That ugly old fart? He has terminal dandruff."

"As long as she didn't wear her glasses, she wouldn't have known. And she never wore her glasses in front of old farts—gentlemen callers."

Bobby squint-eyed the gazebo. "I can see it. She'd be wearing her hoop skirt."

"Reading a romance novel." The shelves in the back room were crammed with them.

"Her bosom heaving under her tightly laced bodice." Bobby threw his arm up over his forehead. "She swoons . . ."

"She'd break her spine," Thea said. "Have you ever tried to swoon on one of those benches?"

Bobby looked pointedly at her. "No. Have you?"

It was good to be with him. He knew her history, had lived part of it with her, been a victim of her aunt's flirtations. He could laugh about it with her as they had ten years ago, as if ten years had never interrupted their friendship. What they were having trouble doing was catching up on the ten years.

They sat in wicker rocking chairs, their feet stretched out in front of them, sipping beer and watching the light ease away. It sank back, disappearing into a dense wall of bamboo and banana trees, cherry laurel and wild hibiscus that enclosed the yard. A passion flower vine grew up over the tall wood fence to one side of the porch. Somewhere in the yard night-blooming jasmine was opening, its sweetness airborne on the light breeze.

Bobby finally broke into the silence of the sweet-thickened dark. "Will Michael be coming?"

"No," Thea shook her head. "No, he won't be coming." And she told him about the breakup of her marriage, a marriage Bobby knew nothing about, that seemed to startle him. She told him how, after six years of living together, the marriage had spoiled their relationship, how Michael had started running around on her and two years had been as much as she could take.

But one thing she did not tell Bobby, could not bring herself to tell him or anyone: she was still sleeping with Michael. He'd been in bed with her the night Aldous Untermeyer called to tell her Aunt Althea was dead and she was rich. She could not tell anyone about sleeping with Michael because she loathed and despised herself for letting it happen.

Bobby thought about telling her she'd broken his heart when she'd gone away, but before he could decide if he should, she asked about his family and he told her that his father had died a couple of years ago. "I lost my best fishing buddy," he said, and Thea could tell he was still quite sad. "I hardly ever go anymore." She asked why but he just shrugged. He couldn't tell her that being out on the boat made him feel such guilt that a case of beer couldn't wash it away. How could he tell her about the stupid, petty problems surrounding his father's death when her parents had been gunned down behind the counter of their grocery store by two black men who'd taken forty-eight dollars and fled? As for his mother, he told Thea that she was confused a lot of the time. "She forgets my father is dead," Bobby said, explaining she had Alzheimer's, advanced to the point that she required round-the-clock care.

But Bobby left something out of this story too: he didn't tell her that his mother sometimes spent hours railing at him, thinking he was her husband, for losing most of the family money; he didn't say that his mother's illness was probably going to take what was left. He was too worried to talk about that. He finished off another can of beer.

The darkness settled around them. Thea remembered how she used to think she felt the weight of the darkness whenever she sat on the porch at night but it was the weight of her grief she felt.

"I used to sit here and dream that I lived in this house with my parents," she told Bobby, her voice modulating itself so as not to drown out the sounds within the darkness but to become part of them. "We had lots of pets, all the animals I never could have because we lived above the grocery store. I put pedestals around the porch for the cats to sit on. From there they would watch the birds, who were in cages hung from the ceiling. The dogs would claw at the pedestals, trying to reach the cats, but after a while they would get tired and lie at the base of the pedestals, waiting for the cats to come down. The cats, of course, would jump from chair to chair, always out of their reach. The cats knew they could never get the birds, and after a while the dogs realized they couldn't get the cats, and finally they all lived peacefully together."

"So now you can have all the pets and pedestals you want," Bobby said. He found he wanted desperately for her to stay in New Orleans.

"I'm going to sell the house, Bobby."

So he told her about the oil bust and people forced to move out of town, out of the state, by the depressed economy. They put their houses up for sale; some of the For Sale signs had been up for over two years. "It'll take a long time to sell your house, Thea." He wasn't used to having to be persuasive. He turned in the rocker, the wicker creaking beneath him, and put his hand on her forearm. "Why don't you just live in it, at least for a while. Stay here."

Her first impulse was to cry out, I already have a life, I must get back to it! But why would she return to a job in a health-food market now that she was rich? What did she have to look forward to there? Being promoted from assistant manager to manager of the store? What else? Fucking Michael once a week, if he showed up, if there wasn't someone else he'd rather fuck? She couldn't even think of anything she'd left behind that she would bother to return to get except her books, a few papers, the photographs of her parents. And Michael could ship all that to her. It was the least he could do. Some life. It could be packed in a few boxes and shipped, then Michael could take the rest of the contents of the apartment he'd once shared with her and dispose of them.

Thea was feeling a bit tipsy from the beer. "Okay," she said to Bobby. "But if I stay, the gazebo goes."

Bobby stood up. "You got it. We'll need a long rope."

They tried the garage but found no rope suitable for the task hanging from the pegs or neatly coiled in one of the cabinets, everything in the garage as neat and organized as everything in the house.

"We could try the attic," Thea said.

Bobby shook his head. "No, I know right where we can find one—my house."

The beer and their sense of purpose made Thea feel a giddy excitement. She'd missed this about New Orleans, the fun, the craziness. She didn't do very many spontaneous things in Massachusetts. Her life there was staid. Dull. Oppressed. She was oppressed by Michael there, either by his presence or because she was waiting for him. As she got into Bobby's car she experienced a sense of freedom that was new, brand new, and it wasn't just Michael's absence, it was also Aunt Althea's. She had moved from one oppression to another and tonight she was free.

The nighttime drive through the neighborhood filled Thea with pleasure. The tree-lined streets were dark, and some of the houses tightly shuttered, but many of them were lit, their curtains pulled back to show intriguing views of interiors through floor windows, alcove windows, or in a few modernized versions, walls of glass. And many of them, as Bobby had said, were for sale.

"All these beautiful houses," Thea said. "I've never seen so many signs."

"Trendy lawn decorations," Bobby told her; then more seriously: "The enclave is seeing some troubled times."

And so was Bobby, Thea decided. He was driving his father's old Lincoln, the transmission sounding dangerously clunky, the right rear fender dented and rusting, the taillight knocked out, and when they drove up in front of his house, Thea was surprised to see that the landscaped gardens had been allowed to grow up all around it, bushes as tall as the windows, a tree limb touching the roof, a piece of gutter loose and hanging. And everything closed up tight, the house completely dark from the front.

Another car was pulled far up into the driveway. Bobby parked in front of the house next door. He came around the car as Thea was getting ready to close the door and did it for her, shutting it as soundlessly as possible. The street seemed abnormally dark and quiet, most of the houses closed up like the Buchanans'. Trees blocked much of the light from the streetlamps. Bobby took Thea's hand and led her to the driveway. Bamboo grew along one side, eight or nine feet high. On the other side, light was seeping through the closed shutters of the house. Bobby stopped at the rear of the car. "We have to be very quiet," he said, his voice low. They went single file between the car and the house to the garage.

The garage was a corrugated, weak-looking structure. Bobby unlocked a padlock and started pulling one of the doors open. It scraped along the concrete. He stopped immediately and cursed, a hiss through his teeth, and looked toward the house. Nothing happened. He lifted the door and opened it just enough to squeeze through, whispering, "Stay here," to Thea.

She could hear him groping around inside, hissing more curses. She was glad she could hear him because all this sneaking about and the dark stillness around her was somewhat eerie, and she began to feel anxious to leave, anxiety altering her mood, her giddiness dropping off. He returned with a thick, coiled rope, closed the door—it scraped again—padlocked it, and hurriedly led her back to the car.

"What was all that about?" Thea wanted to know.

"Oh, it's my mother," Bobby said offhandedly, avoiding her eyes. "She would want me to stay if she knew I was here."

"Who's with her?"

"A nurse."

"Someone comes in when you need to go out?"

He started the car, and for a moment Thea thought he wasn't going to answer her. He drove to the corner, stopped, and then he looked at her. "No, I have someone stay with her twenty-four hours a day." It sounded like a confession. Thea nodded, not knowing what to say. "I just couldn't take it anymore. I decided I didn't care about the money." That wasn't quite true, he thought, but it was true enough.

They drove a few blocks before Thea said, "It's okay, Bobby. You don't have to feel guilty."

The comedian was gone, not there for him to hide his pain behind. "I know I don't have to," he said, "but I do."

But he didn't want to talk about it; he wanted to take the gazebo down for her. He waited while she moved her aunt's Mercedes out of the driveway, then he backed in. Together they opened the wooden gates, and he backed through them, angling into the yard.

Thea watched from the porch steps as Bobby looped one end of the rope around one of the posts of the gazebo and tied the other end to the trailer hitch on the Lincoln. He slowly moved the car forward, taking the slack from the rope, then increasing the tension on it. There was a moment of suspense before the post gave. The crack of wood was a palpable shock to Thea's body.

"No!" she yelled, her hands covering her ears even though the sound had stopped. She stared at the broken post, the roof of the gazebo, its little pink turrets, pitifully tilted, and she felt dreadfully sorry for this inanimate object she had ruined to strike a blow at dead Aunt Althea.

"What? What is it, Tee?" Bobby was at her side, the car still running.

She heard his old nickname for her and she began to cry. He'd called her Tee all through high school and she had hoped it would catch on, but nobody else ever used it, as if it were reserved for Bobby alone. She cried because the nickname, to her, had not been a sign of Bobby's affection or of her desire to be accepted by the group, but a way to reject her aunt. She cried because she'd run away with Michael after Aunt Althea told her he reminded her of her father, though the only way he was like her father was that he refused to cater to her aunt, but Thea knew she meant he'd be the end of her, as her father had been the end of her mother, forcing her to work in a failing grocery store where eventually she was murdered. She cried because she'd never really loved Michael and because she really had nothing against this broken gazebo.

Bobby, taking her hands away from her ears, was saying, "I'm sorry, Tee, really I am. Please don't cry, Tee, I'll fix it if you want."

7

The next morning Burgess rode over to Thea's in the Cadillac with Delzora. To drive them, Dexter had dressed up in a starched white shirt and forgone his vest. Burgess always wore a starched white shirt tucked into tight black pants, and he never went anywhere, day or night, without his wide-brimmed black felt hat and mirrored aviator sunglasses.

Thea had forgotten about Burgess coming. When she got downstairs, the first thing she saw was the black hat, aviator glasses perched on its brim, on a table in the foyer. She went into the kitchen and found Burgess having tea with his mother.

He got up from the table and extended his hand. "Ms. Tamborella," he said in a baritone that seemed too big and round for his long thin body. His voice had changed considerably; she didn't recognize him at all until he smiled. It was the same smile she remembered on him as a kid, his top lip tipping upward and curving back over his teeth to show a line of dark pink gum, the smile he gave every time he won the game with the baseball cards.

They had spent a few Saturdays together, perhaps twenty years ago, when Thea used to spend every Saturday at Aunt Althea's. She loved being in her aunt's beautiful house with its elegant furnishings. It was her palace of pretend; it was her first and most fateful step out of her humble beginnings above the grocery store. Only she sometimes wished for someone to play with, she was always so alone. One Saturday Zora brought Burgess with her. At first they were shy with each other, as any boy and girl of nine or ten would be, and undoubtedly because he was black and she was white. Forced integration had already taken place in the New Orleans public schools, but because most white parents had immediately removed their children to private or religious institutions,

Thea and Burgess both were still going to essentially segregated schools. But more compelling than that, the integration issue had made color differences very stark indeed.

At first they played separately, Thea in the house, Burgess in the yard or on the porch. But gradually Thea became curious. She would take her books or her dolls wherever he was and play near him. Then one Saturday Burgess brought his baseball cards. He squatted down on the porch and began tossing them one at a time at the back wall. Thea watched, fascinated by the flick of his wrist, the skimming of the card through the air, but she didn't understand the point of the game. Finally she asked him.

He said, "See how close I can get," without looking at her.

She didn't understand what he meant, but she continued to watch, getting tired of standing, squatting down beside him after a while. He asked her if she wanted to play. She wasn't any good at all at the beginning because she thought she was supposed to get the cards close to each other, and couldn't understand why he kept saying he'd won. She caught on when she happened to throw several cards right up against the wall and he had to count to see who'd won. Then she couldn't remember how she'd managed to get those cards up against the wall and had to learn all over again. She watched him intensely. Under her scrutiny, he would hardly look at her, but soon they both became adept enough at the game that he would have to count each time. When he won he would give her his wide, friendly smile. A couple of Saturdays of this and he suggested they play for money.

Thea liked the seriousness the game took on once money was involved, even though he won most of her allowance from her. She began to look forward to Saturdays all week. And then he stopped coming. When she asked Zora where Burgess was, Zora just said, "Oh, he couldn't come today, honey." Thea thought he wasn't coming anymore because of her, something she'd done.

Burgess finished his tea and went into the parlor with her. He quickly surveyed the large room. "I got two expert paper hangers can start strippin this old paper off tomorrow mornin."

She nodded slowly; this was going a bit fast. She still had legalities to finish with Mr. Untermeyer before she had access to all the money. But she heard herself telling him to give her a day or two to pick a new pattern, and he said he'd work up a price for her. She didn't ask him any of the questions she knew she was supposed to ask, about being bonded and insured, and she didn't consider getting any other estimates. She had made up her mind, almost unconsciously, something to do with his smile, that she was going to let him do the work.

They walked into the foyer. Burgess picked up his sunglasses, then his hat, holding it upside down by the crown, ready to leave, when Thea thought about the wrecked gazebo. Something was going to have to be done about it; she couldn't stand to see it sitting there lopsided and pathetic. She told Burgess she had something else for him to look at outside. He tossed his hat on the table and followed her back through the kitchen, down a short hallway to the porch and, putting his sunglasses on, out into the yard.

He looked at the tilted roof, the cracked post. "What happened to it?"

She stammered slightly telling him she'd tried to take the gazebo down.

He inspected the broken post more closely. Turning to her, he took off his glasses. "You tie a rope to your car?"

The idea of it was so ludicrous she had to hold her bottom lip with her teeth to keep from laughing. He looked at her squarely, expectantly, perhaps the beginning of a smile on his lips. When she nodded, the smile broke wide open and he laughed, a laugh that rippled the air two backyards away with its resonance.

Inside the house, Delzora heard her son laughing and went to a window looking out onto the screened porch and into the yard. She watched both of them laughing fit to kill themselves, standing next to the gazebo. "That Burgess," she whispered, shaking her head, thinking he could have done anything with his life, he had such charm. She left the window abruptly. Suddenly she was in a bad mood.

"So what you need?" Burgess said to Thea. "Want me to go 'head and level it?"

"No, I want to leave it up. Can you fix it?"

"I got an expert carpenter can do it."

"Okay." Now that she was looking more closely, she could see the pink paint beginning to chip and peel. She eyed Burgess. "Do you have an expert painter—paint it white?"

There was that smile again. "Yeah," he said.

The heat didn't allow too much standing around. Going back inside, Burgess stopped to size up the porch. "Nothin much changed here," he said.

"Nothing at all," Thea agreed. They stood in the midst of chintz-covered white wicker, both caught up in memories of time spent there together, both uncomfortable to be remembering in the presence of the other. Thea finally spoke. "I always wanted to know, Burgess—why did you stop coming on Saturdays?"

He looked at her, surprised, puzzled, as if he thought she might be putting him on. "You sayin you never figured that out?" He grinned, good-natured, and said, "Your auntee, she didn't think you should be playin with no black boy."

Thea wondered how she could have been so stupid.

8

That afternoon Dexter failed to show at the Victorian house to pick up Delzora. She waited over half an hour for him because he escorted other people home besides her; maybe one of them had run late or run into trouble. Burgess had started this escort service when crime was at its peak in the Convent and people, especially elderly people, were being mugged on the street in broad daylight. All of the Convent men who owned cars were asked to participate. They more or less patrolled the area, since the police didn't do it anymore, and soon crime in and around the Convent began to decrease.

As crime dropped in the Convent, it rose in the neighboring rich white district of big houses. People were assaulted on the street, waylaid as they came home from parties, held at gunpoint in their beds. The problem was blamed on drugs. Some said it was the welfare system. Teen pregnancy and lack of education were also cited as factors. The property owners called meetings, established Neighborhood Watch, and stepped up the patrol of the area with off-duty policemen. No matter what they did, crime flourished, and more and more often, it seemed, someone was killed during an armed robbery. People began to hide in their houses. Those who could afford it lived behind bars. They slept within nets of security beams, behind doors wired to explode with sound. They left their electronic cells of safety in fear.

Delzora left Thea's house that afternoon in agitation, however, not fear. She was tired and she was used to her comfortable ride home in the Cadillac. She walked down Convent Street lambasting Dexter under her breath. He was getting more like Burgess by the day. Mr. Big. Mr. Important. Vain as a fighting cock. He was probably at home, standing in front of the mirror, examining that beat-up face of his, no regard for time whatsoever. It's what came of not having an honest job. Driving for Burgess certainly couldn't be called an honest job. Nevertheless, she hoped he'd pull up at the curbside so she could give him a piece of her mind, for one thing, and tell him to spend some of that money Burgess gave him on a wristwatch.

Delzora crossed St. Charles Avenue and walked a block farther, until she was alongside the project. She hadn't seen the Convent up close like this for some time, riding in the Cadillac with its tinted windows, her eyes usually closed, resting. She stopped. The place looked different, spruced up. Part of the yard had a lawn now, and there was the vegetable garden Burgess had told her about. It was quite large. Residents had planted it and took care of it, he said. Everyone who worked in it shared in it, as well as the sick and the elderly and single mothers. That was a good idea, Delzora had to admit. And well off the street, toward the back of this block of housing units, she could see playground equipment. He'd bought it and gotten some of the men to help install it. That must be where the new day-care center was. One woman was paid a nominal amount to run it, and the mothers who could volunteered their time to help staff it. Well, okay, that was a good idea too. And as far as her eye could see, the red-brick dwellings had been cleaned up, new windows put in where she remembered there'd once been boards, the trim freshly painted a bright green. It looked good, she had to say, but as if she and Burgess were arguing again, she was thinking, You can't fool me. The Convent gon always be the Convent, with junkies on the stairs and crack deals in the alleys and gunfire in the middle of the night. Don't matter how many drug centers you got, or how many people you teach to read, or how many painters and carpenters and plasterers you put to work, you couldn't get me back in the Convent that I wouldn't go kickin and screamin, and God willin, I won't never have to go.

One last look and Delzora continued on her way, wondering as she went what all the fuss on TV was about, talk of razing some of the projects in the city and the mayor firing the head of the housing authority, the tenants protesting. Well, she didn't care, she didn't have to care, and she didn't want to care. She lifted her head high and felt a bit superior as she stepped up her pace toward her old mold-blackened apartment house.

Dexter never did pull up at the curbside. At about the time Delzora was lambasting him, he was sitting in a straight-backed chair, his arms cuffed behind him, in a small windowless room in a police station. He winced from the bright light shining directly in his face. The long interrogation about drug activities in the Convent was wearing him down. They asked him over and over again, in a hundred different ways, who the kingpin was in the Convent. They were looking to stick somebody with the cop killing, but Burgess was clean on that. It was out all over the Convent that the cop himself had been into dealing. For all he knew, Dexter thought bitterly, when they gave him a chance to think, the police had decided to get rid of a greedy cop and take a few more brothers off the street at the same time, till pretty soon there wouldn't be anybody left. He'd lay money right now no one would ever know who killed the cop. But still, Dexter knew they weren't going to give up on him until they got something out of him. The longer it went on, the more scared he got. He groped around for something to tell them that would satisfy them enough to let him go. He tormented himself thinking it was bad luck he'd been home that afternoon. He didn't want to say anything at all. He was superstitious; he knew how things like that went: once you gave them anything, the smallest detail, then the big picture was out of whack. Things changed, not usually for the better.

He was thinking along these lines when one of them strolled into the room with a big see-through plastic bag, strolled right up to him with it. Dexter started screaming. They put the bag over his head, and his mind went white with terror. He couldn't even hear what they were saying anymore. He tried to take small breaths, but too soon the thin plastic was all over his face, stuck to it with his own sweat and the force of his need for air, creeping into his nostrils, forming a vacuum seal across his wide-open mouth. He passed out.

When he came to, they were back in his face, all over him, but he was dazed and they seemed far away, until they came at him with that plastic bag again, and he knew he had to find something to say, something to get them to stop.

He pulled his shoulders up, wanting to protect his head, a wasted effort with his hands locked behind his back. "I don't know nothin," he said. "I don't know nothin and I ain heard nothin 'cept he wears a black hat all the time."

They laughed at him, asking him, didn't he know all the bad guys wore black hats, and he began to cry, not because they were laughing, but because it was a betrayal, didn't matter how little, it was still a betrayal.

They said to let the crybaby go home.

9

Dexter told Burgess later, "Don' wear that hat no more, man. Don' never wear that hat again."

The hat in question lay on a blond Formica coffee table in front of a red plush sofa where Burgess and Dexter sat. Janine and Sherree sat on the single bed, which was covered with an old green chenille bedspread and pushed up against the opposite wall. Overhead a milk-white glass light fixture shaped like a woman's breast shielded a low-wattage bulb that merely dampened the room with light. Burgess picked up the hat, balanced it on an index finger, and twirled it around while Dexter, Janine, and Sherree watched in suspense, as if he were performing a circus act of some magnificence.

They were all wondering just exactly what was Dexter's status with Burgess now. They were beginning to sense the change that Burgess knew was already set in motion.

Dexter didn't think he could bear to be in Burgess' disfavor. Burgess had given him something to do, a living, had given him a lift in Sherree's eyes. Now he had money, he drove Burgess' car and spent time with Burgess, he had power.

Sherree wished Dexter could be an independent man, but at least he had a job. And it was true that the job made Dexter a hot shot, made her a hot shot too. She was the envy of many a single woman in the Convent. Just to have a man these days was something; to have a man with money was something else. Of course, she wasn't sitting nearly as pretty as Janine was.

But Janine wasn't sitting so pretty in her own eyes at the moment. She looked at Burgess, his face passive as he took in what Dexter was telling him, and felt a rush of love that quickly turned into a wave of nausea at the thought that he might not always be there. She realized that over the past several months she'd grown dependent on Burgess, and one of the lessons she'd learned, living with a mother who'd been deserted while she was pregnant, was no man is dependable.

Burgess used the momentum of the twirling hat to send it flying across the room.

"No more hat," he said. "You better find a garage for the Cadillac, Dexter. Better do it tomorrow. After that, go buy a cheap used pickup." He lifted his hips off the sofa to dig in his pants pocket. From a gold money clip he unfolded twelve hundred-dollar bills and handed them to Dexter. "We got to lay low for a while."

Dexter took the money and he and Sherree left Burgess' place, Janine's place really, and went home to Sherree's apartment two red-brick buildings away. Dexter felt strangely let down after all the high drama of the day. Burgess didn't seem to hold any grudge against him and was still going to let him drive, but he would be driving a pickup truck instead of the Cadillac. He saw the wisdom of this, but still, it was the consequence of his inability to pass out in the plastic bag as many times as it took before the cops believed he knew nothing.

"I just couldn't take that plastic bag no more," he said to Sherree. "Burgess got to know that."

Sherree was sitting at her dressing table wearing a white chiffon negligee she had danced in back when she worked at the strip joint. The way Dexter was talking annoyed her. If it was at all possible, she was going to turn him into something other than an ass-kisser. "You don't worry 'bout nothin 'cept savin your own skin," she said to him sharply and struck herself on the forehead, chin, left cheek, right cheek, unconsciously using the sign of the cross to leave large dabs of nightcream on her face.

Sherree was something of an expert on the theory of saving your own skin; she was a survivor. The only home she'd ever known was the Convent. She and her two brothers were children of an arthritic mother and alcoholic father. They were victims of terrible poverty. For weeks at a time they would have nothing to eat but instant oatmeal. A pot of red beans on the stove was festive, made it seem like a holiday. The younger brother was frail and did not survive this meager diet. One winter he succumbed to the flu.

Sherree's father was next to go. He died in a barroom brawl, hitting his head on a table and never regaining consciousness. Sherree dropped out of school to take care of her mother. When her mother died, Sherree was sure she'd died of grief, mourning the death of her eldest son, who'd become a crack peddler by the time he was fifteen and was dead by the time he was seventeen, murdered, it was assumed during a dope deal.

Alone in the world but feeling lucky to have a roof over her head, Sherree decided it was time to make something out of her life, to be somebody. She wanted to seek gainful employment, but early on she realized that not being able to read beyond about a fourth-grade level was going to cause her some problems. She thought of going back to school and looked into literacy programs, but she needed to eat and pay her rent quicker than she needed to be literate.

More than anything else in the world, Sherree loved to dance. She decided she was going to be a dancer in one of the nightclubs downtown. She got a routine together that involved a lot of swishing chiffon and high kicks, but she knew that the object of the dance in these clubs was to strip down to a G-string and pasties. She didn't like the idea of this at all. In her own eyes her body was not the ideal of a stripper's body. Her chest caved in and her breasts tended to want to point toward each other. In clothes this made her appear to have some cleavage, but there would be no cleavage with nothing on but pasties. If the ideal breast was likened to a large grapefruit, then she would have to liken hers to small ice cream cones. She took the problem in hand—almost literally.

Without ever having heard of Gypsy Rose Lee, Sherree decided that she would become known as the most modest stripper in the city of New Orleans. Using nothing but a pair of scissors, a needle and thread, and the cheapest material she could find, Sherree made herself a white satin body suit with nylon cutouts that came up over her breasts in the shape of hands. She cut the legs of the suit at the sides to her waist, and as an afterthought added a third, smaller hand with its middle three fingers lost under the curve in between her legs. All in all, a modest little body suit, over which she wore a frilly, virginal negligee of white chiffon.

Sherree was a hit. She became known as the Hands-On Girl; she was modest but provocative, always drawing a decent crowd. Life was a ball for a while, until she got pregnant, got laid off, drew unemployment, then had to go on welfare.

Sherree's baby girl, Lucilla, was only a few months old when Burgess moved into the Convent to live with Sherree's lifelong friend Janine. He was a rich man come to live among the poor people, using his money to buy medicine and a playground for the kids, repairing the Convent buildings when the city wouldn't do it, installing smoke alarms when the city said it couldn't afford to, paying Sherree to run the day-care center, paying Dexter to run for him. And she was learning to read too, at the literacy center Burgess got the nuns from St. Stephen's to start right there in the Convent.

Burgess was a hero to the people in the Convent; he was like Robin Hood to them. So when Sherree, annoyed, suggested to Dexter that he worry about saving his own skin, she was also smart enough to realize that this meant saving Burgess' skin as well.

The next morning she and Dexter both began some serious networking. She got Dexter up early so he could talk to as many men in the Convent as possible before he went off to work. From the day-care center, she passed the message on to all the women who dropped off their children. By the following afternoon, almost everyone in the Convent was wearing a black hat, women as well as men.

Sherree had all the kids out in the yard teaching them a new dance routine when she heard a series of coded whistles, a warning to Burgess and his men that strangers were in the Convent. Burgess wasn't around and the whistle codes were not the ones used for the police, so Sherree was more curious than scared. She kept on dancing, counting out loud to keep the kids moving in time to the music coming out of the boom box next to them on the lawn. Most of the tenants in sight were heading indoors. Sherree looked back toward Convent Street and saw TV trucks parked at the curb. People with cameras and microphones streamed into the Convent yard. Heading the pack was an extremely good-looking brown woman, full straight hair, aquiline nose, thin lips, dressed in a bright blue dress, black patent high heels, and a lot of chunky gold jewelry. The woman came straight for Sherree, undoubtedly attracted by her crimson leotard and tights and the large black straw hat she was wearing. Sherree turned off the box and told the kids to sit down in the grass and be good for the TV cameras.

The woman introduced herself as a reporter for one of the local TV stations. Sherree recognized her but didn't want to say so. She put one hand on her hip and looked hard at the woman, at her two-inch-wide gold necklace, the matching bracelet on the wrist of the hand holding the microphone, earrings the size of silver dollars. The woman asked Sherree a couple of preliminary questions: did she live in the Convent and, laughing, were all these kids hers, not a laughing matter as far as Sherree was concerned.

Two more reporters, both black because it wasn't safe to send whites into the Convent, men from other local stations, put their microphones up close to Sherree as she explained that she babysat with the children while their mothers went to work, that was how she made her living. She was careful not to use the words *day-care center*, since the center was not officially certified by the city. As she spoke, Lucilla ran up and clutched one of her legs. Sherree put her hand on top of the child's head and told the reporters how, prior to her daughter's birth, she'd been a professional dancer.

One of the male reporters asked Sherree if she wasn't afraid in the Convent since the cop had been killed.

"There ain nothin to be afraid of 'cept the cops themselves," Sherree said, getting belligerent. "They come in here and beat up our men. Two days ago they come in and take my boyfriend downtown for questionin. You wanna know how they question people from the Convent these days?" she asked them, pushing her face up closer to them so they had to back off with their microphones. "They put plastic bags over their heads first."

By this time black-hatted tenants were back in the yard, out on the porches, and up on the balconies, watching.

"What were the police questioning your boyfriend about?" the other male reporter asked.

"Whatever they felt like," Sherree said.

The well-dressed woman reporter said to her, "Rumor has it that one of the biggest drug traffickers in this part of the country is hiding out here, in the Convent."

"Girl," Sherree said, her hand on her hip, "a bishop could hide out in this here Convent and no one'd know 'bout it, not even the people that live here."

On the news that night, Burgess, though still anonymous, became known as the Bishop of Convent Street.

10

Janine and Burgess sat on the red plush sofa. They were waiting for the evening news broadcast. Sherree told them to be sure and watch, she'd been pretty good in front of all those cameras.

Janine waited, expectant, excited, her best friend was going to be on TV, telling everybody in the city how the police put a plastic bag over Dexter's head to make him talk. Let everybody know how bad the cops could be, let them know the way it was in the Convent these days: the police didn't protect the tenants, the tenants needed protection against the brutality of the police.

After the news Burgess would feel better. The past couple of days he'd been tense, Janine could feel his edginess, making her edgy too, though she was afraid to show it for fear of getting him angry. As quickly as he'd come, he could go away that fast. He stayed away from the Convent during the day, coming home after five o'clock as if he had a regular job. He didn't say anything to her, but she knew he was busy keeping out of sight.

She was dressed up for him this evening, the black dress with the purple roses on it and the peplum he liked to put his hands under, run them over her hips, down her sleek thighs. He asked her why she was all decked out, her high-heeled shoes on, her hair done, her makeup just so. Not yet, she said, she wouldn't tell him yet. She was picking her time. After the news, when he felt better. Then maybe they could go out to the Solar Club, get something to eat, do a little dancing. Celebrate.

There it was on the screen in front of them, the Convent. There was the rehab center, the vegetable garden, over there the kids' playground, a woman's smooth but businesslike voice telling about the cop killing, the fear in the Convent, how this black community was pulling together to improve the project and their way of life. Telling too about the housing authority's financial problems, the mayor's proposal to raze the project, asking the question everybody was going to want to know the answer to: If the city isn't paying for all this, then who is?

Janine sat forward. Now here was Sherree, looking good in her red dancing outfit, that big black hat, one hip thrust forward, talking to the reporters as if she did it every day. No question about it, a natural-born entertainer. That's right, girl, you tell them.

Now some pictures of the tenants all grouped around, wearing their black hats: Sherree so proud of herself earlier, telling Janine her foxy idea. And now the woman reporter putting the cap on her story, a memorable little twist, making a mystery out of it: So where is all the money coming from? And who is the Bishop of Convent Street?

Burgess hit the off button and fell back on the sofa. "They know for sure I'm here now."

"The Bishop of Convent Street?" Janine said. "Come on, that's just some wiseass reporter making her story."

"That's not what I mean. It's the hats, all those hats, everybody wearin a black hat."

A few seconds lapsed before Janine got it, then the blood left her face. If she hadn't been sitting down, her legs would have gone out from under her, the shock of realizing that Sherree, with all good intention, had told the cops exactly what they wanted to know, what they had not found out for sure from Dexter even though they put a plastic bag over his head.

She couldn't speak, her tongue was like a slab of hide with a thick coat of fur on it. That feeling of dread she'd had the other day when Dexter was talking about Burgess' hat, it was back. And with it came the voice of her mother: No man is dependable, you remember that, especially after he goes and knocks you up and makes sure you got no way out.

No way out. She felt as if she were going to vomit, vomit up those words, vomit up the dread, vomit everything inside her. Because Janine had gone out and got herself a home pregnancy test and this morning it had showed up positive.

She swallowed hard, swallowed it all down. "You got to hide."

You got to hide. Hide as if there would ever be a time that he could stop hiding. Hide as if there were life after hiding. Hide as if his future depended on it. But there was the catch. He was famous now. People who were famous were supposed to have a fabulous future ahead of them, as long as they didn't go and mess it up themselves. It didn't work that way for Burgess; his future diminished in direct proportion to his fame.

Janine was panicking, pulling at his arm, saying, "You got to hide," maybe dragging him out the door next, she was so scared.

He laughed. "I am hidin, remember?"

"Somewhere else."

"They ain no better place to hide," he told her, and was telling her not to be afraid, he'd be all right, they'd be all right, all the while thinking to himself no place was safe, no place would ever be safe again.

The next morning, two bodyguards dressed in workman's white overalls with him, Burgess went over to Thea's house to get the work on the parlor started. He took his time. He had tea with Delzora. He talked to Thea. She'd changed her mind, she wanted to paint, not paper. Was that a problem? No problem at all. He went back to scratch, how much paint would it take, how much would it cost, he'd get his two expert painters on it, the same two guys, it turned out, who were the expert paper hangers. He went out to look at the gazebo again. He had coffee with Thea. He was in no particular hurry to leave.

Because as long as he was at Thea Tamborella's house, he was safe.

11

Thea went with Bobby to a dinner party, a gathering of some old friends at the new-southern-style home of Lyle and Sandy Hindermann. By the end of the evening she was afraid to be alone in her own house.

Waiting for Bobby, she stood in the wrecked parlor surveying the work in progress for the third time that day but really wondering if she were dressed correctly in her basic black dress, pearls, and low-heeled pumps. She wondered if it would be like high-school days when no matter how good she thought she looked before going out, the minute she saw a girl like Sandy she would feel she was dressed all wrong and it was hopeless that she would ever get it right. She could never be like those girls, the golden girls, with the right looks, the right backgrounds, the right credentials, and all the right moves, the kind of one-foot-directly-in-front-of-the-other walk that made them look so sexy and made her look punch drunk when she tried it in front of her bedroom mirror.

She told herself that was all high-school nonsense, but as she and Bobby stood on the portico of the Hindermanns' plantation-like house, the curtains open so that the windows were tantalizing showcases for the tempting life inside, Thea was nervous, her fingers floating on the slick of sweat they left on the black leather clutch she was carrying. It slipped to the brick portico floor. She picked it up quickly, before Bobby could, his movements so slow they might open the door and catch him at it. She tucked it securely under her arm.

The party was for Thea, to welcome her back to town. She was flattered, but besides being nervous and uncomfortable, she was also surprised. The old friends coming to the party were not her old friends: the only one she could remember from their high-school class was Mona Dupre, Sandy's old friend. For that matter, her own friendship with Sandy couldn't qualify as an old friendship, hardly as any friendship at all. Lyle and Sandy and Bobby and Thea had made a foursome back in high school, but that was because Lyle and Bobby were best friends and so they doubledated nearly every weekend. Sandy had been very nice to Thea on those weekends, even making a confidante of her sometimes, but around school she remained aloof, as if a friendship with Thea might lower her social status. Which Thea thought it probably would, so she didn't hold too large a grudge against Sandy.

Sandy opened the door and held her hands out to Thea, then embraced her warmly. Thea was relieved—her clothes were okay. In fact, she and Sandy were dressed so much alike, both in basic black and pearls, that it was nearly distasteful. Lyle came up behind Sandy, echoing her words of welcome—it had been way too long; glad they were neighbors again—as if he could think of nothing to say himself, leaning forward, his head large and bullet-shaped with his hair a closely cropped flattop, to kiss Thea.

They both still had their Waspy, sun-streaked blond good looks. The image of them driving around town in Lyle's father's baby-blue Cadillac convertible was imprinted on Thea's brain forever: Sandy's hair flying, bright and shimmering, she and Lyle waving, the king and queen on parade, important, flamboyant, their smiles a quick gleam shrinking to self-satisfaction.

But now there was something off-key about them, something strange about their eyes, the way Lyle looked at Thea directly when he kissed her yet seemed to be looking inward, the way he wouldn't look at Sandy at all, yet her eyes searched constantly when they were on him.

The eyes. Always she was aware of eyes, a habit left over from long ago when everyone would look at her and say such nice, warm, sympathetic things, but their eyes would not be warm. They would be curious, watchful, keeping their distance all the while they were saying the right things, being so very nice. People were only nice like that if something was wrong with you, if you were crippled or deformed. If your parents had been shot down in their grocery store. Then they became curious: what had it done to you, where were you crippled, how were you deformed?

She looked for their watchful curious eyes. Maybe they would want to know how rich she was and what the money had done to her, was she less crippled, less deformed? Actually, she wondered herself, but she hadn't had it long enough to know.

But their eyes reserved those kinds of looks for something else now, something that was wrong with their own lives, something they looked for deep down in themselves and each other, looking hard for it but not seeing it.

Two small light-haired children, a boy and a girl, came speeding down the stairs, their baby-sitter, an older black woman, running hard after them. They were introduced to Thea and sent off to bed. Then, while Bobby went off to make drinks, Lyle and Sandy showed Thea around as they waited for the other dinner guests to arrive.

The house was a mix of Old South splendor and contemporary showcase—the kind of place magazines call "fabulous"—and it gave them obvious pleasure to exhibit it to Thea. They pointed out the arched leaded windows from a church that had been demolished, the paneled wainscoting—doors, actually, from the old rectory—everything softly glowing under the recessed lighting in the ceilings or spectacularly lit by glass halogen fixtures on the walls. Thea's mother would have called them "house proud," as she had called Aunt Althea, but labels like that don't get attached to confident and beautiful wealthy people who live in magnificently, artistically, redone showplaces.

Thea thought about the way Lyle and Sandy had been in high school, a couple ever since she had known them, but not a couple she had perceived as being in love, or romantic, or caught up in any sort of passion. Instead they were more of a romantic ideal, something quite different from flesh and blood that heated up and pulsated and desired. They didn't touch each other affectionately, not even the way she and Bobby touched each other, friendly, familiar; instead, they huddled together whispering, their eyes darting. Conspirators.

As they gave her their well-practiced tour, Thea realized that their romance had been based on the recognition of their mutual ambition; their passion had been for acquisition, for social power. Lyle's position with the Cotton National Bank was a symbol of their standing in the community, as were the dinner guests they expected, all of whom regularly lit the society columns. And their house was the symbol of their ambition, a true reflection of their old southern family backgrounds and their modern acquisitional ways.

It was all as Thea would have expected, with one exception: on the way over to their house that night Bobby had told Thea that Lyle was banker by day, crimestopper by night, a reserve policeman taking an action-packed Saturday night off to entertain her. Bobby said that Lyle patrolled the neighborhood and had a regular beat as well, answering calls—murders, rapes, robberies—the way any cop would.

And was that, Thea wondered as she stood in the backyard, the final stop on the tour, gazing down into the black-tiled swimming pool, a black lagoon against a backdrop of spotlighted tropical foliage and a gurgling fountain, was that a symbol of whatever was off-key with these two people?

The long dining table was draped with a bone-white linen cloth. Tall, tapered yellow candles, two feet long at least, burned on either side of a large bowl spilling over with yellow daisies and black-eyed susans. The twelve plates, edged with navy blue and gold filigree, held tiny glazed quails from one of Lyle's hunts, wild rice, and a mix of colorful vegetables. Over drinks before dinner Thea had been the center of attention, everyone wanting to know about her life in Massachusetts, and she had surprised herself by saying that living in Amherst had been an interesting interruption. Now, during this reprieve at the dinner table, listening to their scattered conversations about people she didn't know, Thea wondered what exactly she'd meant by that. During the last few months in Amherst she had thought about going to school, getting a degree, though she didn't know in what—something that could eventually release her from her boring, dead-end job—and that thought had followed her to New Orleans. It wouldn't have to be anything practical now; perhaps she could become an expert on the works of Camus and the existentialists, study the meaning of being, or go straight to the cutting edge and study essentialism, write a dissertation on the meaning of meaning, become Dr. Tamborella. She drifted back to reality: the fact that her education had been broken off, although perhaps part of what she meant by an interesting interruption, was not all of it. It would take some reflection.

She found she was staring into the reflection in the dining room's wall of uncurtained French doors. It prevented her from seeing into the yard. She could see only back into the room, the candlelight and the people at the table, the darkness outside turning the glass into a smoky mirror. The effect was eerie, momentarily unsettling, as if they all had become ghosts, even with their voices ringing off the hardwood floors, the high curved ceiling, the wall of glass doors. It seemed that the moment she decided to tune in to the echoey din, someone's name reverberating, it stopped. Now a thick silence pressed against her eardrums, a large silence, everything larger than life in a room like this.

They were all looking at her. Thea swallowed a half-chewed piece of quail breast and felt it stick mid-esophagus.

"He was killed," Lyle said to her, "about three months ago, coming home from work. They shot him point-blank in the back of the head, execution-style. He was the second one in a month they killed like that."

Was this someone she had known? She didn't think so; the name had not triggered any memory. She looked across the table at Bobby, but he offered no help, fairly well plastered, his eyes glowing redly at her, a slight smile parting his lips. The silver fork seemed awfully heavy in her hand.

Lyle's eyes were on Thea, holding her. She was dimly thinking they were so small, their brown reminding her of old dull varnish. He had always been on the serious side, but in the candlelight Thea saw seriousness permanently etched in the flesh around his mouth, across his forehead, a deep cut between the eyebrows, down to the bridge of his nose.

"Most of us are carrying guns now," he said. "Women too."

Mona Dupre said, "I've got mine," her voice sounding oddly chirpy, only adding to the weight in the room. "Lyle taught me how to shoot."

Thea looked at Mona, glad for the release from Lyle, her eyes automatically riveting to Mona's hands, a large opal circled by diamonds on the right hand, a huge emerald-cut diamond flanked by sapphire ring guards on the left. A gun in those hands . . . guns in the midst of all their culture and high society and proper behavior. Imagine those uptown ladies shooting to kill, their legs spread as far as their fashionable clothes would allow, in a policeman's crouch as taught by Lyle, their jewel-bedecked hands clutching their guns . . .

"I carry two," Lyle said. He was talking to her again, forcing her eyes back. But everyone was watching him as he reached behind him, underneath his jacket, and placed a gun on the white tablecloth next to the bowl of yellow flowers, at the base of a silver candlestick. The candlelight reflected faintly, as if it were dying, in the gun's oily blue-black surface. His eyes never wavering from Thea's face, Lyle leaned down and pulled a second, smaller gun from an ankle holster. He let it sit in the palm of his hand, showing her how it fitted, how it could be hidden, before he placed it next to the larger weapon.

Thea felt trapped by his stare. She forced her eyes down, to the quail, their pitiful little legs sticking up into the air, no longer delicacies, just dead.

"I don't think there's anyone sitting at this table who doesn't know someone, more than one person, who's been held up at gunpoint, if not killed." Thea raised her head. Lyle nodded at the guns. "We have to protect ourselves, what we own. You might want to think about getting a gun too, Thea."

Lyle's eyes had become brighter, and Thea thought she could see rage smoldering behind them, giving them the only light they contained; she thought she knew what he was trying to tell her about the anger they all felt, and about the fear, the hate, and the helplessness. He was saying to her, It's been done to us too, now we understand, now we know what it's like to be a victim, to be connected to death by violence.

But there was something they did not understand, something they had not experienced directly, something that had come after she was worn out with anger, fear, hate, and helplessness. It was the sense of confusion that lingered. First there had been the confusion of coming home and finding the grocery store full of police, of not being allowed inside. Then the confusion of displacement, a new home, a new school, people behaving strangely toward her, and later the confusion of her feelings for her aunt. But there was this other confusion, dense and full of questions that refused to make themselves clear, a confusion from which there had been no release, not now, perhaps not ever.

Lyle went on, "They're all armed, so we have to be armed too."

"They've declared war on us," Mona said belligerently.

Thea was beginning to understand that what they mostly empathized with was hate. But she did not hate anymore. As for fear, her fear had never been the same as theirs was now. Her fear had been about the loss of her parents, their love and their guidance, their special concern for her, unselfish concern, not at all like Aunt

Althea's kind of concern; her fear was not fear of all black people. And her helplessness and anger were not their helplessness and anger: she had been helpless in having no one to turn to for other needs besides food, shelter, clothing—the need to talk to someone, to ask questions of someone trustworthy, of someone who knew the answers, of someone who could tell her what had gone wrong; she had been angry at her aunt for not being that someone.

Instead, that someone had been Delzora. She hadn't had all the answers, but she told Thea it was all right to be angry. She couldn't tell her what had gone wrong, but she helped her see it was wrong to hate.

Thea met Lyle's relentless eyes. "You know, my father wanted to protect his family and what he owned too. You may not remember, but the gun he kept in the store was gone afterwards, and the police believed he and my mother were shot with it." It was the first time she'd spoken of the murder with any of them other than Bobby. But everyone at the table, even Bobby, seemed frozen with some kind of prurient anticipation.

Lyle said, as if trying to convince her, "They could have held a gun on your mother and gotten it away from him."

"Yes," she said, "they could have, it could have happened any number of ways. If you'd known my father and his Italian temper, you might think he'd have gotten them first." There were many questions and she'd asked all the ones she knew how to ask, but it was the answers to the ones she didn't know how to ask that she wanted, not Lyle's answers.

Sandy slid gracefully into the tension at the table. "Oh, I don't think we should talk about all this now. Thea will think she should go back to Massachusetts, and we want her to stay."

The other women guided the conversation into safer waters and Lyle slipped the guns back out of sight into the holsters hidden on his body.

Later, when Thea went to the kitchen to help Sandy serve dessert, Sandy said, "Listen, I'm really sorry about all that—Lyle . . ." She hesitated as if she were at a loss for words, a first in Thea's recollection.

"It's okay," Thea said.

But Sandy shook her head, rather violently, the golden hair flying away from her neck. "No, no, it's not okay." Her eyes were too bright. She lifted a hand, her mouth opening then closing, her hand falling. She blinked rapidly three or four times and said, "He's gone mad on law and order."

After the party Lyle walked Thea and Bobby to the car with his big oily blue gun drawn and ready. He clapped Bobby on the back and held the door for Thea, his eyes roaming continuously.

Thea stood at the side of the car. She laughed nervously. "This seems awfully dramatic, Lyle."

His eyes came to rest on her. "It's sad, isn't it, that this is what it's come to. I don't mean to scare you, but the truth is we just can't be too careful anymore." He kissed her cheek and she got into the car. "Well, this was fun," he said jovially, his roving eyes continuing their search beyond the car. "We'll do it again soon." He punched the lock down with his free hand and closed the door.

12

After the Hindermanns' dinner party, Thea asked Bobby to take her straight home. Bobby, even in his inebriated state, could see she was upset.

"Don't pay any attention to Lyle," he said as they stood just inside her front door. "He thinks he's Supercop disguised as a mild-mannered banker." His speech was slower than usual and a bit slurred.

Thea smiled faintly. Encouraged, Bobby bent toward her. He almost lost his balance and took a short step forward as he encircled her in his arms, pulling her in. Thea put her arms in between them, her hands against his chest. "I know he means well," she said, "but it bothers me when someone thinks he has all the answers, that's all."

"He's pretty arrogant about it." Bobby held her more tightly, forcing her arms around him, his lips in her hair, now grazing her face as he said, "I only have questions, like are you going to ask me to come in for a while?"

The smell of bourbon on his breath spread in the air, and Thea turned her head away. She put her arms in between them again and with a slight pressure on his chest pushed him from her. His arms fell away. "I'm tired, Bobby. This wasn't easy for me tonight—parties like that have never been very easy for me, you know that."

"We don't have to go to any more if you don't want to."

She frowned. That wasn't the point. Bobby was too drunk to understand anything except what he wanted. Suddenly all *she* wanted was to be alone. "I need to go," she said.

Bobby understood that he had not pleased her. He kissed her cheek. "Sleep well," he said. With his hand on the door knob, he paused, looking at her, but she was already turning toward the stairs. He let himself out.

She went straight up to the shower. She let the water beat first on her face then on her back. She slicked a fragrant bath oil over her arms, her legs, over and around her breasts, up her neck, sliding across her shoulders. But she was still anxious—jittery, she now realized. Spooked. She wrapped herself up in a big terry-cloth robe and left wet footprints down the hallway to her room.

It was the same room Aunt Althea had given her when she came to live there, a large room furnished with the same heavy, dark mahogany furniture, a high four-poster bed, a dresser and dressing table. Over the dressing table was a large mirror. Thea sat in front of it and began to comb out her hair. Behind her, reflected in the mirror, was a large round curio cabinet displaying a collection of porcelain and bisque dolls.

Thea had never liked the dolls. The collection was Aunt Althea's idea; she thought all young girls should have a collection of some kind. Thea had said she wanted to collect books, but Aunt Althea said, no, she meant a *real* collection, and decided upon the dolls. It was obviously a collection she herself had always wanted.

For a while, with annoying regularity, Aunt Althea had given Thea a doll, the Daughter of the American Revolution doll, the Pierrot doll, the Scarlett O'Hara doll, Dorothy from *The Wizard of Oz*. And there was the Rapunzel doll with her hair to its tiny white-shoed feet.

Thea did not like any of the dolls very much. They weren't dolls she could play with; their cold hard faces were too fragile, their complicated clothes were made for show, not for dressing and undressing. She was not attracted to any of them, but she had no idea why the Rapunzel doll in particular was so creepy to her.

When she came to live with Aunt Althea she took the Rapunzel doll off the mantelpiece in the room designated as hers and hid it in a dresser drawer, covered by soft, powder-puff sweaters with pearl buttons and other sweet schoolgirl clothes she never would have picked for herself, clothes picked for her by her aunt. Aunt Althea found the doll within days, and that's when Thea realized she would have no privacy in the house whatsoever. Yet she didn't protest her lack of privacy, just as she didn't protest when the round curio cabinet was filled with the dolls and placed next to her bed. To have protested would have let her in for one of Aunt

Althea's freezes: no direct communication, no direct looks, an intense and thorough displeasure, disapproval, and disliking.

Thea stopped combing her hair when she caught the reflection of the Rapunzel doll's lifeless yet curiously alert blue eyes in the mirror. They were aimed straight at her, too bright in that white death-mask vitreous face. Thea stared at the eerily white face. It wasn't staring at the face that scared her, but staring at it jelled the inchoate jittery feeling that had begun at the Hindermanns'. And fear of being alone in the house set in.

She lay in bed in the dark, wide awake for a long time. She tried to talk herself out of being afraid by telling herself it was time to get rid of things in the house she didn't like and didn't want. She would give the dolls away, and when Burgess' men were finished in the parlor, she would have them start in Aunt Althea's bedroom, with its window-seat alcove, huge closet, and a bathroom right off a large dressing room. She would make the room over for herself and put in a tub with a Jacuzzi. But thoughts of a Jacuzzi and modern decor and charitable donations couldn't shake her fear or drown out the creaks and groans of the old house. She knew Bobby had wanted to spend the night with her, and she almost wished she had let him. She thought of him driving home with all that bourbon in him and began to worry. Her worry was a relief from the fear for a while and was easier to deal with, since, after all, Bobby had only a few blocks of familiar lamp-lit empty streets to negotiate to get home. Where he would have been for some time now.

Bobby stayed at Thea's front door, his cheek pressed against the tiny squares of beveled glass, watching through one as Thea floated up the wide staircase, her fingers dragging lightly along the varnished wood banister. For a moment he felt those long, short-nailed fingers glide over the small of his back. The hair on his nape rose slightly, his dying erection revived briefly, until she pulled her foot up the last visible step.

He knew he'd turned her off, and he knew it was because he'd had too much to drink. Christ, he hoped it was only because he'd had too much to drink. He wanted to ring the doorbell, make her come back so he could ask her was that it, too much bourbon? He'd admit he'd had too much; he'd tell her he'd stop.

But even in his booze-befuddled state he knew it was better not to push it tonight. She was upset: that damn Lyle and his guns. Bobby was beginning to wonder if Lyle was ever going to talk about anything else, anything besides crime and people getting robbed and niggers in his backyard and shooting to kill. Thea had said she was sick of the cold weather up north; he didn't want her to start thinking that it might be cold but at least it was safe.

He stumbled on the steps, his own shadow blocking the soft light from the gas lamps on either side of the leaded-glass doors, the large oak tree in front of the house making a pattern of dark lace on the brick walk. He went through the low iron gateway and closed the gate carefully behind him. He walked to his car, patting his pockets, getting out his keys, thinking he'd come to see her tomorrow, tell her he wasn't going to drink so much any more, make her believe him. He tripped on the sidewalk where it was cracked from the roots of the old oak pushing up, persistent, impervious, then he tripped again on the thick, gnarled roots themselves, like small tree trunks half buried in the earth. He fumbled with first one key then another at the door of the old Lincoln. Fantasies about the time he would stay with Thea all night rolled pleasantly before his mind's eye, and he could feel her straight smooth hair like inky silk in his hands, he could see her breasts flatten as she reclined, her back arch as he touched her, her small foot on his thigh, and he was starting to get hard again when he thought he heard something, not quite behind him, on the other side of the oak, but before he could turn around to see, Bobby felt a crushing weight on his head, his fantasies went black, and he went down.

Thea slept for a while, then woke from a dream she forgot instantly. She lay rigid, the way people do when they wake in the middle of the night, listening. Had that been a whisper outside her door, was that thud a footstep on the stairway? No, no, it was only her own blood rushing in her ears, the thud of her own heartbeat.

Their fear had spread like wildfire to her stale dread of being alone. One night with them and her fear was like theirs, no longer a fear of being alone in the world, a fear whose character had changed over the years, melting down into sadness; now her aloneness was compounded by a fear of what was outside and what might get inside. And how could she control that? How could

Bobby control that if he were here with her? Ah, yes, well, that was where Lyle's guns came in.

Thea tossed back the covers and moved her feet up and down on Delzora's starched sheets, making noise, daring whatever was there, if it was there, to show itself.

Gradually the fear subsided. She tried to imagine Bobby asleep in this room with her, this little girl's room with the cabinet full of dolls, spending the night with him, how sex with him would be. She wondered if he would start making demands on her, after all these years. Maybe that's what had been the matter, no demands, he'd been too easy. She wanted someone to make demands, but she couldn't make Bobby into that someone. She thought about the letter she'd written to Michael a few days ago with a list of the belongings she wanted him to send her. He would have gotten it by now, but he had not called. She wondered if she was wanting him to call and ask her to come back. She tried to imagine him on the phone, begging her, but she couldn't make that fantasy work either.

She sat up in bed, turning to hang her legs over the side, dangling them reluctantly at first, then swinging them, another dare, finally dropping the few inches to the floor. Old childhood fears—silly, but she couldn't help it. She put the terry robe on in the dark, the fragrance of the bath oil still so strong on it that someone could find her by smell alone. She went out into the hallway, heading for the bathroom, but at the last minute she passed it by to go to the second-story front porch, a small curved screened porch just under the third-floor gable. She unlocked the door to it. The door was swollen with dampness and she had to tug on it to get it open. She pulled at it in something of a panic, hating having her back turned to the hallway, wanting out of the house yet knowing it was absurd to think she would feel safer on the porch.

The door grated open. Thea rushed out onto the porch, dragging the door closed behind her, the porch floor gritty beneath her bare feet. The limbs of the oak almost touched the house. She looked through the dirty screen, the dense leafy tree limbs, and she started. Why was Bobby's car still here? She dropped to her knees, her hands and forehead and the bridge of her nose pressed against the screen, and she saw him on the ground at the base of the tree, his body inert, twisted, uncomfortable, and she jumped up, struggled with the door, cursing it, crying, then running, almost slipping on the stairs, almost tripping herself on the robe but never slowing down, never thinking what might be behind her or what might be lurking outside, waiting. She flung open the front door and sped down the walk.

His face was turned toward her, his right cheek pressed into the rough tree roots. She scraped her ankle trying to get around him and saw the blood on the crown of his head. But she could see also that his chest was rising and falling.

Once she saw that Bobby was alive, Thea ran back into the house. Maybe it was because the number was written on a pad next to the telephone, maybe it was because calling the police emergency number seemed so impersonal, maybe because he was Bobby's best friend—whatever the reason, like a preprogrammed automaton, Thea called Lyle Hindermann.

13

The first time Bobby's father said he wanted to be cremated, he and Bobby were sitting in a duck blind out in the Louisiana marshland about eighty miles south of New Orleans.

It was before dawn, freezing cold, and Bobby had the worst hangover of his life. On the way out to the blind he had thrown up over the side of the pirogue, and now he was huddling sick and weak within the camouflaging brown roseaux surrounding the blind. He felt nauseated from the miasma created by a kerosene-soaked roll of toilet paper slowly burning in an old coffee can. He'd rather be cold than smell it, but he knew that when the toilet paper burned out, the kerosene fumes would be replaced by the stink of the decaying marsh, a swampy brew that made the mud a reeking, gooey mess. His and his father's clothes were already smeared with it. He was telling himself that he was never going to drink again and he was never going duck hunting again, when his father handed him what was left of the bourbon from the night before and told Bobby he wanted to be cremated. After that, the ducks were flying and Bobby was on his feet, taking aim, backing up his father's missed shots, forgetting about everything except the sight of those ducks falling out of the sky.

The next time, they were out in the Gulf of Mexico fishing for snapper. The sun was so bright it was a blinding buttery smear on a baby-blue ceiling. The heat had Bobby pinned to his swivel chair in a state of pleasurable lethargy that he broke every now and then to take a cooling sip of beer or to reach over into the ice chest and grab a couple more for himself and his dad. They sat together in silence, neither of them having much to say, both of them comfortable with that. Nothing on their minds anyway, or so Bobby thought, except knocking back a case of beer and catching a few fish.

When his father spoke, he picked the conversation up where he'd left it in the duck blind. "After they cremate me, put my ashes in a paper bag and bring them out here, to the blue water."

Until that moment, Bobby had forgotten his father's talking about cremation in the duck blind. "Imagine Mother's reaction when she sees me putting your ashes in a paper bag," he said. His father dismissed that by shrugging one shoulder then tilting his head back and draining off the end of a beer. "Have you told her?" His father shook his head. "No, of course not. She'd have every Jesuit at Holy Name praying for you and trying to talk you out of it."

His father tossed the can overboard. "The hell with that. I don't want any wake gawkers or graveyard visitors. Gives me the creeps. They can say their prayers and sing their masses and then you bring me out to the fishes."

"All right, but whatever you want, Daddy, you better write it down."

"Just promise me, Bobby."

There were several such conversations, always out in the marsh or on the water, but a few years later Bobby could find no excuse for himself in his father's failure to either write down his wishes or tell his wife he preferred cremation to burial. Surely his father must have known that Bobby would never be able to override his mother.

Millie McKenzie Buchanan planned the funeral services for Robert Buchanan, Sr., with the same attention to detail that she had applied to parties for their group of uptown New Orleans socialites. She wrote a carefully worded newspaper story and included a picture taken ten years previously. She decided the casket should be closed and ordered nearly a thousand dollars worth of flowers to drape it. She arranged for the opening of the Buchanan family tomb in Metairie Cemetery and called the caterer. All the while Bobby protested that none of it was what his father wanted, that he wanted his ashes carried in a paper bag to the blue water.

"Oh, Bobby," his mother said, "you know your father just said morbid things like that when he was sick." *When he was sick* meant when he was drinking. Millie burst into tears.

"But he made me promise," Bobby said.

Millie didn't answer because she was psychosomatically hard of hearing. There were some things Bobby never could stand up to; one was Millie's tears, another was her deafness. This, however, was a situation worthy of raising one's voice.

"I said, he made me promise."

Millie sniffled and remained deaf.

"Mother, you know good and well you hear exactly what you want to hear." It felt good, accusing her.

She said pitifully, "Bobby, I just can't talk about this anymore."

"Mother, don't you understand, he made me promise. I want to do this for him."

He was quite familiar with the hard look she turned on him, a look of cold determination, something else in her trove of southern matriarchal responses, but he was a bit taken aback by her viciousness. "If you wanted to do something for your father, Bobby, you should have refused to help him drink himself into the grave, which is where he is going to go. I doubt seriously that you could find your way out to the blue water with him in a paper bag anyway."

Two days later, in a drizzle, Bobby stood under a canopy in the Metairie Cemetery, supporting his mother on his arm while his father's body was slid into the tomb, an ornate above-ground room with stained-glass windows on the east and west walls. He went back home and drank his way through six hours of friends and relatives comforting the family, eating tiny sandwiches, drinking, remembering, and suffering.

The following morning Bobby went out to the cemetery alone. He stood in front of the granite and marble vault and said, "Daddy, I told you to write it down."

Besides some guilt, Bobby's father left him with a piece of property, a once-beautiful Greek Revival house that was now cut up into five apartments. It was several blocks off Convent Street in a neighborhood that had been described at the time of purchase as marginal but had since gone all black. When Bobby's father bought it in the early eighties, at the tail end of the real-estate boom in New Orleans, he thought young professionals would move into the neighborhood eventually, fix up the houses, and triple the property values. At the time, renovation was the name of the game in uptown New Orleans, and Bobby's father wanted to cash in so he could replenish the family fortune, which was drying up along with the oil leases held by the Buchanans for three or four generations. What he hadn't counted on was the oil crunch. Property values stabilized, then they fell; nothing was moving. Tenants came and went. Later they came and stayed, bringing so many others with them that Robert Buchanan could never be sure how many people were living in one apartment at one time. Things began to happen to the building. All the outside shutters, the gutters, and a whole section of weatherboards were stolen. A toilet fell through the floor. Two plaster walls were demolished by machine-gun fire in one of the back apartments. Instead of replenishing the family fortune, the apartment house slowly drained more of it.

Late Sunday morning after being mugged outside Thea's house and spending the rest of the night in the hospital, Bobby drove up in front of the apartment house. The For Sale sign was face down in the square of muddy yard between the porch and the sidewalk. It didn't make any difference; the house wasn't salable anyway, too dilapidated, badly in need of a paint job, the wood rotting, but he got out of the car and went over to pick up the sign. When he bent down, the inside of his head pounded against his skull. He stood up, palm to forehead. He didn't know if his head was splitting because of the enormous hangover he had or because it had literally been split open by some blunt instrument, the butt of a gun maybe. He thought he remembered Lyle counting twelve stitches.

The door to the downstairs front apartment was ajar. Bobby pushed it open slowly. As he suspected, the apartment was empty— that is, if you didn't count all the rubble left in the middle of the living room floor. Once again he was out at least two months' rent. It occurred to him that he ought to take the For Sale sign down and put one up that said Free Apartments. And just let the place fall down. If he had the money, that's exactly what he'd do. Then when the city came after him, he'd hire a demolition company.

He stepped inside cautiously. You never could tell what you might find: bodies—starving, sleeping, murdered; rats hiding under the greasy chicken take-out bags; cockroaches, always, everywhere the roaches.

It was dark inside. Someone had tacked pieces of heavy cardboard over the windows. Bobby flicked the light switch but nothing happened. He looked up. The light fixture was gone. Wires twisted like worms out of the cracked plaster medallion of fruit and flowers at the center of the ceiling.

He skirted the trash and went into what had once been the dining room. Shit—the crystal chandelier, a nice piece with long prism crystals, was gone too. His mother had told him to take it down and store it. He'd told her he would. And once he'd told her he would, in his mind he had. He'd catch hell now. No. No he wouldn't. His mother would never have to know. One thing about her illness, her reign of terror—most of his life—when she kept tabs on everything he did or didn't do was over. Problem was, he kept catching himself trying to shirk blame for something or another. Maybe one day he'd get used to his new freedom.

In the dining room, against the inside wall, was a sleeping mat made from newspaper and an old blanket. Some poor bugger had made himself right at home. Too bad. No more freebies. He went into the kitchen, crossing some seriously spongy floorboards, doing his best to ignore the disgusting mess in it, to see if the back door was bolted. A couple of boards gave and he nearly fell through the floor. Cursing, he went to the front room and ripped a piece of cardboard away from one of the windows to lay across the hole. On his way out through the dining room, he picked up the blanket and newspapers, his nose twitching at the stale human smell they released once he disturbed them, and threw them out on the front porch. He locked the front door.

As Bobby was coming down the front steps, Lyle pulled up across the street from the apartment house. He was in uniform, and as he got out of his car, the sun glinted off his badge and off the gold-rimmed aviator sunglasses he always wore on the beat. Bobby could hear the belt and holster leather creak as Lyle crossed the street. There was something tough about the way that sounded. There was something tough about the way Lyle walked when he was in uniform, different from the way he walked in a three-piece suit.

"Had a hunch I might find you here," he said. He talked tough too.

Bobby sat down on the front steps. "Yeah, another tenant vamoosed in the night. Bilked me out of two months' rent."

"Lousy break." Lyle stretched one leg out to the steps and leaned on his knee. "How's the head?"

"It must be all right. I can still eat and go to the bathroom."

Lyle nodded; no laughing matter this. "Mess inside?" In uniform he talked in truncated sentences. Muy macho.

"No worse than usual. I'm putting up a few roaches and other life forms till I can get over here and get the place ready for the Cosbys."

Lyle's sense of humor had taken a fast car out of town. "Doing it yourself?"

"Got to, my man. No dinero, must trabajo. Comprendo?" Lyle's sunglasses showed no sign of enlightenment. "That means," Bobby said, "I can't hire anyone. I'm broke."

"I know what that means. That means you're going to be all by yourself in a goddamn war zone." Lyle straightened up, reached behind him, and pulled a gun from his waistband. He presented it to Bobby.

Bobby pushed it away. "Jesus, Lyle, pull out a gun in a neighborhood like this and you're likely to start the war."

"What do you mean? They already started it," Lyle said. "You're lucky to be alive today; don't push it. Here." He put the gun in Bobby's hand. "I'll start the paper work tomorrow."

"But I don't want it. You're talking about my luck, I'll probably shoot myself in the foot. Or worse—I'll never have children."

Lyle's answer to that was to tell Bobby he'd pick him up at six o'clock the following evening for target practice.

They both went to their cars, Bobby self-consciously holding the gun upside down by its barrel. Lyle started to drive off as Bobby reached over to put the gun in his glove compartment. Lyle slammed on his brakes and backed up level with Bobby's car. "And don't leave it in the car," he said. "You'll just end up arming another nigger."

14

An oxidized-red pickup truck with a bad muffler clattered to a stop in front of the brick walkway, and Dexter sprang from the driver's seat. Today he was wearing a pair of jeans with brass studs in a line down the side of each leg. Sometimes he wore black velour trousers, though his favorites were still the blue leather, but whatever pants he wore, tucked inside them was a fresh starched white shirt. In this way Dexter emulated Burgess, but with his own dandified, high-profile signature.

He rushed to the other side of the truck to help Delzora from the high seat. If he didn't hurry, the old woman would open the door herself and make motions as if she were going to try to climb out backwards, since her stubby bowed legs were too short to reach the street. But he always got to her before she actually started; she timed it so he would. She muttered under her breath as he helped her down. The way she talked under her breath like that so he couldn't hear her made Dexter nervous. The next minute she might be giving him the business about his clothes or about wasting time, or going on about honest jobs, talking as if he and Burgess didn't work at all. He watched her start up the walkway to the big house. Then he drove off with a sense of relief, a feeling that he'd gotten away unscathed.

Delzora's early morning routine varied a bit these days. She still went straight back to the utility room, where she took her wig off and set it on the shelf next to the laundry detergent. She changed into her white uniform, then put the wig back on, adjusting it in the small mirror above the toilet. There were too many people in the house now, too many visitors. It was one thing for Althea to see her nearly bald and what hair was left almost all white, but not these younger people who might think she was old as the hills, too old to do good work.

She barely got her tea on before the workers arrived. She wished they would hurry and get finished, they disturbed her quiet mornings when she read the newspaper, but just when she thought they were finally coming to the end, Thea found something else for them to do. What they did was create a lot of white dust for her to clean up. As far as she was concerned, the house was fine the way it was, just needed a little fixing up here and there, nothing like taking down all that beautiful gold wallpaper, those perfectly good velvet curtains, putting up shutters on the inside that looked as though they should go on the outside, painting the walls dull grays and bleak whites, barren colors. Delzora shook her head as she scrubbed out the kitchen sink. There was simply no accounting for people's taste.

Upstairs, Thea could hear the workers' soft talk and low laughter in counterpoint to the rhythm and blues coming from their cheap, tinny-sounding radio. Distant, their words had a hushed, mumbo-jumboish quality. Once she was downstairs it was pure New Orleans jive. One of them, Jared, liked to sing. He let out a long soul-suffering wail followed by some jazzy vocal acrobatics followed by Zora yelling at him to hush up, he was going to wake the dead. It made Thea smile. She liked all their sounds, they made the house feel alive. It had been deathly quiet when she'd lived here with Aunt Althea.

She went down to the kitchen, where Zora was putting on a pot of red beans. The morning with its slight chill, the smell of cooking, the male voices—Thea was suddenly thrust into the middle of her dream that she lived here with her family, her mother at the stove cooking, her father singing Italian arias in another part of the house. She was overcome with a feeling of warmth, of safety, tinged with the slightest bit of melancholy. The feeling stayed with her as she and Zora started their project for the day, packing boxes of romance novels and bric-a-brac from the den.

Before long Bobby stopped by, procrastinating on his way to the apartment house. He walked in without ringing the bell, since once the workers arrived the front door was kept unlocked because of so much coming and going. Bobby followed his nose, heading straight for the pot of beans, calling out to Thea. Thea came into the kitchen, Bobby kissed her, then he lifted the pot top and began stirring. Bobby loved Zora's cooking, and after a short morning at the apartment house, he always came back to Thea's for lunch.

Delzora came into the kitchen just as Bobby put the spoon to his mouth. "You get away from my beans this instant, Bobby Buchanan, do you hear?"

Bobby paid no attention to her but went on tasting the beans for a second time. "Dee-licious, Zora. What time should I be back for lunch?"

"You be here 'bout one o'clock, they be ready, but there ain't no sense tastin them now, they ain't been on long enough." She took the spoon out of his hand and put the top on the pot with a bang.

"What a tyrant," Bobby said.

"Damn nuisance," Delzora countered.

The two of them sometimes went at each other like the worst enemies, but Thea knew that Zora had always been quite fond of Bobby. She didn't laugh or smile much normally, but she did around Bobby.

Much more than she did around her own son.

Burgess came in, stopping first to talk to the men, joking with them. They were glad to see him. From the kitchen, Thea could hear them telling him what they needed, what problems they'd encountered, what was finished or nearly finished. Already Delzora seemed separated, sullen as she turned her back to them to clean some figurines from the den, though moments before she had been laughing and telling Bobby he was going to break his neck as he described himself working in the apartment, teetering on a high ladder to reach the ceiling and hang a new light fixture, hanging on to a piece of plaster fruit on the medallion to keep from falling.

Once Burgess came into the kitchen, Delzora was silent. Thea watched her. She was angry with Burgess, that much was clear. Thea tried to imagine what Burgess could have done to make her so angry for so long, for she had been angry with him ever since Thea had come back to town. She spoke to him only when necessary. She didn't try to avoid his eyes; on the contrary, she met them defiantly. Yet once Thea invited Burgess to sit at the table with her and Bobby, Delzora placed a cup of tea in front of him, along with cut lemons and a bowl of sugar. He thanked her politely, and just as politely she said, "You welcome," and lapsed again into her detached silence. She was cleaning the figurines quite meticulously even though Thea was going to pack them and put them up in the attic.

Bobby returned to complaining about the apartment house. He told Burgess how he almost fell through the floor, about the toilet that did. "But nothing," he said, "annoys me more than having a new paint job marred by machine-gun fire."

"Damn annoyin," Burgess agreed. "Where's your house?" Bobby told him and he said, "Where I come from, we call that a good neighborhood."

Bobby said, "Well, it's true I haven't been mugged there yet," and then with his characteristic flipness sprung the line he'd tried out on Lyle, about the Cosbys moving in as soon as he could get the place ready.

Thea's stomach went into a clench. Bobby's joke seemed out of place, even cruel. But Burgess slapped the tabletop and let go with his great baritone laugh.

Bobby was pleased. "A man with a sense of humor," he said and asked Burgess where he came from. When Burgess told him the Convent, Bobby said, "Well, hell, man, the Convent's looking better these days than that old rat-infested neighborhood where my house is."

Burgess looked behind him at Delzora. She didn't live very far from Bobby's apartment house. "You hear that, Mama?" But Delzora didn't answer him and didn't turn around to look at him either. So Burgess said to Bobby, "How 'bout I come over and look at your apartment house. I give you a good price on the work, save you a lot of trouble."

Bobby shook his head. "You come on over any time," he told Burgess. "I'd enjoy the company. But the only good price you could give me right now is free. And I'm the only person I know who works free." He got up and put his hand on Thea's neck, under her hair, as he passed behind her. "I'm off, Tee, but I'll be back. One o'clock, right, Zora?"

"That's right," Zora said, but later, when Burgess was leaving, she didn't tell him to come back for the beans. Maybe she didn't feel it was her place to do so, so Thea made the invitation herself.

But Burgess didn't come back for lunch. Instead, Lyle stopped by just before noon. He rang the bell, then opened the door, waiting on the threshold until Delzora came. Thea heard him ask for her and followed Zora into the foyer. She knew that Zora didn't like Lyle. When he was in the same room with her, her body posture changed. She became bent, meek, shrinking into invisibility. She wouldn't meet his eyes, wouldn't speak to him if he didn't speak first, which he didn't always, and then she only mumbled in answer.

Lyle was on his way to a business lunch. He'd been dropping in daily in the week since the attack on Bobby, sometimes on his lunch break, wearing his banker's suit, sometimes after hours, in his police uniform, checking on Thea and her house. He eyed the workmen warily. He wanted Thea to have a burglar-alarm system installed. He still wanted her to think about getting a gun. He wanted her to keep her doors locked at all times, monitor the coming and going of these untrustworthy black men. Every time he came over and found she had not heeded his advice, the lines of seriousness on his face were carved deeper by disapproval. Yet he doggedly and patiently repeated himself, telling her again today in his by-the-book monotone that she should have an alarm system put in as soon as possible.

"But with all this work going on . . ." she began her excuse for not complying.

"All the more reason," Lyle said.

They stood in the hall near the front door. Zora had returned to the kitchen, but the workers were only a room away, in the second parlor, which was going to become a library. Thea did not want them to hear Lyle, who had not bothered to lower his voice. She took him out to the front porch.

"But Lyle, I know these people. Burgess is Delzora's son. These men work for him; he trusts them. I," she put one hand on her chest for emphasis, "trust them."

With his stony policeman's eyes he said, "Drop a twenty under your hall table. See how long it stays there."

Thea did not like Lyle's shoot-now-ask-questions-later attitude toward black people, yet she saw that in his self-appointed role of protector he allowed no room for error because of misplaced sympathy, compassion, or trust. He took no chances. The part of her that was afraid, that came close to panic when she thought Bobby could have been killed out in front of her house, appreciated Lyle's vigilance, as did her neighbors, people she felt a growing sense of community toward, but Zora, Burgess, the workers, these were people she knew and liked.

His sincerity aside, Lyle still made Thea uncomfortable when he was around, especially if Bobby wasn't there, and it was always with relief that she watched him retreat down the brick walkway. Even if she were willing to agree that someone had to be the watchdog, she did not want the watchdog mentality thrust upon her. Even when she was willing to concede that she might like the security of a burglar alarm, his doggedness called up her resistance. She did not understand her ambivalence. It made her uncomfortable too.

She went inside and closed the front door behind her, still not bothering to lock it, perversely not wanting to. She started back to the kitchen, passing the hall table, her purse and keys on top of it, as Lyle, always the detective, the watcher, had no doubt noticed.

She hesitated, then abruptly turned. She picked up her purse, put her keys in it, and brought it with her to the kitchen. Indeed, her actions were perverse and she knew it, for if Lyle had said anything to her about keeping her purse on the hall table, she wouldn't have moved it.

15

Five o'clock, everyone gone, the house to herself, what to do. Thea was tired of making decisions about furnishings, about things that were now hers but belonged to her chiefly because they were part of her childhood memories. How was one supposed to decide which memories to keep, which to use, which to store, which to sell or give away? She could not view these things with any objectivity, could not decide which of them fitted in with the way she wanted the house to look. Part of the problem was that she had no clear-cut vision of exactly how she did want the house to look. As long as it had Aunt Althea's possessions in it, it was Aunt Althea's vision.

So the third floor had become a large attic, a place to store anything she had the least doubt about keeping, a cluttered space with covered furniture and sealed boxes and locked trunks.

A perfect hideout for a ghost.

Thea wandered the nearly empty front rooms of the house in search of a vision. The rooms seemed enormous now without their little groupings of furniture, isolating rather than intimate, their thick curtains suffocating and claustrophobic, their copiously patterned wallpapers repeating designs like fences.

The light walls and open spaces should have offered possibilities, but no vision was forthcoming. Instead the walls seemed stark, the spaces desolate. Her feet struck hollowly on the wood floors. The sound of emptiness was beginning to grate on her.

She stopped in the living room, where she'd temporarily left the red brocade sofa, a matching chair, and the coffee table with the beaded border off to the side of the room, no longer a group but at odd angles to one another, as if at odds and hastily left to their bad humor. They told of abandoned old lady.

She went to the gray-veined marble mantel. Above it hung a huge mirror framed in rosewood, the old glass beveled to follow the curves in the wood. It was a beautiful piece, the only thing in the room she'd been certain she wanted to keep, rehung on freshly painted walls. Across from it, in the next parlor, was another mirror. The two mirrors reflected each other, mirrors inside mirrors, nothing but emptiness between them to break the infinite see-through images, as if the house itself were made of glass.

Thea stood in front of the rosewood mirror in the empty space and half expected her reflection to be transparent, emptiness inside emptiness, left blank at the end of each day. The nights, unless Bobby came over, and even sometimes when he did, made her restless, as if the day had promised something and then eased out, taking its promises with it.

The last time she'd spent the day anticipating the night was a year ago, well over a year ago, when Michael had started coming to see her again before their divorce had been final. She would be at work, perhaps taking an inventory of vitamins or stocking the shelves with the latest health-food craze, and suddenly there would be that funny prickling sensation at the back of her tongue, and the roller-coaster wave of expectation at the pit of her stomach, traveling down deep, making her legs weak.

She had thought they would get back together. But the divorce proceedings had continued, Michael saying to her, Let's see what will happen; and slowly, too slowly, she began to realize he was only coming for some measure of comfort, perhaps, but that he no longer wanted to be married to her. The divorce had gone on to completion.

And so the excitement was lost, the anticipation was gone. And yet . . . and yet she had continued to sleep with him.

What was it she'd always said about Bobby, the reason she still wouldn't sleep with him? That he was too easy. Just as she'd been, though she knew so well that the rush of excitement Michael had produced in her this second time around was caused as much by his elusiveness, his refusal to be pinned down, the challenge he presented, as by the sex itself.

If she wanted to, she could call up that feeling now, that rush, but the memory of it produced a dull ache, a well of loneliness that dropped away into deep disappointment. She saw that disappointment reflected back at her in the mirror and she closed her eyes against it, against the disappointment of having been abandoned, and against the disappointment in herself too.

The doorbell rang and startled her. Through the leaded glass on the front door she could see a black man, young, a student perhaps, in his wire-rimmed glasses, faded jeans, and T-shirt, hip-looking with a battered porkpie hat on his head despite the lingering heat from the afternoon.

As soon as she opened the door he started talking. "My name is Sonny Johnson, ma'am." He held a driver's license at her eye level. "I'm with an envir'mental group called SAFE." He held up another card showing member identification. "I'm not sellin anything and I promise—I'm safe." He gave a short nervous laugh as he handed her a sheet explaining the purpose of his visit, which he was telling her himself as well. He talked fast, as if he were afraid she would slam the door in his face. Thea knew about talking fast. She used to talk fast too, at school, afraid that if she took too long, whomever she was talking to would turn away, leave her in midsentence.

As close as he was to her, she could feel his nerves. "Maybe you heard of SAFE," he was saying. "We're a group of more than two hundred concerned citizens who want to make New Orleans a better—" another short laugh "—a safer place to live. What we concerned 'bout right now is them trucks carryin hazardous chemicals down Convent Street to the river."

"But I thought trucks weren't allowed to use Convent Street anymore," Thea said. That battle had been fought while she was in high school, but it wasn't over hazardous chemicals; it was because the homeowners said the trucks were cracking their houses, causing the foundations to sink.

She'd made him more nervous. He nodded quickly. "Yes ma'am. That's true. There's a city ordinance against the big trucks, but what they doin is carryin the chemicals in small trucks, like delivery trucks. You know, vans. We wouldn't've knowed about it 'cept for an accident. Maybe you saw it in the paper. Twelve blocks was evacuated, right down there." He pointed toward the river. "An accident could happen anywhere," he said, rattling on as if his words could stop the door from closing. "Be specially bad over there by the project"—he pointed in its direction away from the river—"where they's always kids playin in the street, or here, right in front your house." As he talked his eyes had grown large and round, magnified by his glasses, his eyebrows creeping up his forehead.

Thea didn't want him to persuade her, she didn't want to watch his unease, his just-under-the-skin distrust of how she might treat him. She signed the petition asking the city council to rewrite the ordinance so that no hazardous chemical could be conveyed by any means on Convent Street. He held out his sheaf of explanatory materials so that she could use them as a support while she signed. He had perhaps twenty signatures, but she recognized only a couple of the names above hers. Most of the addresses were on the other side of Convent, near the project.

"Thank you, ma'am." He took the petition and papers from her. "Uh, it ain necessary or nothin," he said, nervously hitting the side of his leg with the papers, "but if you want to make a contribution so we can keep on with our work, it'd be tax deductible."

She smiled at him. "Sure," she said and stepped back to the hall table for her purse, but after Lyle's visit, she'd put it in the kitchen. She asked him to wait, felt awkward closing the door on him, and went back to the kitchen. She started to pull out a ten-dollar bill, thought better of giving him cash, and took out her checkbook instead. In compensation she wrote the check for twenty dollars.

She shook her head as she walked back to the front: she was letting Lyle's distrust propel her, making her actions contradictory, absurd.

She handed him the check. "Thank you, ma'am," he said enthusiastically, as if the sum were so great, yet, ridiculously, making her feel cheap. He sped off in the direction of the river.

She watched him, waiting to see if he went to the house next door, then caught herself double-checking to make sure the door was locked, though she knew Zora always locked it when she left. She closed the door as he was going up the steps to her neighbor's house. What was she doing? Why was she watching—like Lyle? What had Sonny Johnson done? He had committed the crime of being too nervous.

Thea wanted to shake herself free of Lyle, and Aunt Althea and Michael too, like a dog shakes off water; they were getting to her. But it wouldn't be that easy. It would be more like a crab shedding its too-small shell: struggle, rest; shudder, ease out a bit. Once her father had gone crabbing and brought her back a crab just about to crack its shell and shed. He put it in a bucket so she could watch it become a soft crab. It was already partially out. She watched for over three hours, until all at once the crab took a swift step backward and was free of its confinement. Her father told her that once the crab's struggle is over, it has used up its excess weight; it is free and light and vulnerable.

What to do. There was no point in brooding about the past, about what she had done. There was the future to think about with its many possibilities. She would finish the house, and if she still could not release it from Aunt Althea's powerful presence, then she would leave it. She must not become paralyzed by her many choices. If she got tired of thinking about the house, she would think about the garden. With that thought she gathered up some copies of *Architectural Digest* and a couple of Aunt Althea's garden books, poured herself a glass of vernaccia, and went to sit in the gazebo.

It was quite pleasant outside late in the day like this, still warm but the sun beginning to go down. The gazebo itself, though, was just as uncomfortable as ever. Maybe if she had some cushions made for the benches it would help. Even so, nothing would help one's spine. She situated her backbone against the side of one of the posts, her legs stretched out along the seat. She sipped wine and leafed through the magazines, making dog-ears on the pages with ideas she liked.

The first garden book she picked up opened automatically to an English cottage garden, borders of perennials flanking a curving walkway of grass, a garden densely planted with flowering shrubs and trees. She imagined her pain-in-the-back gazebo at the end of such a walkway and finally recognized what she had never liked about it: it had no setting; its placement seemed purely accidental, and so it looked out of place. It needed just the sort of intimate, romantic setting shown in the picture. She could plant more azaleas, perhaps a flowering plum . . .

Thea shuddered, someone walking across her grave. The way the book had fallen open to this page, the crease on the binding faded to a thin stripe . . . she leaned forward to see past the roof of the gazebo. Was it possible that Aunt Althea's ghost was dictating to her from the third floor of the house?

She laughed aloud at her superstitious thoughts—and hoped her laugh would break the spell. The doorbell rang inside. She jumped and spilled wine on the picture. Such a peculiar feeling this gave her, this bell ringing as she laughed . . .

There must be bats in the belfry, Aunt Althea used to say to explain strange noises, eerie coincidences. And other people's lunacies.

Thea opened the front door and Burgess said, "Hey, I know it's late, but I got two carpenters can start on your bookcases tomorrow, and I want to be sure I'm clear on the plans."

"That sounds like a polite way of asking me if I've changed my mind again," Thea said.

"You can change your mind when we finish if you want. We be glad to start all over again."

"Come on in," she said. There was something slightly arrogant about Burgess. Maybe it wasn't arrogance but that trace of irony he always spoke with, his self-assuredness. She liked the way he didn't take everything she said with deadly seriousness. If she'd made the remark about changing her mind to any of the other men, there would have been a lot of Oh-no-ma'am protests.

"I was just out back looking at magazines," she said. "I can show you what I want."

"Good."

They reached the kitchen. "A beer?"

"Sound real good."

She got him an Abita Amber from the refrigerator, took her bottle of wine as well, and led him out to the gazebo.

It was strange that these two should be sitting in as unlikely a place as the gazebo. They leaned into the center of it, holding a magazine between them.

"Something like that," Thea said.

"But your room is shaped entirely different." Thea's room was chopped up with windows and doors and a fireplace.

"Well, I know, but I mean the detail work on the edges of the shelves, the columns in between the cabinets. See? It's sort of a—" she didn't know how to describe it; she thought of the Hindermanns' house "—an updated traditional look."

He laughed, slow and lazy. "Yeah. Updated traditional."

In the fading light she hoped he couldn't see the heat she felt along her jawline, rising to her cheeks.

He said, "We gon have to buy a new saw to do that." He let go of the magazine and sat back.

"Is that a problem?" she asked, holding the magazine suspended a few seconds longer before she closed it and sat back too.

"Findin extra money's always a problem."

"Well, maybe I could front the money for the saw. We can work something out."

There was, for Thea, an embarrassed silence before he said, "Yeah, but first you got to decide where you gon put the shelves."

"I know. I'm just not sure yet."

"Well, look." He leaned across to get the magazine and took an invoice folded lengthwise from his breast pocket. On the back of it he roughly sketched the room, talking about narrow spaces and corners, but Thea was finding it difficult to concentrate, her mind racing with thoughts totally unrelated to what he was saying: he didn't wear his black hat and mirrored sunglasses anymore; Zora didn't call people ma'am or sir either; Zora was angry at Burgess about something big, important; there was something oriental about the way his eyelids folded down at the corners; the way he was leaning forward now, his shirtsleeve riding up as he showed her his sketch, she could see part of a nasty-looking scar on the underside of his forearm. And then she was thinking about his life in the Convent and wondering if the scar was from a knife fight, if there were other scars, her mind leaping to guns, it was gunfights you heard about: had he ever been shot?

Burgess was saying something about limited wall space for a library. He stopped talking and looked at her quizzically. "You with me?"

"Um, Burgess," she said, "No, I'm not with you. I can't seem to focus on this right now. Let me think about it overnight and get with you in the morning." Maybe Sandy could help her with this, with the renovation. All these decisions, it was getting entirely too complicated; his presence, the life he led when he was not here, that she could not get herself to stop thinking about, was making it too complicated.

But he didn't get up to go right away. He sipped beer, she sipped wine, the evening lingered on.

And from the third floor of the house, Aunt Althea's ghost raged at these two intruders drinking and talking and laughing low—the nerve, using her gazebo like that.

16

They sat in the gazebo way past dark, longer than Thea thought it was possible to sit in the gazebo without spinal injury.

They talked all around things. She wanted to ask him what his mother was so angry at him about. He wanted to ask her about her parents and why she wasn't afraid to be sitting in the dark with a dangerous black man; except, of course, she didn't know he was dangerous.

Burgess heard the commotion in the street first. He and Thea went to the tall wooden gate, unlatched it and opened it a crack, but all they could see was blue light careening from the oak leaves overhead, to the side of the house next door, the front of the one across the street. They eased out of the gate, Burgess first, to get a better look.

The police car was in the middle of Convent Street, and two policemen had Sonny Johnson spread-eagled against the side of it.

First Thea was confused: why were they doing this to him—because he was caught mugging someone, breaking and entering, trying to commit some crime? She realized she didn't believe he had committed a crime. And there was no one around that she could see, no victim. So why?

Because he was black? Had one of her neighbors seen him going from house to house and called the police? It was carrying things a bit far. Thea looked at the houses across the street. Windows were dark or curtains were drawn. How many pairs of eyes were watching from behind dark windows and peeking from behind curtains?

She moved closer to Burgess, whispering to him that the man was with an environmental group called SAFE. He smiled—there was that irony again—and nodded, never moving his eyes from the scene on the street.

They watched. One cop was on the radio, sitting halfway in the car. They couldn't hear him, though they could hear the crackling of the radio and the metallic, indecipherable voice coming from it. The other cop stood behind Sonny Johnson.

From his spread, stretched position against the car, Sonny turned his head toward the policeman on the radio. When he moved the cop behind him moved too and slammed his head down on the top of the car. Sonny cried out, his hand automatically seeking his wounded head. The cop picked his head up by the hair and slammed it again.

An involuntary cry rose from Thea and she began to move forward, but Burgess stopped her, his hand on her arm, pulling her back at the crook of her elbow, shushing her.

"But, Burgess, this is making me sick."

"Not yet," he said softly, and they stood there, his hand at her elbow, hearing low moans whenever the radio cut off the incoherent, tinny words, metal twigs that snapped with a protest of harsh static.

After another few minutes the police let Sonny go and drove off, leaving him without help. He was dazed, both hands going to his head. He took one lurching step and sat down on the sidewalk, rocking slightly back and forth.

Burgess went after him with Thea at his heels. Together they led the punch-drunk black man across the street. Who had called the police? She hoped whoever it was watched them now.

They sat Sonny Johnson on the den sofa in between them but finally had to lay him down. He'd been cut twice by his own glasses, a lesser cut in his eyebrow, a deeper one that Thea thought may have gone through his eyelid. He held a piece of gauze to his eye. The bent wire rims with one lens cracked into opaqueness sat on an end table laid out with peroxide, iodine, a box of cotton balls, packages of gauze, everything in the house Thea could find for first aid.

But Sonny obviously needed to go to the hospital. Thea volunteered to take him, but Burgess said he would take care of it and made a phone call from the den phone. "I'm ready," was all he said. Thea was disappointed; she wanted to go with them, but she didn't want to intrude on what suddenly seemed something between the two black men.

Sonny began to rally, feeling well enough to get a bit heated over his ordeal. SAFE, he said, would press charges of police brutality.

"You better get yourself checked out first, brother," Burgess told him.

"Look here at my glasses," Sonny demanded. "They coulda put my eye out."

"Yeah, but they didn't."

"Don' matter."

"Sure it does," Burgess said. He grinned at Thea. "SAFE ain exactly an envir'mental group." He asked Sonny, "What's SAFE stand for?"

"Serious Advocates for Equality," Sonny answered, and Thea didn't know how he accomplished it, but he stated the name of his organization with boyish pride, enthusiasm, and anger.

"Yeah," said Burgess, "serious."

It wasn't long before the oxidized-red truck pulled up in front of the house, the muffler's coughing and putting sounds announcing it half a block away. As Burgess was following Sonny through the door, Thea reached out and lightly touched the back of his white shirt sleeve.

He turned around in the doorway, a look on his face not unlike that quizzical glance he'd given her in the gazebo.

Thea had no idea exactly what it was she wanted to say to him. Something was different between them; they had a different sense of each other. And there had been a shift in power, to his side. She said, "Look, I don't mind being a witness."

She half expected his amused expression, as if she were so naïve, but he smiled, genuine this time, none of his irony. "I know," he told her, "but I doubt it will come to that."

He hesitated with his smile another moment, then was gone into the night with its hidden eyes.

The nights were becoming like some sort of prison, a punishment—for what? For her ambivalence, for her doubts, for her aloneness.

Bed especially, like solitary confinement. And all of her thoughts would come together there, keeping her awake so it could come prey upon her eventually, the fear . . .

The events of the day kept turning in her mind, image after image: Zora, her shoulders rounded with meekness; Lyle, the lines of worry deep in his face; Sonny Johnson, his nervousness making her nervous, turning her into a watcher; Burgess, his hand on her arm, stopping her, shushing her, shifting the power between them.

She lay in the dark trying to understand this shift. He understood the nature of street violence better than she, he had been the one in control, but that was not getting to the heart of the matter. She could only think that before Sonny Johnson she had the power because she was the property owner, she was the employer; because she was white. After Sonny Johnson, her being white meant she shared the burden of guilt with the white policemen.

If that were so, then why didn't her parents' being gunned down by two black men give her the right to hate all black people, make all black people share the burden of guilt? She had never thought she had that right.

She wondered if some blacks felt guilt for the fear incited by others of their race. And then she realized that this was Lyle's excuse: make all black people the enemy; they were guilty of inciting fear if nothing else.

She tried to imagine talking to Burgess about these matters but couldn't. Why not? Why couldn't people talk to each other? She turned irritably in the bed. It was because of Burgess that she was thinking about these things at all. And then, she wasn't sure how she jumped tracks, but she began to suspect that the shift in power between her and Burgess had not so much to do with black and white as with male and female. Here was the heart of the matter, but the problem was that she knew of no way to separate and remove the black and the white from the male and the female.

It must have been Lyle, intruding into her thoughts, who was the wedge, the chink, that let in the fear. Once the fear entered, her body became smaller, this small vulnerable speck of life in the darkness. In the dark her thoughts raced through absurdist associations: if she were small, then she couldn't be seen, couldn't be found, but if she couldn't be seen, she could be snuffed out before she knew it, like an animal on the Interstate or an insect under a shoe.

Sleep moved farther away. She took a deep breath and let it out audibly, playing her childish game, come and get me if you dare.

The darkness teemed with more images, the kind you see flashing across the undersides of your eyelids, burning themselves out in a momentary burst of invisible lights. Thea remembered waking once, or dreaming of waking, in the middle of the night when she was a child and seeing an old woman standing by the side of her bed, bathed in a supernatural light, a Gypsy woman in a long dress and shawl, her braided hair wound around her head. She made no menacing move toward Thea, but Thea could not tell if she was friend or foe.

In the teeming darkness now a form began to materialize by the side of her bed. No Gypsy woman this time, he was wearing a porkpie hat and glasses with one cracked lens, both lenses made opaque, the eyes shot out, by the strange suffused light. He stood there, he made no menacing move toward her. Thea could not tell if he was friend or foe.

17

Janine and Sherree had it out. Not right away; it took a few days for the tension to build, a few days before it became crystal clear that nobody outside the Convent gave a rat's ass if the cops put a plastic bag over Dexter's head or anybody else's; they were much more concerned over the media legend of the Bishop of Convent Street; a few days, too, of the housing authority snooping around asking a lot of who-is-responsible questions; a few more days before Janine realized Burgess was spending an awful lot of time over at the rich white bitch's house.

Janine told Sherree she didn't want her talking to anybody from the housing authority.

"What you think, girl, you can tell me who I can talk to and who I can't?" Sherree said.

"Sherree, I jus don' want you messin things up for Burgess anymore than they already are messed up."

"I didn't *mean* to mess nothin up for Burgess," Sherree snapped. "I was trying to tell that bitch about what they did to Dexter."

"I know what you were trying to do, but that ain't what you did, is it?"

Sherree said, "Your attitude is for shit, you know that? Or you just pissed cause I was on TV and you wasn't?" She had that hand on that thrust-out hip, her head cocked, her chin tilted, taunting.

Janine knew if she got into a yelling match with Sherree, she would lose. From the time they were kids, Janine was no match for Sherree's mouth. She couldn't always summon it up at will, but she reached deep down into herself now, so deep down that it sometimes seemed it wasn't a place inside her at all, but outside, yet could only be reached with her mind, and only when her mind was as strong as it could be, and she summoned up that strange quiet power that was so physical it could shut Sherree up and make her hand fall off her hip. She brought it up and said, "I'm tellin you, don't go messin around where you don't belong messin around. Anybody comes from the housin authority, I want to talk to them. I hope you got that straight, Sherree."

Janine didn't mean it as any kind of threat, but she didn't care if that was the way Sherree took it either. There were plenty other women would jump at the chance to run the day-care center.

Sherree's head stayed cocked, but her hand fell from her hip and she turned and walked away, no more argument about the housing authority, no more argument about anything. That had been days ago, and the two women were still avoiding each other.

Janine was going to have to handle the housing authority very carefully, and if she did it right the Convent might be the first project in New Orleans to have tenant management. Other cities had it; she didn't know why New Orleans always had to be the last on the list for progress. Black progress especially. Even the black mayor of the city would rather talk about tearing the projects down, the worst idea Janine had ever heard. Where was everybody supposed to go while they waited for the new fancy townhouses to be built? Anyway, if you looked hard enough at the Convent, especially with its trim all painted fresh and bright, you could imagine it was fancy once too.

But nobody was moving on that either. It was all a bunch of talk to keep from having to do anything. Bunch of talk and a lot of studies. The big shots in New Orleans loved studies. They spent all kinds of money to do studies on how not to spend all kinds of money. Like the smoke alarms. The city bought them and stored them because they had to do a study to figure out how to keep the tenants from stealing the batteries once the alarms were installed. Some mastermind thought wire cages would do the trick. Where did the dude come from? Not a New Orleans project, that was for sure. Or he would have known how the junkies sell the wire right off the clothes poles. When Burgess put in alarms, he ran an electric wire to them and that was that. Meanwhile, the city was still paying a storage fee for the other alarms. If Janine wasn't careful about what she said, they might want to raise rents to cover it.

Or if she wasn't careful, Burgess might decide he had to go away. She didn't think he'd take her with him. He'd never said it to her before, but she could hear him saying, "After a while baby, when I'm settled in. You and the kid, I'll send for you."

She could hear him saying it because that's what her own father had said to her mother when she was pregnant with Janine. That was right before he took off for Detroit or Chicago, maybe New York, wherever he could find work, he said. She could hear it because her mother had told her the story till she knew it by heart, like some kids know *The Three Little Pigs* or *Goldilocks*, how her father had called from Jackson, then Memphis, as far as Cincinnati, telling road stories, saying he missed her, he couldn't live without her, running up big phone bills until the phone company took out the phone. And after that he was never heard from again.

Her mother didn't tell the story so much as Janine got older, but then sometimes, when there was whiskey on her breath, she would cry. Too much whiskey and she would yell and throw things. Whatever her mother was so angry about, Janine knew it was all her fault. If she'd never been born, her mother would be in Detroit or Chicago, maybe New York, big glamorous cities where ladies wore tight dresses with fringe on them and shiny high heels and went to nightclubs with their men and listened to bands playing jazz and drank tall pink drinks out of little straws. She knew her mother would rather be in one of those hot jazzy cities than stuck here in this poor town, in this tiny apartment with her. She was afraid when her mother started to throw things. Janine knew she deserved to have them thrown at her, but she was so afraid when her mother got like this that she would wait until her mother was looking around for something else that would break into a thousand pieces, whatever was left that she could smash up against the wall, leave a stain like a star exploding, and Janine would crawl off to the bathroom and squeeze between the toilet and the bathtub and wait there until the raging stopped.

Janine didn't usually think about these things, but since she'd been pregnant there seemed to be a lot of skeletons raging in closets. There were times, like tonight, that she could feel anger swelling up in a hole right above her stomach. It would swell until it seemed she would burst with it, but she never did. Burgess would usually come home and it would slink back down like a snake into its pit.

She wondered if that was the way her mother's anger had been, almost to the bursting point so many times that when it finally erupted it did so with a fury that sent things flying. She wondered if it would help to throw things, to scream at Burgess while he wasn't there, shout about how miserable she felt sitting here all dressed to kill, waiting for him, dinner on the stove, in this same tiny apartment where she used to shiver up against cold porcelain in the bathroom.

Janine didn't think that would help at all. She would just get into a habit of screaming and throwing, and it wouldn't change a thing. Neighbors would come at first, then they would stop coming. Eventually she would get tired of screaming and throwing, just as her mother must have, and then she would get sad, just as her mother got sad and started to use the needle until the needle killed her. That was no way to end up.

She decided to go over to the Solar Club so she wouldn't feel she'd gotten all dressed up for nothing. Otherwise there wasn't going to be much else to do except go to bed, alone, and lie there in the dark thinking gaudy thoughts about where Burgess was and what he might be up to—and get more and more afraid that tonight was the night he wouldn't come home anymore.

She went to the hall closet where he kept the Corn Flakes box stashed with emergency money. Janine hardly ever went into it because Burgess gave her money every morning, but today she'd spent it all on groceries.

The box felt light, nothing in it maybe; she could hear a few corn flakes rattling around the bottom of it. So, fine, if all the money was gone, there'd be a few guys over at the Solar Club willing to stand a couple for a foxy lady in a blood-red dress with fringe on the shoulders, coming down the sleeves.

She took the box into the kitchen and put it on the counter where she could unroll the top of the paper bag lining it. She reached into the bag, pushing her red fringed sleeve up out of the way. The waxy paper crunched. The fringe fell down around the opening of the box, all its long fingers tickling her arm just below the elbow, her own fingers touching the money, a few bills at the bottom of the box, and something else, fringe, brushing her hand, circling her wrist, and all of a sudden the box teeming with life. She ripped her arm out of it. All over her arm, on her hand, running down her fingers, up her sleeve, little shit-brown cockroaches, their tiny legs brushing up against her skin like soft, whiskered kisses.

Janine flung her arm and there was fringe flying and cockroaches flying, and her neck bulged with the scream stuck in her throat.

The roaches scurried across the floor and the counters and the sink and the clean dishes while Janine did her best to shake out her tight red sleeve.

She began to cry and went into the bedroom. She fell across the bed, her high heels still on, her dress pulled up taut around her hips, and cried out all the tightness in her throat. She lay there a long time in the dark, her head cradled in her arm, the fringe making furrows on her wet cheek.

Her crying subsided and as she became still, the rushing sounds of silence up against her ears were amplified in the quiet around her. She listened and they calmed her, and she was aware for the first time of her abdomen pushing against the material of her dress, making it tighter than it had been. She wouldn't be able to wear it much longer. There was a slight surge of panic at the thought of how her body would change, that she would lose her attractiveness, but the calm took over again as she remembered how she and Sherree used to play babies when they were little.

They took turns being the baby. Being the baby was supposed to be the preferred role because then the other person had to do everything for you, feed you, rock you, cradle you in her arms. But Janine remembered how she started looking forward to her turn as mother so she could do the feeding and the holding. It would be as if some switch had been pulled and the power cranked up on her imagination. She would cuddle Sherree and rock her back and forth, sitting on the hard ground, and imagine scenarios in which bad men were trying to harm her or her baby, or take her baby away from her, and she would find ingenious ways to outwit them, hiding with the baby under the house behind the gas meter until they gave up trying to find her, putting the baby in the dumpster inside a pink satin-lined box until the men went away.

Lying there, her eyes closed, she frowned. That was such a silly idea, a baby in a miniature coffin hidden in a dumpster, and she remembered that it came from hearing about a woman who had put her newborn baby in a dumpster until some men—it must have been the garbage men—found it. She was so little when she heard that; she didn't understand; she thought it was bad that the men found the baby. If the woman had only put the baby in a box . . .

Hiding from the men—it was the only time she ever imagined men in her stories.

She didn't share these stories with Sherree; she was afraid Sherree would laugh at her. But the stories, half-baked, without beginnings or very good endings, were not what she enjoyed. It was the feeling that she was able to protect her baby, that she and her baby were one, that because she was such a good mother she would be able to watch her baby grow and be happy. She had the power to do that, and that was not pretend.

They played babies without any props, only pretend bottles and pretend diapers. Then one Christmas her mother took her and Sherree to the auditorium across town where there were Santa Clauses giving toys away. They stood in line with lots of other children, and they each got dolls. One of the dolls, dressed in a pink diaper shirt and a diaper that snapped on, came with its own bottle. You gave the doll water from its bottle and it peed in the diaper. The other doll was bigger and was called a walking doll because its legs were jointed at the hips and moved. But the doll walked creakily, not much better than a doll without joints would have moved.

Janine and Sherree were thrilled with their dolls at first, but playing babies wasn't the same without a real live baby. They stopped playing as much until one day Janine suggested that Sherree be the baby and she would give her water in the tiny bottle.

Janine, in her dark bedroom, drifting at the edge of sleep, turned so she was lying on her back. She put her hands over her stomach. She remembered how secretly excited she'd been when Sherree had told her she was going to have a baby, secretly because Sherree was so angry at first, knowing she would have to give up her act at the nightclub.

"I'll take care of the baby at night so you can go back to work," she heard herself saying again to Sherree, this time echoey, as if in a dream, but Sherree had decided not to go back to stripping, said she couldn't live both lives.

Janine, her half-conscious dream continuing, held Sherree's baby girl in her arms. She loved this baby, as much as she would her own.

And now she would have her own. When she found out she was pregnant, she told Sherree before she told Burgess. Sherree shrieked—in her living room they jumped up and down, holding hands like schoolgirls, in slow motion now so she could hang on longer to that feeling of such pleasure, such closeness. Sherree said she hoped it was a girl. But Janine hoped it would be a boy who looked just like Burgess, only she didn't tell Sherree that. Sherree would have argued, and she didn't want to argue just then.

Sherree is jealous, Janine thought dreamily. She was sad; she missed Sherree. She didn't have anyone to laugh with anymore, no one to tell her secrets to, oh sure there was Burgess, but it wasn't the same as with Sherree. They had been like sisters; they had been like mother and daughter to each other too. They had said they were going to be better mothers than their mothers had been; they'd give their children candy every day and buy TV sets.

She was putting Sherree in the past and she didn't know why, she was too sleepy. They had fought before, plenty of times. They could be friends again, couldn't they?

Janine opened her eyes but they closed almost right away and she slept for a little while, lightly. When she woke briefly she was filled with that feeling she had when she used to pretend she was hiding her baby: that power she had to protect, the strength she had to give, and she was struck with the realization that it was the same power she had called up with Sherree, that this time had changed their friendship forever, and she didn't understand how the power to nurture was the same power to destroy.

Janine slept until the sounds of Burgess coming in woke her. She was wide awake immediately but she didn't move, her body still weighted with sleep.

"Janine musta gone to bed," she heard Burgess say. Thinking he would come check on her, she forced herself to turn over, so he could see she wasn't asleep. The bed groaned softly.

Feet shuffled in the hallway into the kitchen. The refrigerator opened. Beer cans popped. Feet shuffled back to the living room. Janine felt a small rise of anger: he must be with Dexter, dumb, pain-in-the-ass Dexter, hanging all over Burgess all the time so she hardly got to be alone with him anymore.

She got up slowly so the bed wouldn't creak. She took off her shoes and crept to the doorway to listen. She was so close to them that if she stepped out into the hallway the overhead light would cast her shadow into the living room where they sat.

Nothing for several seconds, then Burgess said, "So what you got on your mind, Dexter?"

"I was wonderin if you heard 'bout Ferdie yet."

Ferdie was one of Burgess' sixteen-year-old recruits, a gang leader from down on the other side of the project.

"You mean the trouble last night?"

Dexter nodded. "Ferdie's gone."

"Dead?"

"Naw. The only body they found wasn't nobody from the Convent. They say he was from across town, Desire or St. Bernard."

It was the first shootout in the Convent in so many months that the residents had actually begun to believe maybe there wouldn't be any more. It had happened in the middle of the night, in a vacant, boarded-up apartment down where Ferdie lived.

Dexter turned the bottom of the beer can around on his jeans. "Another crack deal gone bad—I guess they gon blame it on the Bishop."

They might have meant the cops but it might have meant anybody in the Convent, the way Dexter was giving Burgess that look out of the corner of his eye. Burgess' safety depended on the people in the Convent keeping quiet about him, and he knew if they got too scared, the only way to make sure they didn't talk, didn't inform, was to use more fear.

"So where's Ferdie?" Burgess wanted to know.

Dexter just looked at Burgess. They both knew what this meant: Ferdie, like most of the boys his age, wasn't interested in painting or carpentry or masonry or plastering. Not enough money and too much work. Burgess remembered how he'd been at that age. Nobody could talk to you about tomorrow, there was no tomorrow, except for tomorrow's deal. You believed you'd die young; he still believed it. It was the big flaw in his plan.

"So where's he gettin rock from?" Dexter asked Burgess, but he knew Burgess had no one answer; there were lots of answers and they were all trying to move in on the Convent. And the Bishop.

"Well, okay," Burgess said. He was ready for Dexter to leave now. He didn't want to think about all this; he was tired of these problems. But Dexter didn't get up. He kept turning that beer can into his jeans, fidgeting, killing time.

It was true, Dexter was stalling. He had something else to say to Burgess, something he'd primed himself to say, something unrelated to Ferdie or any drug problems. He had primed himself to say it but now he was having trouble getting it out.

"Listen, about your mama, Burgess," he finally said.

"What about her?"

Dexter pulled one shoulder up, half a shrug. "It's the truck. She havin a hard time gettin up and down, you know? She cusses under her breath an you know she don' like for no one to help her."

There, he'd gotten it out and it wasn't such a big deal. He hadn't meant to say Burgess' mama was cussing—he didn't know what she was saying when she talked to herself like she did. What did it matter anyway? This was just a little thing, nothing like that day in the police station.

Burgess was laughing, keeping his mouth closed so that deep rumbling laugh was kept down. "Yeah, okay," he said. "Let Mama ride in the Cadillac." He laughed some more and said he'd get Janine to take care of the paper work the next day. He kept the Caddy in her name. "You just bought yourself a car, Dexter."

Dexter left Burgess, having gotten more than what he'd gone after. All that business about Ferdie—that was just a lead-in; he didn't figure Burgess expected much more from the kid. He swiftly crossed the grass to Sherree's, anxious to tell her the news. But Dexter was getting wiser. He jumped ahead, anticipating Sherree's reaction: her face would be stern, she'd find something wrong.

He slowed his pace, thinking hard. Sherree, somehow, would make it seem his plan had backfired because Burgess gave him the car. So he didn't have to tell her about that.

Dexter glanced furtively over his shoulder and walked faster. It might not be such a good idea to linger in the Convent yard these nights. But his feet felt leaden, as if they were carrying a bad boy home to face the music.

What the hell, at least he would be driving the Cadillac again.

After Dexter left, Burgess sat where he was on the sofa, his hands resting loosely on his thighs, his shoulders drooping, his chest sunken. He felt a bit as if the wind had been knocked out of him. It was happening; the shit was coming down. Before long the Convent would be the same killing place it had been when he got there, shootings every night, more dead every week, too many pushers, everybody wanting control and nobody strong enough to take it, but plenty enough guns to come after him. He had a couple of choices: he either went back into business big time, got Ferdie and his gang making runs the way they used to so maybe they thought they were making enough money that they didn't have to deal in the Convent, or he got out, tried to get Janine out too. What his mama had been telling him to do.

Janine came in quietly on her stockinged feet, the undulating fringe on her dress catching his eye first. She stood in the entrance to the hallway.

"Hey, baby, what you doin all dressed up?"

"Waitin for you, Burgess. I been waitin for you."

"Aw, baby, I'm sorry. There was some trouble over at the house where Mama is."

"What kind of trouble, Burgess? White woman trouble?"

Her face was like stone, her jaw muscles clamped hard with anger and jealousy. He didn't answer; he held his hand out to her. She came to the sofa and sat beside him, and he ran his fingers up and down her arms, combing through the long silky fringe. He kissed her neck but she sat rigid, not responding. He didn't stop. He put his hand on the upper part of her back, bared by the scooped top of the dress, then let it drift down and pull the zipper. He pushed his other hand into the front of the dress, over her breast, taking the hard nipple between his fingers, and felt her sink toward him, her breath on his face.

Janine drew her shoulders in and let him push the top of the dress down around her waist. Both of his hands were on her breasts now, his head was bowed. She knew he would start to kiss her breasts soon, pulling on her nipples with his teeth, and she could feel the anticipated pleasure opening her up to him. With the little resistance she had left she pushed on his chest until she forced him to look at her.

"Burgess," she said, and her breath caught involuntarily, "tell me what's goin on over there."

She felt his deep laugh vibrate the wall of his chest. "You want to know what's going on, you gon have to come over there with me and see for yourself."

He started bending toward her neck, but she stopped him. "What's all this stuff Dexter's talkin about, with Ferdie and that killin? What's all that mean?"

He laughed again but this time moving on her, his breath hot on her neck as he spoke: "It means they know when you ain got no teeth left."

He pushed her back on the sofa and bit into her dark, goose-bumped areola.

18

Sandy fell into her old way of making Thea her confidante. She talked as if there were no one else she could really talk to, no one else who would quite understand. Thea knew how seductive women with highly developed social skills could be and that it was possible Sandy confided in all her friends this way. But not about Lyle. When Sandy talked about Lyle, her words rushed over Thea as if a long-stoppered bottle's fecund contents, grown too large and squeezed too long into their confined, well-guarded space, had been suddenly released. Talk like this would pass around Sandy's social circle like an infectious disease. Thea was certain that it was only her status as an outsider that made her privy to Sandy's intensely private world gone horrendously wrong.

The morning Sandy came over to help Thea with the bookcases there were no workers downstairs at the house. There were two painters in Aunt Althea's old bedroom and a third man replacing rotten wood and ripped screen on the second-floor porch. Zora was also upstairs, running the vacuum cleaner. The motor droned directly above them as Sandy stood in the center of the room that was to be the library. She made a slow pivot as she scanned the room, a forefinger resting at the side of her mouth.

She narrowed her eyes at a corner. "It *is* a difficult room," she said to Thea, but after more thought, accompanied by pacing and squinting, she came up with an ingenious solution: window seats, cushioned seats that were also cabinets, so the motif of the columns could go all around the room, unbroken except by the doors.

Sandy had other ideas too. She walked to the door of the living room. "The mirror's okay," she said, "but you've got to get rid of that chandelier. You should have pitched it out with those Gone-with-the-Wind curtains." She told Thea she had a catalog of the most marvelous contemporary light fixtures.

Thea was disappointed to hear Sandy say this about the chandelier. She'd gotten up on a ladder and cleaned each of the crystals, nearly two hundred ovals and balls cut like faceted jewels. She'd shined the brass structure, taking the better part of two days to do the job, and she'd been pleased with the results, the crystals sparkling and catching the afternoon sun coming through the long, uncovered living room windows, throwing color on the white walls and ceiling until twilight. She thought the chandelier was so beautiful and such a part of the room that it would look good no matter what else was in the room. Now Sandy was saying the chandelier wouldn't do at all.

"I thought you liked the idea of blending the old with the new," Thea said.

"Oh I do, but you have to be very careful about what you keep. The chandelier is so big and fussy, and the room has clean, tailored lines now."

"But I like the chandelier," Thea said, and she had a sudden longing for her memory of the room, with all its fussy furniture and the red velvet curtains like the lining of a womb.

"Oh well, if you like it . . ." Sandy said, but she sounded disappointed with Thea.

Sandy walked farther into the room, her flowered tea-length skirt touching lightly against her legs. The sofa and chairs were off to the side, pushed there so Thea could clean the chandelier. Sandy went to the center of the room and stood under the huge, heavy fixture. She held her arms out, swinging around to face Thea. "Don't you just love it when a room is empty like this?" she asked. She looked around with an expression that approached beatific ecstasy. "So full of potential!" She turned her face upward as if at any moment she would be struck with a vision coming down out of the cut glass.

It was Thea instead who was struck with the vision: she saw Aunt Althea's furniture back in the room, but reupholstered and refinished, leaving the dark-stained wood and worn red brocade to the past. The second she thought of it, she knew it was right, the right way to fold her memories into her present life, to turn her former childhood palace of pretend into a place where the memories of her future could happen. She was about to suggest to Sandy that they go up to the third floor to look at the furniture, but at that moment the vacuum cleaner went off, and as if deflated, Sandy's arm fell limp to her sides. She said, "Thea, really—" and came back to the doorway where Thea stood "—you should call my architect. He'll do everything for you, design the bookcases, the window seats, do the contracting. He'll show you things you can do with this house you never would have dreamed you could do."

Thea was very aware of the silence upstairs, their voices, so loud in these empty downstairs rooms, carrying up the stairwell straight to Zora and the workers.

"I've already hired a contractor. I thought you knew." Thea pointed upward.

Sandy missed only a beat. "Oh, you did tell me. I forgot."

Thea suggested coffee. As soon as they reached the kitchen Sandy lowered her voice considerably, though no one upstairs could hear them now. "Sorry. I completely forgot you hired Delzora's son. I wish you would have talked to me first."

"I don't need an architect, Sandy. After these bookcases are finished, I want to stop working on the house, settle into it, try to feel that it's mine and not Aunt Althea's."

"I understand," Sandy said, "but you need someone really good to do your library."

Thea was pouring coffee. She put the pot down and asked Sandy, "Is there something wrong with the work that's been done?"

"No, no, of course not, but it's just some painting, floating the walls, hanging shutters—you need a really good finishing carpenter for those bookcases."

Thea handed Sandy a cup of coffee and walked out to the back porch. She turned on the ceiling fan and she and Sandy sat in the wicker rocking chairs, side by side, across a small table with inlaid green tiles.

Thea took a sip of coffee, put her cup on the little table, and said, "Burgess has a good finishing carpenter."

"You've seen his work?"

"No, but—"

Sandy flipped her hand, dismissing whatever else Thea had to say. "The carpenter my architect uses has his work in at least a dozen houses right in this neighborhood. He'll show you."

"And if Burgess and his carpenter never get any work, how will they ever have anything to show?"

"That's their problem, not yours. You should hire the best you can get."

"And what if they're as good as the best?"

Sandy made a face as if Thea were talking utter nonsense. "You won't know, will you, until the job is done and paid for."

"So far, Burgess has gone out of his way to make sure I've been satisfied," Thea said. Sandy indicated with a shrug that this cut nothing with her, so before she could argue anymore Thea told her, "I'm already committed to Burgess anyway."

"Yes, I can see that. Well, just be careful and—"

Thea held up one hand. "Please. You don't need to tell me. Lyle comes over at least twice a week to tell me to be careful."

Sandy's voice rose with exasperation. "I was going to say, don't let them take advantage of you; don't front them any money—it causes them to disappear, like magic. Until they need more."

Thea thought about the saw she'd told Burgess she'd front the money for, not exactly what Sandy was talking about but close enough that she was sure Sandy wouldn't approve. She frowned, annoyed that Sandy and Lyle's approval always seemed to be an issue these days.

Sandy didn't notice her frown; she was frowning herself, staring off toward the gazebo. "Lyle comes over here that much?" she asked.

For a moment Thea feared some sort of accusation of an illicit relationship. "He's just trying to get me to install a burglar alarm," she said. When Sandy didn't react, she added lightly, "Are you sure he's not moonlighting for one of those security companies?"

It was as if Sandy had not heard her. "Has he told you that if you don't get an alarm, Burgess is likely to break in one night and slit your throat, or better, shoot you in the head—execution-style—before he takes everything of value in your house?"

She shot this out rapid-fire. Thea, thrown back into her confusion about Burgess, didn't answer.

The heat in Sandy's eyes died down in the silence, and she suddenly looked horrified. "Oh, Thea, I'm sorry. I didn't mean . . . your parents . . ."

Thea, distracted still, touched Sandy's forearm. "No, no, it's not my parents, not that. It's . . . I can't explain it." It was not her parents' death but something bigger. She did not know how anything *could* be bigger, but she knew that she was being compelled to look at something and to look hard, and that looking frightened her.

Sandy was crying softly. "I'm becoming as morbid as Lyle is, saying things to you that are terrible to say, the same way he talks in front of the children about terrible things." She stopped to wipe her tears away before her words were rushing again. "He talks in front of the children about the murders he's seen until they can't sleep anymore, then he takes off in his police car, Mr. Tough Policeman," she spat, "and leaves me to deal with their nightmares."

She had been speaking out toward the gazebo but now she turned to Thea. "They're so little, Thea, they don't know what he's talking about when he talks about crack and ghetto violence and little children getting shot with assault weapons. It just scares them."

She looked intently at Thea, asking for understanding. Thea nodded. Sandy went on. "I asked him the other night please not to talk in front of them." She stopped, biting her lips to keep her crying under some control. "The bastard," she said with barely controlled rage. "I asked him not to talk in front of those babies, so he stopped talking. He comes in with that horrible scowl on his face just long enough to change his clothes, and he won't talk to me at all. That's how he gets back, the coldest, the meanest—I hate him. I'd divorce him but he'd force the sale of the house. He'd ruin everything we've worked for, everything we've built. He'd tear it all down to nothing without a second thought. Everything would change. I'd have to start all over again."

"That might not be such a terrible thing," Thea said.

Sandy's lower lip trembled. "But I like my house. I want to stay there. Except for the way Lyle is acting, I like my life the way it is. I don't want to lose it."

Sandy cried again, and as Thea tried to comfort her she realized she would not know who Sandy was if Sandy were without her house and her marriage, one as much a possession as the other, together providing an answer to the question, Who is Sandy Hindermann?

Sandy was what she had.

19

Thea had another night of waking in a sweat, the sheets twisted around her legs, her heart sending vibrations down through the bed. A dream had waked her, a dream that began with the realities of her days and nights. She dreamed of going to sleep, and she slept on the cusp of waking, drifting in and out, never quite certain what was real and what was not.

The dream was real enough at the start, beginning with a man coming to see her about installing a security system, the same man who had come to the house that very day to give her an estimate, but in the dream his eyebrows were arched peculiarly, drawn up nearly to triangles, the eyes underneath them mad, spittle foamed white at the corners of his mouth.

In the dream she was nervous. She wished the man would hurry and finish, but he seemed to be delivering a canned sales pitch, determined not to miss a word. She kept glancing toward the door, and every time she did, the speed of his delivery would slow down and his voice would deepen, as if he were a record being played at slow speed. She wanted him to finish before Burgess arrived. But his words came slower and slower, his eyes got madder and madder, and she began to feel an urgency and a frustration that centered itself in her groin, as if at any moment an orgasmic explosion would lift her right off the red brocade sofa and send her crashing into the crystal chandelier.

What had actually happened that day was that Burgess and his girlfriend had arrived as the salesman was leaving. As Thea was showing him out, the man remembered a brochure he'd meant to give her and put his briefcase on the hall table to rifle through it. There were some awkward moments, the four of them in the hallway, Burgess introducing Thea to Janine, and Thea not certain whether to introduce them to the salesman or not. If she did, it would prolong his being there and her embarrassment—an irrational feeling that Burgess had caught her doing something wrong. If she didn't, they might feel she was in some way slighting them. In the end she didn't because the salesman snapped his briefcase shut, told her he'd send her the brochure, and departed hastily enough to make Thea think he was uncomfortable too.

It was Burgess, that way he had of always looking amused by whatever was going on around him. It was, Thea decided, another way of being inscrutable, and inscrutable people always had such a commanding presence, drawing people to them, at the same time intimidating them.

"Getting one of them alarms put in, are you?" Burgess had said in front of the salesman. When he said that, his girlfriend smiled a tight, rather contemptuous smile, as if Burgess had said one thing but implied another.

Thea looked from one to the other of them before she said, "I'm thinking about it," but she was thinking this had turned into a ludicrous situation: she'd been scorned by Sandy for hiring Burgess and his not-very-expert men in the first place, frightened by Lyle because she'd even let them in the house, now laughed at by Burgess and his girlfriend for putting in a burglar alarm to keep them out, because it was *them*, all of them, the alarm was supposed to keep out; it was, after all, *them* against *us*.

She offered them tea, but Burgess declined, saying he'd just come by to talk about the bookcase and check on the upstairs work. She gave him money for the saw. He folded it and it disappeared into his pants pocket. Then he and Janine left in the oxidized-red pickup truck, the putt-putting of the muffler growing louder by the day. A little while later the workers left and the Cadillac came for Delzora.

Yes, it was all ludicrous, nothing more so than Burgess' buying a flashy, souped-up Cadillac so his mother could be chauffeured to her job as a maid while he himself drove a beat-up old truck that needed a new muffler.

Her dream was full of these realities given an odd, sinister twist— Burgess and his girlfriend arriving while the salesman, determined, was finishing his slow-speed pitch, the two of them laughing openly at her, though Thea did not think they were at all amused, herself babbling incoherently, trying to be heard over the loud rumbling of the salesman's deep voice, trying to explain to them it was all Lyle's idea, since Bobby had been attacked in front of the house. Janine said, "Burglar alarm won't do much good out there," and she and Burgess laughed some more. Thea kept trying to explain, but she was speaking so fast they could not understand her.

And then there was a leap in the dream to herself asleep in her bedroom, next to the cabinet full of dolls. She dreamed of a deep sleep brutally interrupted by a sudden and insistent shrieking, a sound so loud and intense that it seemed three-dimensional in its ability to grab her body and make her fight to be released, all of her muscles bunched and pulsating against its huge and pervasive force. It was the new burglar alarm going off in the middle of the night. As her eyes snapped open, the glass of the curio cabinet shattered and the frightened faces of the dolls cracked into spidery black lines from the high pitch of the Gestapo-siren wail of the alarm.

She dreamed that Burgess, Janine, and the salesman being there before was only a dream, but that now she was really awake, wide awake, and someone was either in the house or trying to get in. She must do something: first, get out of bed.

She felt her way across the carpet of her room, her toes digging in, holding on for dear life, and made her way down the stairs—so many stairs, she didn't remember so many flights—the darkness filled with the scream of the alarm, so that if she screamed, no one could hear her.

She groped her way down, down endless flights, cowering, expecting an attack, to the panel where she shut off the alarm. Outside the front door she could see the police already there. She ran to the door and down the walkway in her long white gown, the light from the police cars casting supernatural blue on the street, the houses, and the foliage. She thought she saw Bobby lying under the oak tree, but it was only the light playing tricks.

She ran to the nearest policeman, whose head was bent as he wrote in a small booklet he held in his hand. He stood in the shadows of the big oak so she wasn't sure at first, but yes, it was Lyle. She began to laugh with relief, to tell him how glad she was to see him; she wanted to fall on him, have him hold her.

He cut into her laughter. "We've checked the premises, ma'am."

He spoke as if he did not know her, his hard impassive face showing no recognition of her. "No sign of entry, all doors and windows closed and locked. It is the responsibility of the homeowner to make certain the security system is in proper working order." He tore a page from the booklet and handed it to her. It was a ticket for improper use of a burglar alarm and disturbing the peace.

She started to reach out to him, to say, Lyle, don't you know me, but he turned and went back to his police car, only it was Burgess' customized Cadillac he got into instead. He stuck a blue light on top and he was gone, his siren blaring, his light flashing, the chromed Cadillac streaking off into the night.

The other policemen left too, and the lights went off behind the neighbors' windows. All alone again, Thea walked slowly back to the large foreboding house, gloom settled on it so that it looked for all the world like one of those scary Victorian houses on the covers of the Gothic novels in the supermarkets, and she, like the heroine standing before the house in her thin white gown, was caught between whatever sinister forces were inside the house and the unknown, invisible ones outside. The only thing missing from the picture was a man.

She went back inside, locked the door behind her and started down the hallway. And there, standing in the shadows, waiting for her, was a man.

Was there something familiar about him? The way he held himself? The cock of his head? His thinness—or was that just the darkness camouflaging his bulk? She couldn't be sure, the shadows pitching his face into blackness, his features, as long as he stood back, remaining unknown. Her heart pounded wildly. Outside, in the distance, was the putt-putting sound of a bad muffler. Thea woke up.

The dream had been so real, and she'd been so certain she was already awake, that she lay in bed thinking the man must be in the room with her. She strained to see into the darkness, a block of ice in her stomach, her skin cooling rapidly without covers over her. She was too afraid to move. She remembered the sound of the muffler and wondered if that had been part of the dream or if she'd really heard it. She wanted to get up and look outside but she couldn't.

It took a long time to calm down, to feel that there was no threat in the house. It took until daybreak. And as she lay there Thea tried to understand why she was so frightened so often. She'd never been frightened like this in Massachusetts. Of course, there were no ghettos where she'd lived, no housing projects; in fact, hardly any sign of poverty, and hardly any sign of blacks, some students, a few professors, a poet or a musician in town every now and then. It was not the way it was here in New Orleans, people living so close together, their lives intersecting and connecting frequently, more frequently than anyone liked, if they would admit it. Take this neighborhood, so many of the blacks dependent on the whites for jobs and not enough jobs to go around, some of those same whites dependent on the blacks to keep up their huge houses, their lawns and gardens, even their children, and not wanting to give up their easy way of life.

But there was something that reached farther than that, beyond the exteriors of everyone's lives. Thea could hear Sandy referring to *them*, and alone now, she heard all the fear and hate, the racism, that one word carried. There was no denying the fear, no denying it was real, and easy enough to see how such fear could turn into hate. There was no denying, either, the unjustness of that hate and the basic unfairness of the often vast differences in the way the two races lived, the haves having so much, the have-nots having it always in their faces. No one had been concerned about the people in the Convent and their lives of violence and deprivation and misery. No one had been concerned until they came out, threatening and dangerous in their poverty and need.

Her dream had cleared some of her confusion and left a small crystal of understanding about what she was trying to come to terms with: not only the lives of blacks and whites, but the fates of both races were connected by their dependence upon each other. No matter how either race would try, there could be no separation. What one did affected the other; neither could thrive unless both did. Her parents' death forced her to face the fact that their fates, all their fates, were connected, and that this truth transcended her personal loss.

Yet she was struck by a piercing aloneness, as if these thoughts were more responsible for her aloneness in the world than any death. She got up and pulled back the curtain, letting the first light of day into the room. She found herself wishing Michael were there, but he had not even called, just boxes arriving now and again, no letters, no communication, as if he were the one offended, the one who had been abandoned. She cried thinking about him. But Michael was only another kind of aloneness. She stood at the window and pressed her eyes with the heels of her hands until her tears retreated, catching in her throat.

20

Thea did not know what she was going to do about getting a security system. She could imagine herself lying awake at night waiting for the alarm to go off, in bed cringing against the anticipated blast of noise. On the same morning after her dream, Bobby solved her dilemma. He arrived at the house and surprised her with a dog. He also brought a cat, a canary in a cage, and a Corinthian-style plaster pedestal.

Thea hung the birdcage so that the canary had a view of the trees from one of the living room windows. She put the pedestal on the porch so that when the kitten was old enough to get on top of it, he could jump to it from the backs of the wicker rockers. It seemed unlikely, though, that he would ever use it to escape from the dog: on the afternoon of the first day the kitten curled up against the dog to take a nap. The sight made Thea so happy that her throat got tight and her chest got full. The dog, no longer a puppy but not yet full grown, looked comfortable. When she stretched out she was like a tawny bear rug. She was a mixed golden retriever and Labrador with a rich chestnut coat.

"That dog jus the color of a nice dark roux," Zora said.

So Thea called the dog Roux.

She stayed busy getting the animals adjusted to the house—and the house to the animals—and she forgot for a while how irked she'd been that the carpenters had failed to show up that morning. Neither had Burgess called or come by to tell her why. It had never happened before; nevertheless, all she could hear was Sandy saying, "You front them money, they disappear."

Later that afternoon she asked Zora to help her clear out the last of Aunt Althea's personal belongings from the closet of one of the unused bedrooms upstairs.

Roux followed them up, behind her the kitten, who stopped to mew every couple of steps and had to be coaxed to come along.

As they reached the upstairs hallway, one of the painters, Jared, the one who sang, came out of what had been Aunt Althea's bedroom, paint can in one hand, brush in the other. He saw Roux and froze just outside the doorway. Roux rushed forward, the hair raised on the back of her neck. She stopped about the middle of the hall, planted her front legs, her hind legs ready to spring, and barked fiercely. The kitten, not to be left out of the action, arched its back and hissed. Jared stepped backward, his free arm held out in front of him as if to ward off an attack. He tripped on the threshold and the paint can swung on its wire handle as he jerked his arms upward to maintain his balance. Paint sloshed onto the hardwood floor.

"Roux!" Thea yelled, but Roux rushed forward again, stopping short of stepping in the paint, but barking louder and more insistently.

"Miss, please," Jared said, his voice a plaintive whisper.

Thea moved up beside Roux, telling her it was all right, running her hands over the dog's head and neck. Roux backed off but continued a low growling until she let Thea lead her into the spare bedroom. Thea closed the door behind them and hugged the dog, glad that she'd won Roux's loyalty already but feeling bad about Jared. She went out to the hall. Jared was cleaning up the spilled paint, Zora watching.

"I'm sorry my dog scared you, Jared," she said. His eyes darted up at her and back to the paint spill.

"Liked to scared me to death too," Zora said.

The other painter working with Jared came to the door grinning. "All dogs scare Jared," he told Thea. "They all want to eat im up." He laughed.

Jared turned and said something to him that Thea didn't catch but didn't sound too nice. The other painter didn't stop laughing, but he moved back inside the room.

Thea tried to think of something else to say to apologize. Before she could, Jared said, "I don' like dogs."

"I understand. I'll keep her away from you."

"I'd 'preciate that," he said and went to get more clean-up cloths.

Thea and Zora went into the spare bedroom where Roux sat waiting. She jumped up to lick Thea's face.

"Bobby Buchanan done give you a good watchdog," Zora said. Roux jumped on Thea again. Thea patted her and told her to get down. Zora closed the door and said, "Maybe she don't like them black mens."

"No," Thea protested. "That's not it. She knew Jared didn't like her. She knew he was afraid of her too." She didn't know if it was true, nor was it her first concern at the moment. She said, "I wonder if she would have hurt him."

Zora, crossing the room to the closet, stopped and turned to Thea. "Hard to say," she said. "When somebody's that afraid, I guess they be pretty scary themselves."

Zora had such a way of saying things, a way of making Thea think about something differently, from a viewpoint she would never have thought to take. Roux, of course, had meant to frighten Jared, but Thea had latched onto another idea—what a person who was frightened looked like to someone who didn't necessarily mean to be frightening. She thought about Sonny Johnson's nervousness making her so nervous. It would be much the same, wouldn't it?

But the moment to reflect on this idea vanished when Zora opened the closet door and out of it came that odor that was so overwhelmingly Aunt Althea. The odor of plaster and paint had moved it out of the rest of the house, but it spilled from the closet, a powdery evocative odor that Thea might have called "old lady" smell except that she remembered it as always being there, even when Aunt Althea was a much younger woman. In that odor Thea smelled part of her childhood. It was such an integral element of those years that she had never thought to decide if it was pleasant or unpleasant until the day she arrived in New Orleans after such a long absence. When Zora had opened the front door that afternoon, the smell had lunged at Thea, distinctly unpleasant, not only an odor but a powerful way of summoning feelings that could not be summoned so immediately or so succinctly through any of the other senses. She had recoiled from it then as she recoiled from it now, only to be drawn toward it, as to a memory not fully remembered or an experience not fully understood.

She stepped into the closet. Against one wall hung a row of dresses. On the other side were shelves with boxes of old shoes stacked on them, and higher up, on the top shelf, a row of well-worn handbags. Aunt Althea must never have thrown anything away. And all of it was drenched in that powdery odor. It was flowery, yet it also had a metallic quality to it, as if you'd stopped to smell the roses, expecting a floral perfume, only to find that the roses were sculpted from tin.

Thea wrinkled her nose. "This room will have to be painted," she told Zora. "It's the only way to get rid of that smell."

"That's that talc Miss Althea liked," Zora said. "She used to get it over at the K & B. I 'member one time she went over there and someone tole her they wasn't gon be gettin it no more. She bought a whole box and brought it home. She told Mr. Dum'ville 'bout buyin it and he says, 'A whole box? I never liked the stuff.'" Zora shook her head. "Lawd, lawd, they went round and round 'bout it, Miss Althea sayin he never tole her that before and him sayin she never asked him. She was mad with him for a week."

"But she didn't stop wearing it," Thea said.

"Yeah she did, for a while. Then she said Mr. Dum'ville never noticed nothin even when it was put under his nose, and she started wearin it again."

"Did he notice?" Thea wanted to know.

"No. Sho didn't. Least, he never said nothin. Miss Althea said he wouldn't say nothin 'bout nothin 'less them sisters of his said somethin."

Thea handed Zora some of the dresses. "Those sisters. Aunt Althea did not like Uncle Cecil's sisters."

"Who could blame her? They never treated her like fam'ly. She weren't no sister-in-law to them womens, she were a rival."

Thea dumped another load of dresses on one of the twin beds in the room. "What do you mean, a rival?"

Zora leaned against the bed, one hand on her hip. "I mean them sisters never treated Mr. Dum'ville like a brother neither. They treated him more like he was a husband or somethin." Thea raised her eyebrows at what Zora was telling her. "It's the truth," Zora said. "They come over to this house fussin all 'round him like a coupla old busybodies and flirtin with Mr. Dum'ville too. That ain't no way to be treatin a brother."

This was definitely a new slant for Thea, who had seen her aunt as culturally, socially, and articulately inferior to the dangerously sharp-tongued Dumondville women, not as a victim to them, not as rivals from whom she had to win her own husband's affection. Now she couldn't help but wonder if maybe it wasn't by watching Uncle Cecil's sisters that Aunt Althea had learned how to flirt herself. Do unto others what has been done to you.

Thea and Zora had spent hours side by side going through Aunt Althea's things, talking about Aunt Althea's eccentricities and about Uncle Cecil and his peculiarities. Zora was the only person left for Thea to share family history with, a springboard for her memories. She felt close to Zora, talking to her about these things, but of course, her closeness to Zora went back to the time that her parents died, since it was Zora who had comforted Thea and given her the sympathy she needed, Zora who had understood her loss while Aunt Althea made the audacious move to replace it, busying herself with Thea's clothes, prying into her friendships, eager for her to make friends at her new school, break off with her friends from the old school, leave off with her old life, begin a new one, meddling, not ever giving Thea the privacy to be her own person or have her own thoughts. But now Zora was telling her that her aunt had had her meddlers too.

"God, she was an exasperating person," Thea said. "You'd think she would have tried not to be such an old busybody herself, especially after my parents died. She was on me about everything from my clothes to those damned dolls."

"Well, honey," Zora said, "she was jus dealin with her grief, doin all that."

Thea stopped folding a dress. "She never acted like she was grieving. The way she talked about my mother . . . like she was mad at her. She'd say something about her, then snap her mouth shut, you know, Zora, the way she did that, like she was furious."

"But she missed your mother, honey. You musta known that. They was close, them two, talked about everything under the sun."

Yes, Thea knew her mother and aunt had talked, mostly over the phone, sometimes for hours. Her mother would ask Thea to leave the room sometimes, and her father would tell her mother that whenever she talked to her sister, she was always upset afterwards, and her mother would say that wasn't true. She would defend Aunt Althea, but her father would say that her sister thought she was superior because she was older and she had married money.

Thea sat on the bed, holding her aunt's dress, thinking that her father, the way he'd talked about Aunt Althea, had somehow convinced her that her aunt had only used her mother, had bullied her. And after her mother was gone, Thea had assumed that Aunt Althea was angry that her mother was no longer there to be used and bullied. She had never thought of her aunt as grieving for her mother, missing her in any way similar to the way Thea missed her. Or that she might have grieved when Thea left as well.

"Is that why she couldn't bear to see me leave?" Thea remembered that awful day, her bags packed and waiting in the hallway, Michael driving up to get her, and Aunt Althea closed up in her bedroom in a sulk, refusing to say good-bye. It was Zora who'd stood on the front porch waving, wiping a tear away as she and Michael drove off. "I was the last one," Thea said. "She didn't have anyone else."

"She took it hard," Zora told her. "Mighty hard."

It was the only time Delzora had ever had much sympathy for her employer, a malcontent who was so unhappy all the time about small things that she didn't know how to be unhappy about the large things. Delzora knew it had nearly broken Althea's heart to see the girl go, yet Althea had never been able to let her niece know that, just as she'd never been able to grieve properly over her sister's death.

Thea sat there a long time, holding the dress, while Zora folded the others and put them in boxes. She thought about her aunt growing old all alone, no husband, no children, no relatives left, despised by her in-laws, a classic southern story of an old woman whose maid and gardener were the people in the world she was closest to, but who could not be true friends even with them because, in her mind, they were not equal, could never be, it simply wasn't possible in her frame of reference. They were servants first and finally, who did things right most of the time but not all of the time and had to be told when they didn't.

Thea put her hand on Zora's shoulder. "I think I understand it now, Zora. I understand why she just decided to die."

Zora straightened up from one of the boxes and said, "Why's that?" She was in fact very interested in why, since she couldn't understand it at all.

"Well, look," Thea began. "She was old and she was tired and she didn't have anyone left to care about. All she had to care about was this house, but a house can't care back. She just didn't have anything to look forward to anymore."

Zora was looking hard at her. "That ain't no reason to decide to die," she said belligerently. "I'm old and tired and I ain't got nothin to look forward to neither 'cept comin and takin care of this house every day. And it ain't even mine." She went back to packing.

"But Zora . . ." Thea put her hand on Zora again, to make her stop and look at her. "You have Burgess, Zora."

Delzora said nothing. She reached for another dress, folded it, bent over to put it in the box, her movements a little slower, her bones feeling a little older. She'd been angry, but it was silly to be angry with the girl, she still thought of Thea as a girl, who meant well but didn't understand, not about Burgess—she didn't want her to understand about Burgess, didn't want her to know—and not about the rest of Delzora's life either.

Thea wanted to see through Delzora's eyes, but for Delzora, that was only another way Thea had of looking at her own self, feeling her own feelings and putting them on someone else.

They's them and they's us, Delzora thought. And she wished they would just realize that and stop trying to make us into them.

Burgess finally did come that afternoon, to tell Thea that the carpenters would be there the next morning. He came after Zora had left, as if he were trying to avoid his mother.

When he rang the doorbell, Roux barked once and bounded to the door. Thea was making her way slowly down the stairs, carrying one of the boxes she and Zora had packed. When she saw Burgess through the leaded glass she was afraid there would be a scene similar to the one with Jared, that Zora could possibly be right in thinking Roux might not like black men. But Burgess came in without hesitation, with his wide friendly smile, talking easily to Thea, and Roux sat relaxed watching them.

"Decided to get yourself a dog too?" Burgess asked, his irony making a seemingly casual statement uncomfortably poignant. He patted Roux on the head and Roux's tail brushed lazily back and forth across the floor.

"Yes," said Thea, "and bars on the windows and over all the doors and invisible light beams that trigger alarms and guard snakes patrolling the grounds."

"That's good," Burgess said. "The only place I see you still be vulnerable is up on the roof. I got a retired fightin cock you can borrow, pretend he a weather vane, do some serious damage to them UFOs."

Thea had meant to light into Burgess about the carpenters the moment she saw him, but that smile of his had disarmed her immediately. A good thing too, since "We get on it tomorrow" had meant just that: Burgess had been out buying the wood, picking up a load of it along with the new saw, and now was hauling it into the house, Roux shadowing him, romping alongside him to the red pickup and back, Burgess pausing now and then to play tag with her in the front yard.

He was putting the last of the wood in the library when Bobby arrived. Roux saw Bobby and left Burgess to jump up on him and lick his face.

"Down!" Bobby yelled. Burgess came out of the library and into the foyer. "Hasn't she got this dog trained yet?" Bobby asked him. He brushed off the front of his clean polo shirt. "I just got out of the damned shower. Sit," he commanded Roux. Roux stood there wagging her tail. Bobby shook his head at Burgess. "I gave her the dog this morning. She's had all day."

Burgess started with his deep, rumbling laugh. "She been too busy with them guard snakes outside."

"Guard snakes, of course," Bobby said. "I didn't think it could be the DT's." He and Burgess strolled back to the kitchen and were popping beers open when Thea came down the rear stairway. "First beer of the day, Tee," Bobby called out to her. He lifted the bottle toward her as she joined them in the kitchen, then he said to Burgess, who was mopping his sweaty forehead with the sleeve of his dirty white shirt, "Looks like you've been working hard, my man. Showing an awful lot of energy for a brother, aren't you?"

Thea made a sound of disgust, which they both ignored.

"Yeah," Burgess said, drawing out his words, his upper lip tipped back as he grinned. "Guess I should learn to conserve energy like you rich white boys. Try not to work at all."

21

About thirty years earlier many white people had felt it necessary to flee the inner city and move to Jefferson Parish, which in some places is a stone's throw across a drainage canal from New Orleans. It seemed far away then, a new frontier being conquered by developers who built modern brick bungalows atop what previously had been a salt marsh on the southwestern shore of Lake Pontchartrain. If it was hard to leave the exotic charms of the old New Orleans neighborhoods, huge oaks and magnolias, wrought iron, high-ceilinged houses, it was easy enough to move into a neighborhood where the neighbors were all like you: white.

The white flight out to the Parish was caused by the integration of schools and by blacks' inching their way into middle-class neighborhoods, either by moving in or breaking in. The blacks out in the Parish lived in small, isolated areas; they kept to themselves, or it was easy enough to see to it that they did. Out in the Parish, too, there were lots of new private schools for whites being started by various Protestant and fundamentalist religious organizations.

Everything out in the Parish was new and safe and mostly white. And the people in the Parish meant to keep it that way.

Thirty years passed and the Parish changed considerably, growing larger—more people, more houses, more high-rises, more commercial enterprises—becoming a small city unto itself, but still it was safe and mostly white, and still the people meant to keep it that way.

No one understood this better or believed in this more than the sheriff of Jefferson Parish. But as Christmas neared, there was an unprecedented, parishwide rash of burglaries. It caused fear, anxiety, and a general feeling of violation. The people demanded action. The sheriff, in response, called a press conference to announce that any suspicious-looking black males seen in all-white neighborhoods would be stopped and questioned, especially those driving shabby, disreputable cars.

It was early evening, but already the atmosphere in the Solar Club was smoky. The patrons, most of them men, were doing some serious drinking, some hunkered down over the bar, some sitting at small tables lined along the walls of the large, low-ceilinged room. Christmas-tree lights were strung up around the lounge, not because the Christmas season was approaching but because they and the edging of silver tinsel hung just below the ceiling and running the entire width of all four walls were never taken down. The lights twinkled and blinked and seemed more numerous than they actually were because their twinkling and blinking was reflected in the large sheet of gold-veined black mirror behind the bar.

Burgess and Dexter were at the bar drinking beer. The TV above the bar was tuned to the evening news. They had already seen the sheriff of Jefferson once on the local news, and now they were hearing his statement to the press again on the national broadcast. The bartender turned up the volume, and all the men in the club gathered in a tight group around the bar to listen.

Sherree walked into the Solar Club just as a spokesman for the NAACP labeled the sheriff and his mandate racist. Sherree was tired from fooling with the kids all day and she wanted a drink but she could see that no one was going to get her anything until they were finished watching the news. She went up beside Dexter, who slipped his arm around her and, his eyes glued to the TV set, absentmindedly patted her rear end. Irritated, Sherree bumped his hand up against the edge of the empty barstool behind them to get him to stop. Dexter hardly noticed: a plan was beginning to form in his mind.

As soon as the report was over, the men shuffled back from their tight knot around the bar and began grumbling, an angry voice rising out of the low growl of protest every once in a while. Dexter remained silent until his plan worked itself out. Burgess listened to what the men had to say. Sherree told the bartender to get her a margarita.

All of a sudden Dexter stood up from his barstool and shouted above the drone of discontent, "So they gon stop any suspicious-lookin black man in a beat-up car? How many men an how many cars you think they can stop at once?"

116

The men drew back in to listen to Dexter. After he told them his plan, the mood in the Solar Club changed. The grumbling turned to laughter as they all got behind Dexter's idea. Drinks were ordered and there was the sound of their palms slapping the bar and one anothers' backs. They started listing all the people they knew who had especially *bad* cars. A line formed at the pay phone.

Sherree was the only person in the Solar Club not caught up in the spirit of fun and protest. "I don' like this, Dexter. You jus screwin around, an it's gon be nothin but trouble."

"Aw, relax, Sherree," Burgess told her. "Let em have their fun."

Sherree said emphatically, "I ain't gon bail him out."

"It ain't gon come to that, you'll see. An anyway, if it does, you know I'll take care of it."

Sherree shrugged, flipping Burgess off with one shoulder. She turned to the bar and her margarita. Sometimes Burgess really pissed her off. If he hadn't liked the idea, one word and it would have been dropped. He was like the goddamn pope, and the minute she thought that, a little laugh rose inside her: the Bishop of Convent Street—she'd called it right.

But that one little laugh was all Sherree was going to get. She sat sipping her drink and feeling a kind of uneasiness. Or maybe it was irritation, being tired of their childishness—all she ever did anymore it seemed was fool with children—or maybe it was discontent, being just plain tired sometimes of everything. She rested her elbows on the bar and tried to concentrate on the taste of the margarita. She licked at the salt around the lip of the glass. She read the neon-pink lipstick writing slanted across the gold-veined mirror behind the bar—The Solar Club, So Hot It's Kool!—and tried to feel pleased that she could read it. She looked at the little Christmas-tree lights framing the mirror, the edging of silver tinsel. She tried to feel the way she did sometimes at night when the place was jumping and the jazz was playing and looking at the lights and tinsel made her happy, excited, made her think life was all right after all.

So big deal. If they wanted a parade, let them have a parade; if they weren't doing that, they'd probably be up to no good, drinking their lives away like they all seemed to do if they weren't on drugs, like her daddy did, drinking and banging his head on a table corner—dead drunk. Everyone in this city was parade-happy anyway. She'd just keep doing what she'd been doing. Maybe she didn't dance anymore, but that didn't mean she couldn't have her secret ambitions, that she couldn't be somebody again someday.

Sherree finished her drink and felt her misgivings begin to wash away. She told the bartender to get her another.

At noon the following day Dexter's parade of cars lined up on Convent Street across from the Solar Club. Some of the cars were shabby and disreputable—pitted and rusted, bumpy Bondo jobs, fenders and doors that didn't match, fenders missing altogether, peeling vinyl tops, hoods that wouldn't close all the way, cracked windshields, broken windows replaced with plastic held on with duct tape. And some were disreputable in other ways: rolling works of street art, graffiti on wheels, murals, swirls of color, licks of fire, Malcolm X on the side of a van, midnight-blue velour carved with gold stars and slices of moon, a Volkswagen with a Continental kit and the grillwork of a Rolls, and at the very head of the parade, Dexter in the customized Cadillac. Streamers and balloons flew from the antennas.

The caravan moved slowly down Convent Street toward the river, to take River Road out to the Parish. There the drivers would cut through the black Shrewsbury section—so they could show off—then work their way across the white suburban neighborhoods of Metairie until they got out to the big posh houses on the lake.

Burgess and Janine watched the parade leave, nearly twenty cars, waving them on their way from the Convent Street Housing Project. But Burgess didn't like the idea of hanging around the Convent on that particular day. In spite of what he'd said to Sherree the day before, he was afraid there might be trouble, if not in Jefferson, then after the parade. He didn't want to be at the Convent then and he didn't want Janine there either.

"I'm feelin jumpier than usual," he said to Janine.

Janine thought maybe that was because he had the baby to think about now, and she thought that was the way it was supposed to be. She left in the pickup truck with Burgess, feeling more in love than ever. She didn't know how she'd gotten so lucky, to have somebody like Burgess in love with her, glad she was going to have a baby. He wasn't like other men, lazy, indifferent to babies, living off women, men who were drinkers and dopers, who got hold of money and had to be hot shots, pissing it all away like there was no tomorrow. Never mind how Burgess got his money, he was doing something with it. He had a plan, he told her, for the baby. For our son, Janine said; Janine was sure the baby was a boy. And she would make sure the boy grew up to be like Burgess, not like those other men, not like Dexter, that ass Dexter, thinking he was such a rebel because he had dreamed up this parade of cars as a protest against some honky's racism, as if that could make any difference. Burgess was the real rebel, the one who made the real difference. All you had to do was look at the difference in the Convent.

No, Janine thought, moving across the seat closer to Burgess, not a rebel: a revolutionary.

Burgess the revolutionary, the Bishop of Convent Street, his conviction growing stronger by the day that it was time to get out of the Convent altogether, took Janine to a sandwich shop for lunch, for a stroll through the Audubon Zoo to kill time, and then headed over to the cloistered safety of Thea Tamborella's house.

"Damn nuisance," Delzora said, armed with a broom, fighting her ongoing battle against sawdust, "keepin this house in a uproar." All around her was chaos and noise: the shrill of the saw, the pounding of hammers, men shouting, the radio blaring, Jared wailing, the dog barking to be let in, the cat mewing and clawing at Zora's legs, trying to climb up her as if she were a tree.

She took the broom and went back to the utility room to get some peace and quiet. She might as well change her clothes anyway; it was getting late, almost quitting time. She took off her wig and pulled the white uniform over her head.

While Delzora was in the back, Burgess and Janine arrived. As soon as Burgess was in the house, Jared was at the head of the stairs, yelling down to him, "They headed back, Burgess!" He meant, of course, Dexter and the cars, their route having been reported all afternoon by WYLD radio.

"Nothin happened yet?" Burgess asked.

"Nothin!" Jared yelled, overly excited. "No sheriff, no deputies, nothin. Dexter's been on the radio callin it a parade of protest, and the TV station's been there too. Ain't like that sheriff to miss a photo opportunity."

Burgess went up to see the work, then came down to talk to the carpenter, an older man everybody called Mr. Robert. Jared and the two men working with him began cleaning up so they could get to the Convent to meet the parade. Thea came down from the third floor where she'd been trying to decide what pieces of furniture to reupholster and put downstairs. Bobby came in with house supplies, a case of Abita and some bags of Zapp's chips. He was heading to the kitchen when Jared began shouting from upstairs, "Burgess, they comin! I can see em from the window—they headed this way!"

Jared and the other two men came flying down, their feet clattering on the wooden stairway, their hands squeaking on the banister, out to the front porch. Mr. Robert's helper went after them, then came Burgess and Thea, Bobby and Janine, Delzora bringing up the rear. The only one who hadn't rushed outside was Mr. Robert.

They could see the line of cars coming down Convent Street. They pressed against the porch railing as if they were behind police barricades at a Mardi Gras parade, craning for a view. They heard the sounds of Mardi Gras parades too, the dull thuds of big brass drums and the music, but it was coming from the cars' radios turned up so loud they could be heard two blocks away and felt deep down in the chest.

Thea looked around and saw that Mr. Robert hadn't come outside. She went back into the house. He was still in the library, his head with its tight salt-and-pepper curls bent over his work.

"Don't you want to come outside with us, Mr. Robert?" she asked.

He looked up quickly, as if she had surprised him. "Oh no," he said, his voice old and gravelly, "I don' mess aroun with that stuff," and he went back to measuring a piece of wood.

Thea stood there a few seconds longer, admiring what she could already see was going to be a beautiful library. My library will be the equal of anything in Sandy's house, Thea thought, and wondered at this competitiveness, so firmly in place within her, that before this moment she had not known was there. She watched Mr. Robert. He worked slowly and steadily, handling each piece of wood sensuously, stroking away the dust, fitting it perfectly.

"It's going to be the most beautiful library anyone's ever seen, Mr. Robert." This time he did not look up, but he smiled and nodded once. "And they'll all want you to build one for them."

He measured and marked one plank, put it down, and picked

120

up another. "I won't never build another like this one," he said. He glanced up to see her smile before he made another mark.

Thea turned to go back to the porch. Through the open door she could see Bobby handing beer around, passing the bags of chips. As Thea started out, Delzora came in muttering under her breath, passing Thea as if she were not there. She almost passed Mr. Robert too, but she stopped abruptly and said in a tone that would have been hostile except for what she was saying, "Mr. Robert, you want some tea?"

The old carpenter set down the piece of wood he was holding. "Yes ma'am," he said, "some tea would be mighty fine," and he followed Delzora into the kitchen.

Thea returned to the porch. She stood back from the others and watched Janine and Burgess together at the railing, closely together, the sides of their bodies sealed like Siamese twins. Their closeness separated them from the rest of those at the railing. Now their bodies moved apart, but only so their heads could come together as they whispered and laughed. They faced each other, quite apart from everything that was going on around them. They weren't laughing anymore; Janine smiled, a smile with the serenity and inner certainty of the Mona Lisa. Burgess touched her stomach, just his fingertips on her slight roundness, lightly, reverently, then his arm went up around her shoulders and they turned away, their attention back to the street.

The moment that Burgess' fingertips reached Janine's body, Thea knew that Janine was pregnant. This knowledge traveled clear through her, a sudden sexual pain burning her insides, intensified by the loud music coming from the cars. It was not a pain to double you over, but a pain to make you want to move, to ease the pain by moving, to run, to dance in a frenzy. She could not move.

Bobby turned, as if only now missing her, and saw her standing there, planted there on the porch. He came to her, mercifully saying nothing. He touched her hair, then circled his arm around her back and she moved into his embrace, easing the pain by touching as much of the side of his body as she could with hers, sealing herself against it.

And so they were standing as the Cadillac pulled up even with the house, the music shaking the very foundations, rattling the glass of the tall windows facing the porch. Jared and the other guys crowded the space at the top of the steps, but stayed there instead of going down the walkway.

Dexter stopped and got out of the car. He had on his leather outfit, pants and vest, and in the spirit of rebellion, he'd worn the vest without a shirt on underneath. He elevated himself on the edge of the car's floor next to the driver's seat and fanned his bare arm at the cars behind him to get them to turn down their radios. Once they did he yelled, "Hey, Burgess, I come to pick up your mama!"

This was greeted with a great deal of hooting and laughing, and Burgess yelled back, "My mama goes with me."

Dexter raised a triumphant fist high and shouted, "The Solar Club!" He got back in the car. As soon as he did, the volume of the music climbed to its former pitch.

All the loud music, the excitement, had driven Roux nearly to a frenzy on the back porch. She also heard the sirens before the people did. She clawed at the door and yelped and whined and barked until Delzora couldn't stand it anymore and finally let her in. Roux tore through the house, through the open front door, nearly knocking Jared and another man down the steps. She flew down the walkway and out the gate to the street. The cars were moving again and she ran alongside them, jumping and barking and threatening, mostly to catch herself under their wheels.

They heard the sirens now, coming up through the loud music, creating, along with confusion, a concussion on their eardrums and on the windows behind them. No one noticed the crack across the upper pane of one of the living room windows. Bobby put his hands over his ears and went after Roux, and as he did the line of cars came to a stop, but stopping from the rear to the front, leaving wide gaps between the cars. Next to them came a line of police cars, some of them pulling into the wider gaps. The assault of noise stopped, but gradually, an extra warning wail from a siren here and there, the radios losing volume as one after another was turned off, Dexter's last, one last moment of knowing no fear. Uniformed officers soon had all the occupants of the cars on the street, cuffed and waiting to be picked up by police vans.

Bobby had grabbed Roux by the collar, and seeing a friend of Lyle's, a cop called B.T., get out of one of the police cars at the front of the parade, walked over to him.

"What gives, B.T.?"

"Parading without a permit," B.T. said, putting one foot up on the car bumper and crossing his forearms over his knee. The position reminded Bobby of Lyle; he wondered if they taught it at the police academy.

"You got to be kidding. How come they didn't arrest them in Jefferson Parish?"

"Beats me."

"What an asshole." Bobby meant the sheriff of Jefferson. B.T. knew who he meant. "Just got a big mouth," he told Bobby. He looked down the street, surveying the action as the police vans started picking people up. "Should've just done it and kept his mouth shut."

"Jesus, B.T. . . ." But suddenly they were both distracted by a skirmish at the nearest police van. In the middle of it was Dexter. Bobby recognized him, his blue leather pants and vest being hard to miss.

Dexter was struggling against the two policemen who held him and tried to push him into the van. His leather vest was ripped down the back. "You takin my car," Dexter yelled. "I ain't never gon see it again."

One of the policemen whacked Dexter across the middle with his sap. Dexter doubled over and vomited, part of it hitting the policeman's shoes. The officer cursed and shoved Dexter into the van head first.

Roux was straining against Bobby's hand as if she wanted to bolt in the direction of the skirmish. Bobby pulled her back, saying to B.T., "That's the kid who picks up my girlfriend's maid every day. Can't you get them to cut him some slack?"

B.T. stood up and turned in Dexter's direction, as if to go to him, then nodded toward Roux. "You better get your dog on home before there's any more trouble."

He sounded just like Lyle when Lyle was using his cop's voice. Disgusted, Bobby walked off; B.T. did too, but he went over to the Cadillac and began rifling through the glove compartment looking for the registration papers.

Bobby walked Roux back to Thea's. As soon as he got her in the gate, he let her go, pushing her ahead, telling her to go on.

Thea saw Jared getting out of Roux's way, putting Burgess and Janine between himself and the dog. She called to Roux and took her by the collar. "What is it, Bobby? Tell us."

Bobby, coming up the steps, said with anger and disgust, "Oh, they're arresting them for parading without a permit. Looks like they're impounding the cars too."

But he was the only one who was angry. The rest of them were let down, and their silent acceptance made anger seem the healthier, better response by far. They were defeated—surrender without a fight.

The group began to break up, Mr. Robert's helper going back inside, Jared and the other painter leaving. But as Jared started down the steps, Roux lurched out of Thea's hand and rushed to him. He lost his footing, tripping down two steps before catching himself on the side rail. Roux took advantage of this short fall to put herself right in Jared's face, so he could smell her dog's breath, feel its warmth on his skin.

Bobby grabbed Roux roughly, reprimanding her, and brought her into the house. Jared pulled himself up. He was shaking. "That's it," he said, "I ain't workin no place with no dog." With that, he struck off down the brick walkway.

"Jared," Thea called after him, and when he did not respond, she turned back toward Burgess, putting her hand up, lightly touching Burgess' sleeve. "Burgess," she said, "don't let him leave like that."

Burgess shook his head, refusing, so Thea moved to go after Jared, but Burgess caught her and held her at the crook of her arm as he'd done the night she'd tried to go after Sonny Johnson. "Let him go," he told her, pulling her back the same way he had that night and letting his hand rest there inside her elbow. "Won't do no good to go after him now."

Janine's eyes were riveted to his black flesh on Thea's white flesh, to a touch that, without having to think, she could tell had some familiarity in it. She felt the skin along her cheekbones burn. Her long curved nails bit into the palms of her hands. Burgess' hand slid from around Thea's arm. But not before Thea saw the look in the other woman's eyes.

She could not get it out of her mind, even after everyone but Bobby had left. Janine's jealousy had done something for her that no man could have achieved nearly so quickly or so easily: for the first time in many months Thea felt strong sexually; she no longer felt like a sexual victim, as Michael had made her feel, nor was there any of the hopeless longing she'd felt since Michael was no longer around to sleep with her. She was strong and she was driven, and here was Bobby coming toward her, his hips looking narrow inside his baggy khakis, walking in a way she'd never seen before was so sexy. She took him by the hand and led him up the stairs and pushed him back on her bed. She released his belt and opened up his pants quicker than he could have done it himself.

"At last," Bobby said, and closing his eyes, he put himself in her hands.

22

There was some satisfaction in knowing things were going to go to shit, then watching it happen.

This thought came to Burgess after he woke in the middle of the night and lay for a while listening. He thought he'd heard gunfire, but maybe he'd dreamed it because he heard no more now and Janine slept undisturbed beside him. Of course, these days, ever since she'd gotten pregnant, Janine slept like the dead.

No, it wasn't one of his bad dreams because there it was again, a short burst of automatic-weapon fire. It was far away, the other side of the Convent, where there were still a lot of abandoned buildings, where he'd heard Ferdie was holed up, come back to the Convent, young blood claiming his territory.

Shit was happening all right: they had the Cadillac too, and that meant they were one step closer to him.

Burgess walked in on Bobby Buchanan late the next afternoon at the apartment house and found him sprawled out on the floor of the front room. He was eating a Hubig pie and drinking a Diet Coke.

"Funny you should catch me trying hard not to work," Bobby said around a mouthful of pie.

"Yeah, hard work not workin, ain it."

Bobby got up. "Now, now, my man, let me show you exactly what has been accomplished here."

He started in the living room, pointing out the freshly painted walls, the polished floor, the new light fixture, though it was hanging a bit crooked, not screwed properly into the plaster. "I have to throw the I Ching and consult my astrologer before I get up on that ladder again," Bobby said.

"I send over a Voodoo woman I know," Burgess told him. "She keep you floating right up there next to the ceiling till the work's done."

"Thanks, bro. I assume she'll stick around while I put a new light in there too." He showed Burgess into the dining room and pointed at the hole above them. "Used to be a fancy chandelier there, nice piece. Wish I'd had the sense to take it out first."

"Stripped the place, did they?"

"Down to the plumbing," Bobby said.

He took Burgess through the two bedrooms, their heels on the floorboards echoing through the apartment, then into the bathroom, where he'd put in a new vanity, ornate but cheap because he didn't expect it to last long. Nothing ever did. "I guess they dropped the sink," Bobby said, telling Burgess that he'd found it on the floor cracked in half, all the pipes gone. "Plumbing's a bitch," he added.

Burgess looked around the bathroom with its claw-footed bathtub, the fancy sink cabinet and tiny tiles, the grout in between them stained black in the middle of the floor. It was a big bathroom, much larger than the one in the Convent. Janine would like that. He opened the medicine cabinet. "Brand new," Bobby said.

Burgess snapped the glass door closed. "How much rent you askin?" he wanted to know, and when Bobby told him, he said, "I'll take it. When will it be ready?"

"Wait a minute, that wasn't even the hard sell," Bobby said. "You haven't seen the kitchen yet—you might change your mind. It's going to take time and a strong stomach to get it done."

"How 'bout you let me off the deposit and the first month's rent and I send over a man to help you do it," Burgess said. He'd send Jared.

"Sight unseen? You got yourself a deal, my man."

They shook on it there in the bathroom, then Bobby led Burgess into the kitchen. Most of the linoleum was pulled up, exposing floorboards slick with grime around the hole where Bobby had fallen, the piece of cardboard laid over it. Bobby lifted the cardboard so Burgess could see that the hole went clear through to the ground. He told Burgess that the plumbing, all of it, even under the house, had been ripped out, not a pipe left, and showed him the holes in the walls where cabinets had hung. Over the rest of the walls, rutted like streaks of fingerpaint, were brown smears, undeniably fecal in appearance.

"It could be shit," Bobby said, "but I prefer to think of it as the last battleground of the red bean wars."

Burgess was busy eying up the work to be done and seemed not to hear him. "We do this and be in here in 'bout a week," he calculated, then he said, "You ain *seen* shit if you ain never seen the Convent."

Bobby had never seen the Convent up close, not any more of it than the edge running along Convent Street. First Burgess took him through the front part, the part they'd done over, pointing out places of special interest: Janine's apartment, the building he'd lived in as a child, the vegetable garden with some collard greens about ready to harvest. He told Bobby how his mama had grown herbs and vegetables, and flowers too, out on her balcony all those years ago and shared them with the neighbors, her thumb was so green. "That's what give me the idea for the garden," he said.

They drove slowly along the streets of the Convent in the red pickup truck, its windows down, both of them enjoying the coolness of the early evening. The putt-putting muffler announced Burgess as if he were the ice-cream man making rounds in his musical truck through a suburban neighborhood at twilight. The kids who were still outside waved, and Burgess leaned out of his window and called to them, "You all get on inside now."

The streets in the Convent were fairly wide but scarred with potholes that Burgess avoided as best he could. The red-brick buildings were set back from the streets and grouped around large yard spaces. A maze of cracked sidewalks connected them. But as Burgess drove deeper into the project, Bobby saw the big green spaces give way to large tracts of desolate, putty-colored dirt; out of this loose, lifeless-looking surface, up close to the buildings themselves, grew clumps of dry brown weeds, like hair sprouting from a corpse's head.

Many of the buildings in this part of the Convent were in ruins, with windows boarded up, some of them blackened all around as if they'd been scorched. The balconies of some buildings were gone; holes gaped in the roofs. The desolate earth and the strangely scorched buildings reminded Bobby of pictures he'd seen of European cities after the war: the entire area looked as if it had been bombed.

"We didn't get a chance to get back here and fix up these buildings," Burgess said. "Don' guess we ever will now." He switched on the headlights of the truck, and as he turned a corner the lights shone for a moment on broken glass that lay like a lustrous, opalized covering of frost over the ground. The illusion was jarring in the midst of all this devastation and ruin, nothing to break the monotony of row after row of what could have been burned-out bunkers in a war zone. "War zone" was what Lyle had called the neighborhood where the apartment house was; it was also a phrase Bobby had seen used in the newspaper to describe the projects, not just the Convent but all of the projects citywide. It came to him now, though, not as some tossed-out descriptive phrase or a term of disgust and hostility, but because the reality was right here in front of him in all its ugliness, with all the horror of its implications.

He stared out of the truck's window trying hard to imagine how his own reality would be changed if he had to get up every morning of his life and face this barren, disconsolate landscape, live through what made it this way, what kept it this way. And he failed; he could not imagine it, could not fully grasp what difference it would make, only that it would make a profound difference, that it would change the way he looked at the entire world, that he could be exactly the person he was and yet he would not be at all the same.

Bobby glanced over at Burgess, who was scrutinizing the second stories of the buildings they passed on his side of the street. Many of the buildings were in total darkness, obviously vacant. Streetlights, which should have come on by now, could not—most of them were broken, very likely shot out or stoned out, the darkness deliberate. Looking at Burgess, Bobby thought he was a strange one, to have wanted to refurbish a place such as this, where people who preferred darkness lived.

"Why did you take this on, Burgess, fixing up the Convent?"

Burgess, distracted by these apparently vacant buildings, said, "Seem like a good thing to do."

"That's it? It seemed like a good thing to do?" Bobby sounded incredulous.

Burgess did not answer Bobby right away. He had slowed the

truck to a crawl, the muffler gurgling and coughing, his attention caught by one particular building. But when they passed it, Burgess turned to him, grinning broadly. "Yeah," he said, "that's it—was a good thing to do."

They reached the top of a T intersection. In front of them was another large empty dirt tract, a playground, Bobby supposed, if there were any kids around this part of the project to play in it. But even as he thought that, he saw lights in some of the distant buildings behind the tract. Burgess made a left turn and for a brief moment they were enveloped in darkness again, then something caught Bobby's eye, a light coming from one of the back buildings but now obscured by the building in front of it. It had been but a flash in his peripheral vision, but there was no mistaking what he had seen.

"Hold the phone," he said to Burgess, and when Burgess did not immediately stop, Bobby said, "I mean, whoa. Did you see *that?*" He pointed over his shoulder with his thumb.

Burgess backed up until they had a view down one of the cracked sidewalks. It was in a building with scorched, boarded windows upstairs, but downstairs, through an open door, they could see straight into a living room that was flooded with light from a large crystal chandelier hanging at its center.

"You remember that chandelier I told you was missing from the dining room?"

Burgess leaned over to look through Bobby's window and a rumbling began in his chest that erupted into laughter that shook the truck and drowned out the muffler.

Bobby, his arm propped in the open window, drummed his fingers on the roof of the truck and waited for Burgess to run down. "Of course," he said, "I can't be absolutely sure that's the same one, not without a closer look."

"You want a closer look?"

"No thanks. I'll just let my imagination take flight."

"You want me to find out?"

Bobby shifted in the truck seat to give Burgess a level look. He was vaguely aware of a skinny man wearing ragged clothes, standing on the other side of the street. "You could do that?" Bobby asked, his curiosity piqued.

Burgess answered that by asking, "You want me to get it back?"

"It's up to you," Bobby said. "I hadn't planned to replace it with anything that fancy." He shifted back around to assess the incongruity. "Looks pretty good there, don't you think? Just the kind of thing this place needs." They looked another long moment.

When Burgess straightened up to drive again, the skinny man was standing at his window, right up close, leaning on the truck. Burgess was startled and just barely managed not to flinch. "What you want?" he said harshly.

The man probably wasn't as old as he looked, with his gray skin, his body emaciated from drugs. When he opened his mouth to speak, teeth were missing. "You want some rock?" he asked. The missing teeth caused him to lisp.

Burgess grabbed him by the shirt front, nearly pulling his frail wasted body through the window, his head bouncing off the top of the truck door. "Who tole you to come say that?" Burgess demanded.

"Nobody," the man said. Burgess pulled him in harder and felt the shirt rip in his hand. Blood oozed from a gash in the man's forehead as he said miserably, "It jus Ferdie saw you passin, no harm meant."

Burgess got closer in his face and said quietly, "You tell Ferdie I ain't dead yet." He pushed the man away. "Get on," he said.

The man backed off, holding his shaky hands out in front of him. "Didn' mean no harm, man. No harm meant," he said once again.

Burgess put the truck in gear and rolled forward, no longer indifferent to the muffler's noise making it so he couldn't hear anything else around him. "Let's get goin," he said to Bobby. "Gets dangerous out here at night." He got no argument.

He drove through the front part of the Convent again to get to Convent Street and Bobby was glad for the sight of grass, for the buildings with lots of lights on inside them, for what looked like a normal neighborhood in spite of the sameness of it all. That's when it struck him, the enormity of what Burgess had undertaken, and how far he'd actually gotten. And that Burgess had said they weren't going any further with it.

"How come you didn't get to the back?" he asked. "How come you're not going to finish?"

" 'Cause a cop got killed," Burgess said.

Bobby didn't understand everything, but he decided that with this brief tour of the Convent he understood more than he wanted to: he asked no more questions.

23

Early in the morning Burgess went out to the vegetable garden and picked an armful of greens. Their color had deepened and they'd doubled in size in the cooler fall weather. He knew his mother liked them best after the weather changed. He gathered them while the dew still glinted off their broad leaves, which pushed back the weeds that had grown up around them. The whole garden looked as if it could use some attention. But he couldn't do anything about that now; he was bringing his mother a peace offering.

It was quiet at Thea's house; none of the workers were there yet. He wasn't sure his mother was there yet. He knocked softly, timidly, on the leaded-glass door, and before long he saw her, her body broken in his vision by the cames that separated the panes of glass. She rocked as she walked, from one foot to the other, and as she got closer he could hear her shoes, like brooms sweeping along the bare floor.

She opened the door and peered outside around him like some kind of lookout, then stood aside to let him in. He followed her down the hallway to the kitchen. On the table was her cup of tea and the newspaper. She filled the kettle and put it on the stove.

"I brought you some greens," he said to her back.

"You bring them bodyguards with you?" she asked.

He'd known she wouldn't make it easy for him. He'd come to tell her she was right after all, and he was getting out of the Convent, but she wouldn't be accepting yet: she had to have her say first. He breathed deeply as if to fortify himself with patience before he said, "I know you don' like seein them bodyguards here, Mama. I ain brought them for a while."

"Ain't nothin but a bunch of thugs, that's what," she said. She busied herself getting out a cup and saucer, the canister of tea bags. He held his tongue but the effort made his jaw muscles ache. He hoped she wouldn't go on like this too much longer.

Upstairs, Thea had heard the pickup truck putting along Convent Street. If Burgess was coming this early, he might not show up again all day, and she wanted to talk to him. She left Bobby sleeping soundly and slipped on a pair of jeans and a T-shirt. She brushed her teeth and splashed some water on her face and went downstairs.

When she got into the hallway she could hear Zora talking, her voice slightly raised. "Don't matter," Zora said. "You still actin like a thug." Thea stopped where she was, shrinking back into a dark corner of the hall.

"Why you say that, Mama?" There was supplication in Burgess' voice. "You the one always said we should help our neighbors, share what we had with em. We got to act like ever'body in the Convent is a part of our family—that's what you said."

"That was a long time ago, Burgess."

"Don' matter. All I'm doin is actin like you raise me up to act."

Delzora spoke to him testily. "I never raise you up to be no dope dealer, Burgess." She poured water over the tea bag and set the cup on the table. She sat down.

Burgess did not sit down. He stood there, still holding the greens. "I ain sayin that. I'm sayin you never raise me up to be like every other dumb fuck in the project neither—stupid 'cause I'm so poor, mean 'cause I ain goin nowhere." He put one hand down on the table, leaning toward her, clutching the greens with the other hand. "I done some good in the Convent, Mama, fixin things up, makin sure ever'body's got what they got to have."

Delzora was about to tell him he better watch his mouth but she got sidetracked, suddenly picturing, as clear as any photograph, Burgess as a little boy, the way he'd been full of spirit, headstrong, refusing to be squashed by the burden of life in the Convent. Now she saw his spirit, his exuberance for the project as an affront to her, his being headstrong as stubbornness, a refusal to see that he had become part of all the bad things she'd tried to warn him against, get him away from, that he'd taken everything she'd taught him about living in a Christian way and turned it all inside out, so he didn't know anymore what was right and what was wrong.

"Tell me, Mama," he was saying. "How could I do all that without no money?"

"You think 'cause you do good with all that money, it don't matter anymore where it come from." She tilted her head back, looking at him through the bottom of her glasses. "Why all of a sudden you worried 'bout doin good, Burgess?"

Burgess stood up straight again. He laughed a soft, low laugh. "Maybe I want to see if I can get away with it."

"It jus be another way for you to be Mr. Big, Burgess, to make everybody think you walk on water, that's what."

His jaw muscles were aching again. "I got what I got the only way I was ever gon get it. I ain livin like no millionaire. I ain livin like they ain no tomorrow." He was talking like Janine now, using her words. Janine, who believed he could do no wrong. But this was his mother he was talking to, and she didn't believe that, not at all. He told her truthfully, "The way I see it, they wasn't much of a tomorrow any other way."

"You wrong about that, Burgess," Delzora said. "They's always tomorrow, and they's the day after that, and the day after that."

He stood there a minute longer and then he said, "You want these greens?"

She didn't answer for so long that he was about to walk away. Then she said, "Yeah, gimme them greens." She held her hands out and took them, not looking at his face but at his shirt, wet and clinging to his skin where he'd held the bundle of dewy leaves up against him.

Burgess turned away from her without ever telling her what he'd come to say. He walked into the hallway and was startled to see Thea standing there. The look on her face told him she'd heard it all, or enough. He hesitated, then went past her, his body turned slightly sideways even though there was plenty of room, as if he understood she wouldn't want to touch him. Thea waited until he closed the door behind him before she went into the kitchen. She sat at the table with Delzora, in front of Burgess' untouched tea. The two women looked at each other in silence.

Delzora finally got up, removed the two cups from the table, and began washing the greens.

24

It didn't take Thea long to put it all together. Since she'd come back to town there had been an article in the newspaper every week about the city's housing projects, several of them focusing on the Convent. There had been speculation about where the money had come from to finance the turnaround in the Convent. Most of the residents said they thought the city had supplied it. No one said they thought it was drug money. No one believed there was any such person as the Bishop of Convent Street. Thea remembered reading that someone had said if there *was* any such person, then he was just a step or two below Jesus Christ. From what Zora had said to Burgess about walking on water, Thea thought she must have read that too.

Zora stood at the sink, still working on the greens. Thea spoke to her back. "I heard—I couldn't help but hear . . ." She broke off. She wanted to say something but realized that she didn't know what it was. "I'm sorry Zora," she said finally. "I truly am sorry."

But Zora, her voice raised above the running water, said harshly, "Don't you be feelin sorry, I don't want no one feelin sorry for me."

It was as if Zora, for pride's sake, had dropped a wall of glass between herself and Thea. Thea felt the separation acutely, as if her knowledge of Burgess now alienated her from Zora. The thought of any kind of change in her relationship with Zora, any sort of permanent alienation, made her feel sick and slightly panicky. She forced herself to leave the kitchen and went upstairs to talk to Bobby.

He was just waking up. She sat on the bed. He put his hand out to her and tried to pull her down, but she said, "No, not now."

"Burgess was just here," she began in as neutral a voice as pos-

135

sible, not wanting to sensationalize what was already sensational enough. "When I went downstairs, I heard him and Zora talking—actually, I eavesdropped. Zora's been angry with Burgess for a long time, and I wanted to know why."

She paused; Bobby was rubbing his eyes. He yawned. She went on: "You know all the work being done in the Convent? You know this person who doesn't really exist, the one the media like to call the Bishop of Convent Street?"

Bobby nodded.

"It's Burgess," she told him.

"What did he and Zora say?" Bobby sounded curious, not surprised. Thea repeated what she had heard.

Bobby had told Thea about going to the Convent with Burgess, but he had told it as a lark, describing only surfaces, mainly telling an anecdote about the chandelier. Now he said, "I knew it when we were in the Convent the other day. People are scared enough of him that he could have gone into that apartment and taken that chandelier." He stopped, as if deciding whether to say more. Then, "And that guy I told you offered us crack? Well, Burgess told him to tell somebody—he said, 'Tell him I'm not dead yet.' He deliberately hurt that guy even though the guy was so wasted from drugs. He wanted to let him know."

Thea frowned. "Let him know what?"

"That he could hurt him bad if he wanted to, I guess. That he could hurt whoever he was sending the message to. I got the impression there's some sort of power play going on."

"You didn't ask Burgess about it?"

"Hell, no. I don't want to know that shit."

"Whether we like it or not, Bobby, we *do* know that shit."

Bobby sat up. "It's none of our business," he said. "Whatever Burgess does in the Convent, whoever he is, it's none of our business."

"But it is!" Thea protested. "I don't mean we have to tell anyone what we know. We don't have to decide whether we're turning Burgess in or not, nothing like that, but it *is* our business. We know about it, so it is."

"Okay." Bobby held his hands palms up. "So what do we do about it?"

"I don't know. I mean, it's not that we have to do anything about it." She flipped a hand in exasperation. "I don't know what

I mean. It's not our business exactly, except it is, because we're involved with Burgess."

"Maybe we should get uninvolved, get rid of him."

"That's probably what he's thinking we're going to do. Is that what you want to do?"

Bobby shrugged.

"Do you feel threatened?" Thea asked him.

"Sure. It turns out he could shoot out a wall of the apartment house as quick as the next guy. The question is, do *you* feel threatened?"

"I don't know," Thea said slowly. "I really don't know. Maybe we should talk to him."

"And say what?"

Thea didn't answer.

"Well, all I know right now," Bobby said, "is he's your contractor and he's my tenant." He glanced at the clock. "Christ, I'm running late. I'm supposed to meet Jared at the apartment house, and I need to go by the hospital first." His mother had been at Touro for several days with a bad case of bronchitis. He got out of bed and started dressing.

Thea said, "Maybe we should ask him if he's afraid of us."

Bobby laughed.

Thea stayed sitting on the bed until he left. She had kept her feelings about Burgess veiled, a shadow of disbelief here—except she did believe it—a shade of disappointment there, and something else flickered behind the veil, a spark she was keeping tamped down for fear it would catch and consume her. But consume her with what?

Who could think with all the noise in the house? Mr. Robert and the other workers had arrived. Thea retreated to the third floor. She went with a well-worn copy of *The Stranger,* thinking she was going to read. But she was really going to commune with Aunt Althea's ghost.

The ghost lay low for a while, waiting for Thea to become distracted from her book. After reading the same paragraph three times without comprehension, Thea finally put the book face down on her lap. She was stretched out on an old chaise longue that had been in her aunt's bedroom. Next to her, a floor lamp with a fringed shade lit the corner of the slope-ceilinged room. She used an old trunk as a table, her cup and saucer sitting on it, the coffee left in the cup cold. Around the room were pieces of furniture covered with sheets that stirred now and again in the brisk breeze that came through an open window, as if the ghost fluttered from one to another, restless and impatient to assert its will and the guilt of a long and intolerant past.

The ghost let Thea drift back through her memories for a while, recent ones first, a picture of Burgess and Janine on the porch, a thrill of sexual excitement triggered by the image and by the idea of Janine's being pregnant. Seeing them together had led Thea into bed with Bobby, and for that she was not sorry. She and Bobby had been friends for a long time, and Thea had loved him as a friend first. That was good; she believed that would make their sexual relationship strong and deep and lasting. And when they were making love, her eyes closed so she could only hear and touch and taste and smell, then she could imagine for a time he was that dark, shadowy man who had been in her dreams for many years, dark because she always thought he would be an Italian like her father, shadowy not so much because she could never see his face clearly but because a part of him was menacing, dangerous. Exciting.

Lying there on the chaise, she closed her eyes, willing this dream man to come to her, and what came to her instead was the man in the hallway in her dream about Lyle and the burglar alarm. She quickly opened her eyes: she didn't want him to be quite that menacing or that dangerous.

She drifted back again, to the night that she and Burgess sat out in the gazebo together. The ghost was poised now and very still; this was where it wanted Thea to be. Thea remembered the warmth of the air on her skin, the feeling of comfort in the uncomfortable gazebo. Her eyes closed again and she smelled the night-blooming jasmine and heard the soft rustle of nocturnal life in the banana trees. As long as they were in the gazebo, she had been in control, she was dominant: it was her gazebo, the jasmine and the banana trees were in her yard, Burgess had entered her life. And then there was the intrusion of Sonny Johnson. But no, it had started before that, the subtle shift had started when she began thinking about his life, the scar on his arm, what the rest of his body looked like. Then it was his black life and her white life, and after Sonny Johnson she was no longer in control because of the outer trappings of her life, no longer in control because from the street his life had entered hers and with it came her danger, his power, and the possibility of death. And from the darkness of that possibility came the dominance of the male and the female over the black and the white.

The spark she had kept tamped flared, and that's when the ghost made its move. The ghost shamed her for her attraction to this dangerous, powerful man. The ghost told her she had been used, duped. And, yes, disappointed too: the ghost spoke to her of generosity and caring and told her that goodness in others was expected as a result of those acts. The ghost made her think that all her feelings for Burgess had been negated because she had found out who he was. And then the ghost sat back triumphantly, its work done, expecting Thea to run with these notions.

Right then Thea understood that her parents' death and her aunt's intolerance had left within her a place of doubt and confusion, and that her befriending Burgess had been an attempt to find this place of confusion and to confront it and eradicate it. Instead, she found herself wanting to turn her back on Burgess because that is what her aunt would have done, what her parents probably would have done too.

She wished she'd never found out about Burgess, and it occurred to her that Burgess probably wished she'd never found out either, the way he'd passed her this morning, removing himself from her. She wished she never had to see Burgess again, and the moment she thought that there came the pain of loss, and this loss was not just about Burgess, it was not about the male and the female, it was about the loss of humanity.

A sudden gust from the window caused the bottoms of the sheets to dance along the floor, and the ghost of Aunt Althea had a small, ineffectual fit of rage.

Sandy rushed up the walkway to Thea's house, catching one of her expensive high heels between two bricks. It snapped off like a dead twig.

She limped into the foyer carrying the heel, nails sticking up out of it. "Absolutely nothing is going right," she said, her fury carrying her voice above the scream of Mr. Robert's saw.

Thea led her to the back den and closed the door. Sandy sat on the sofa and tried to stick her heel back on her shoe. "What's wrong?" Thea asked.

"That son of a bitch," Sandy said hitting the side of the shoe on the sofa cushion next to her for emphasis. "He's taken a week's vacation from the bank. I had no idea until I called this morning to remind him we had parent conferences at school today." She put the shoe on her foot and stomped on it a couple of times. As soon as she put the slightest pressure on it from the side, the heel came right off. "Bastard. He didn't come home at all night before last. He got in at two this morning and when I asked him where he'd been, he practically bit my head off, told me to go back to sleep, then he was gone before I woke up."

"What do you think's going on?"

Sandy looked at Thea with disgust. "Do you have to ask? It would be better if he was obsessed with some woman. At least I'd know how to fight." She paused, fighting anger. "I had to go to school alone today. Evan has started biting the other kids. The teacher wanted to know if there were any problems at home." Her lower lip trembled. She stood up quickly, wanting to pace away her helplessness and fury, but there was a sound of material ripping where the heel of her good shoe caught on the bottom of her silk skirt. "Shit!" she cried and sat down to inspect the damage. She flung the skirt hem away from her. It fluttered to the floor again.

"Let me see," Thea said reaching for it.

Sandy motioned her off with one hand and let her tense body fall back against the sofa. She breathed deeply and turned to Thea. "You know, there was something about the way that teacher asked me if there were problems at home that made me think Lyle Hindermann is the talk of uptown New Orleans."

"What do you mean?"

"Oh, you know, Lyle Hinderman, the great protector of the elite. Their own personal blue-blood cop. And behind his back I'll bet they call him crazy and racist. They're a bunch of hypocrites."

"People seem to like what Lyle does, Sandy. He makes them feel safe."

And he made them feel justified. Yet Thea did not doubt that what Sandy said was true. She had seen them at parties talking to Lyle, asking him questions, listening to his answers with great interest, and she could believe that they took Lyle's seriousness and used it to fuel their gossip. But if they wanted to carry a gun, they talked to Lyle; if anything bad happened, if their houses were broken into, if they were robbed or mugged, they called Lyle. She had done it herself the night Bobby was attacked.

She heard Zora calling for her and went to the door. "Mr. Robert's done gone," Zora said, "and them other two boys too. They said they be back sometime tomorrow to finish cleanin up." She was in her street clothes, getting ready to go herself. Thea walked with her to the front of the house and watched her go out to the Cadillac where Dexter waited, dressed in the new outfit he'd showed up in yesterday, all black leather, a column of gleaming onyx studded with silver, the jacket zipped because he had no shirt on underneath.

Sandy came up behind her. "Well, I guess I can die now: I've seen everything."

Thea was so used to Dexter and the Cadillac that for a moment she didn't know what Sandy meant. "Oh," she said, "Burgess' car. He sends it for his mother every day."

"But that's not Burgess?"

"No, that's someone who works for him."

"He must certainly do well for himself."

"Yes," said Thea, "that's what I thought too."

As they watched Zora leave, Thea imagined that Zora, too old, too tired, and too afraid to turn down comfort, convenience, and safety, must nevertheless find her ride in the Cadillac every day rather distasteful.

Thea was glad when Sandy left so she could indulge her empathy with Zora and, while she was at it, indulge her disappointment too. She could be angry at Burgess for his mother's sake, for the one person who had ever told her it was all right to be angry over her parents' death. But she had not been angry in those days; she'd been too bereaved, too frightened over her own fate. And whatever anger there might have been had ebbed away into sadness, a sadness she now imagined was not unlike Zora's.

She went into the living room to cover the birdcage for the night, but her own face stopped her as she passed the rosewood mirror. She would have expected to see sadness there, but what she saw was fear. She did not like this fear; it seemed to her a vile thing. Was she afraid of Burgess, or was she afraid for him? Or was she afraid for them all, for their collective fate? For she was quite certain that such a thing did exist, bigger than any one person's fate, or even one race's fate, bigger than them all.

25

On the night of Dexter's parade, Lyle sat over a couple of beers with his partner and friend B.T. in a bar frequented by off-duty policemen. B.T. told Lyle about the parade and how it had all gone down, and about the soul brother who'd headed it up. He acted out, not once but twice, the fit Dexter threw over his car being impounded. "I ain never gon see my Cadillac again," B.T. wailed in the barroom, and all the cops in the place yelled like Dexter too. B.T. described the car in great detail, the red velour interior, the tinted windows, state-of-the-art sound system, the gleaming chrome, and the way Dexter was dressed, his bright-blue leather outfit, expensive glove-soft leather split down the back as he resisted arrest.

"Threw a fit over the clothes too," B.T. said. "Said they was ruined and what we gon do 'bout it?" B.T. imitated Dexter's agitated, belligerent state, taut muscles, tough, hostile face.

"Was he on drugs?" Lyle wanted to know.

"Clean," B.T. said. "Car too. Clean as a whistle."

"Interesting," Lyle said.

"Yeah," B.T. agreed. They mused on it and drank some more beer. Then B.T. said, "Saw your friend Buchanan over there. Thought I should cut the nigger some slack just because he picks up his girlfriend's maid every day."

Lyle probably would have said it was just cop's intuition. At the same time, he didn't want to mention it to B.T. quite yet, afraid the pro might laugh it off as amateur hour. Lyle's idea was that the white Cadillac was exactly the kind of car that the Bishop of Convent Street would drive. So instead of going home that night, he headed down to Central Lockup. He went over the Cadillac inch by inch even though B.T. had already seen to that. He found nothing in it to indicate anything about its owner, the car itself seeming to make enough of a statement.

He got a look at Dexter, but he didn't want Dexter to see him. He found the officers who had questioned Dexter earlier, found out Dexter had been questioned after the cop had been killed in the Convent, and learned that Dexter's only alibi for that night was his girlfriend.

Lyle ended up spending the entire night at Central Lockup. Before the sun rose he had decided to take a week's vacation from the bank.

The next morning he watched a flashy young woman wearing a wide-brimmed black hat pay Dexter's fines from a roll of money and go with him to get his car out of the pound. Then he watched Dexter go over every inch of the Cadillac.

Dexter drove the Cadillac back to the Convent. He parked behind one of the Convent apartments. He and the woman got out of the car. They were having quite an argument, though Lyle was too far away to hear what it was about. They spoke angrily to each other over the top of the car before the woman began walking up the pavement to the back steps. Dexter walked behind her. Abruptly the woman turned around, one hand on her hip, and said something that must have been rather scathing to Dexter. As if she'd hit his funny bone, his arm jerked up and he slapped her hard across the face. The blow knocked the hat off her head. She picked it up and said something else, and he took off his ripped blue-leather vest, threw it down on the concrete and stomped on it. The woman, holding the hat with one hand, the side of her face with the other, turned and went on inside. Dexter kicked the vest off the sidewalk and followed. After a while he came out dressed in a pair of jeans with studs down the sides of the legs and a white shirt. He got in the Cadillac and drove back downtown to Rubenstein Brothers, an expensive men's store, where he bought himself another leather outfit, black this time, with a bomber jacket instead of a vest. He wore it out of the store.

Dexter returned to Convent Street and went to the lounge across the street from the project, the Solar Club. He left the lounge at four-thirty and drove into the affluent neighborhood off Convent Street, where he picked up three women at three different houses. Two of the houses had been burgled within the last six months. Dexter drove the women into the Convent and dropped them off there. He went back to the affluent neighborhood to Thea Tamborella's house, where he picked up Thea's maid. He stood at the door of the Cadillac like a sentry, formidable in his black leather. He drove her to an apartment house right off Convent Street a few blocks beyond the project.

From there Dexter drove back to the Convent, to the apartment where he lived with the woman. Nearly three hours passed with no action. At approximately seven forty-five, two men arrived at the apartment. They stayed for about fifteen minutes. Between eight and nine o'clock three more men came to the apartment, two together, one alone. None stayed more than five minutes. Lyle assumed Dexter was dealing drugs from the Convent apartment.

At two o'clock in the morning, Lyle called it a night. He went home and got into bed next to Sandy, who lifted her head to say his name with a question mark behind it and ask him where he had been. He told her to go back to sleep.

Lyle could not sleep. He lay very still, his hands clasped behind his head, and thought. There might be no way that he or anyone else would ever be able to find out for sure who had killed the cop that night in the Convent Street Housing Project. If they couldn't, it meant no one would ever be punished for the worst crime of all. If no one was punished, it would happen again. And again. There would be no stopping them. These people had to understand they couldn't kill a cop and get away with it. There had to be some sort of retaliation. Every cop in the department believed that too. Lyle knew that whether Dexter was a cop killer or not, he had too much money to be innocent.

He stayed in bed a couple more hours, and left the house as dawn was creeping in through the windows. He needed to find B.T. They had a busy day in front of them.

That night after her reading class, Sherree walked across the Convent to pick up Lucilla at a neighbor's house. It was quiet tonight, too quiet, only ten o'clock and no one at all around. It was funny how quickly things had returned to normal, because this was normal, everyone afraid to come out of their houses, prisoners in their own homes waiting for the sound of gunfire, the bad guys shooting at each other as if it were the Old West. Burgess either couldn't do anything about it or didn't want to do anything about it. It didn't matter; he wasn't doing anything about it.

Sherree walked alone. Dexter usually met her, but tonight she'd told him she would get one of the men in the class to walk with her. Only there weren't any men in class, no one at all except her and the nun. That was fine with her, meant she got all the attention. The sister had even spent an extra hour with her. She'd made some real progress tonight.

She was still angry with Dexter. First he had to go get himself put in jail, then he had to take the rest of the money Burgess had given her, and no telling how much more, and go buy himself those fancy new clothes. She didn't care how much she had, she wouldn't spend it on expensive clothes like that. She remembered seeing a black businessman on TV once who'd said, "If it's on your ass, it's not an asset." That made sense to Sherree; she still shopped at the thrift store. If that was good enough for her, she didn't know why it couldn't be good enough for Dexter.

They had argued about the money. Dexter was furious that the cops had ripped his blue vest; the only way he was going to get over it, he told her, was to go buy a new one. She told him it was his own fault for driving his black ass around in that Cadillac to begin with. He said she didn't seem to mind getting her black ass driven around town in a Cadillac. She told him it didn't matter what he drove his black ass around town in or what he covered it with, it was still one puny little old black ass. He hit her. And Sherree hadn't gotten over that. She was about ready to tell him to get his puny black ass out of her house.

But she didn't. She contented herself with telling his friends to get out, all the ones who'd come over after she'd gotten Dexter out of jail, to tell him what a great show it had been, on the news, in the paper and everything. And Dexter sitting around all puffed up, that brand new black leather creaking like the bones of an old millionaire and making the apartment smell like a lawyer's office.

She didn't tell Dexter to get out, because she liked his male presence there. It made her feel safe.

Sherree got Lucilla at the neighbor's house and walked home quickly. There was a chill in the air, a cold front coming through, bringing with it perhaps a bit of frost. Sherree cradled her sleeping child, holding her close to keep her warm. As she approached her building, she could see the tail end of the Cadillac parked behind the apartment. She let herself in and called out to Dexter, but there was no answer.

She went down the hallway, past the bathroom to where the two bedrooms were, and put Lucilla in bed in the first one. She woke up as Sherree put her down, and Sherree spoke softly to her, smoothing back her hair, soothing her back to sleep. Then she went into the second bedroom. The room was dark and she groped around until she found the lamp sitting on the night table next to the bed and switched it on. Dexter was not in bed as she had expected. He had probably walked over to the Solar Club so he could be a hot shot some more.

Sherree took off her clothes and went to the bathroom to run a bath. The bathroom was so small she had to close the door to get into the tub. She put a couple of drops of baby oil under the tap and lay back to feel the warm water slowly cover her body. Lucilla, who hadn't really gone back to sleep, hopped out of bed as soon as she heard the water running, picked up two of her dolls, and went into the lighted bedroom, where she crawled up on her mother's big bed to play.

Outside, Lyle, B.T., and three other uniformed policemen stalked the building, their weapons carried low at their sides. Two covered the back door while Lyle, B.T., and the other one took the front. B.T. kicked the door in. Wood splintered with a sharp crack. They rushed into the apartment and as the third man went through the kitchen to open the back door, Lyle and B.T. went into the hallway. They stopped in front of the bathroom.

Sherree was sunk deep in the tub, up to her earlobes. Her eyes were closed and she hummed softly to herself, feeling the hum vibrate her body against the water as she let the running tap tickle her toes. Inside this warm sensual envelope, the crack of the door splintering was a muffled but intrusive sound. Sherree sat up and turned off the water. She heard the rustle of movement outside the bathroom. She stood up in the tub and pulled the string on the overhead light to turn it off. In the bedroom down the hallway her daughter let out a nearly inaudible cry and slipped silently from the bed to crawl under it.

Sherree reached over from the tub and slowly swung the door open. In the light from the bedroom down the hall, she saw Lyle and B.T. framed in the doorway, their guns pointed at her, and her hands automatically went up over her breasts, cupping them protectively just as the nylon net cutouts in her white satin body suit once had. As she opened her mouth to scream, Lucilla crawled over the lamp cord and snagged it on her foot, causing the lamp to topple from the night table.

Lyle heard the crash, the apartment went pitch, B.T. hit the floor yelling, and Lyle opened fire. He sprayed the empty bedroom doorways, the walls, the bathroom, moving his weapon from side to side, covering the entire space. When he finished, the only sound penetrating the ear-splitting silence was the water lapping at the sides of the tub and the whimpering of the child under the bed.

26

During the night that Sherree was shot, the wind rose and brought with it a bone-chilling dampness. The old homeless man who had slept for a time in Bobby's empty apartment house wandered over to Convent Street to a liquor store, where he spent his last money on a bottle of cheap red wine. He needed something to keep him warm. All he had was the thin flannel shirt he wore over a thread-bare, holey undershirt. He couldn't remember what had happened to his blanket; in all his moving about he'd lost it.

The man in the liquor store gave him a pack of matches and a couple of day-old newspapers. He went back out on the street to scrounge along the sidewalk for a few cigarette butts. He walked in the direction of the Solar Club, his head bent to search, stopping when the cold got to him to take a sip of wine and carefully screw the top back on the bottle. He didn't want to drink too much before he found someplace warm to settle in for the night.

He was close enough that he could hear the music from the Solar Club, muffled until the door opened and there was a blast of brass, guitar, and drums as a young couple came out, laughing and huddling closely together once they felt the sting of the damp icy wind. As they came up even with him he said, "Can you spare a cigarette, brother?" He said it low, as if he expected to be ignored.

But the man stopped, the girl fitted under one arm, and reached inside his jacket. He took a pack from his shirt pocket and expertly shook it so two cigarettes popped up in the opening. "Yeah, sure," he said, "have a couple."

He took them quickly and squirreled them away in his own pocket, muttering his thanks, already moving down the street. He was anxious now to find a place where no one would bother him, where he could drink his wine until he was drunk and go to sleep.

He walked, having no particular destination, but retracing ground he'd walked many times before, until he saw an alleyway that seemed familiar, the kind of narrow, sheltered space he liked, between two dark houses. He went deep into it. He spread one of the newspapers on the concrete and folded the other one, stuffing the inside of his shirt with some of the sections. The rest he used to cover his legs. He propped himself against one of the cinder-block pillars and took a long pull at the bottle. His body was shaking with cold and he didn't want to smoke until he'd warmed up a bit.

After a while he realized he wasn't warming up. The dampness had seeped into him and he was so cold he could hardly feel the effect of the wine even though he'd drunk better than half the bottle. He thought the wind must be coming right down the alley. He had a brief memory of being on a train track once, the wind coming down on him like a locomotive, but he forgot it instantly. He folded the newspapers and pulled them along with him as he crawled under the house.

He didn't like to sleep under houses, didn't like that he couldn't see what was under there with him. He fumbled for the matches and lit one, looking all around, up and down, his hands so cold he smelled his fingers burn before he felt them. He let the match drop and lit another. Above him he thought he'd seen a hole. The match flared; there it was, a good-size rent in the flooring. He stood up into it, pushing back a piece of cardboard someone had covered the hole with. He looked around and thought he remembered climbing through this hole before, and that he remembered this house. He put his wine and his newspapers up on the good part of the floor and hoisted himself through. He found his place along the inside wall of the dining room, spreading the newspapers again, drinking again, this time feeling warm enough to light one of the cigarettes. He finished the wine before he finished the smoke and lay down on the mat of paper to take the last few puffs. He was warm and drunk and sleepy now. He reached over to put the cigarette into the empty bottle, thinking he was glad he'd saved the other one for tomorrow. He thought he slipped the still-glowing cigarette end into the bottle but he missed. It landed on the mat of newspaper. He pushed the bottle away from him, closed his eyes, and was out. The newspaper caught fire and the flames quickly spread to a can of paint thinner. He woke up long enough to think he was burning in hell, and then he was gone, along with most of Bobby's apartment house.

Burgess walked. He walked head bent, shoulders rounded against the cold, hands jammed into the pockets of an old sweat suit jacket. He walked Convent Street dressed in his old clothes, and he looked ordinary.

It was as much habit as it was any instinct for self-preservation that got Burgess out of the Convent early that cold and overcast morning. He was going to work, this time to Bobby's apartment house, so he could move Janine, and now Lucilla too, as quickly as possible. He had left them asleep, finally, mercifully asleep after a long and traumatic night.

He walked because he couldn't stand to hear the muffler on the pickup truck anymore. It seemed to shout, "Here I am! Look at me!" in a way the Cadillac never did. Oh but the Cadillac had, he just wasn't remembering, couldn't remember much in the aftershock from the horror of the night before. If he could have listened just then, listened hard, he would have heard the Cadillac whisper, "Here I am; come find me."

He walked until the morning cold had numbed the outside of his body as much as the violent night had numbed the inside, until it was time to go to the apartment house, work off the numbness. He walked right up to it before he saw it; he smelled it first, the burned wood, ashes still floating in the air. And when he saw it, his legs went weak. So weak he had to sit on the fender of a car parked in front of the next-door house, its candied paint job covered with ash, but he didn't notice that. He tried to think but he couldn't think, his shock compounded by yet another plan gone awry. He sat for a long time, he didn't know how long, staring at the ruined building, until a tough young dude came out of the house next door and told Burgess to get the hell off his car.

Silently he complied, head bent, shoulders rounded once again as his feet moved him in response to a command he didn't know he had given, back to the Convent. Instinct took him past Janine's building, to the other side of the yard so he could see what was going on at Sherree's from a distance. He didn't see any more cop cars. There was no one around; it was quiet, abnormally quiet.

He skirted the edge of the garden, no thought for it now. His eyes were drawn, his whole body was drawn to the scene of Sherree's death. Her murder: he didn't know why it had happened yet, but he was sure it was no accident. Habit, once again, made him cautious. He walked slowly in front of the buildings opposite, watching, and when he saw that the door to Sherree's was open, he backed into the shadowed space between two buildings so he was out of sight. He didn't see the children at first, and when some sound or movement made him aware of them, it caused him to jump. They were behind him, deep into the space between the two buildings, sitting in a tight circle, talking softly to each other. He tried not to let them draw his attention from Sherree's, but he couldn't help it. He watched their furtive movements, a head bobbing every now and again, their voices too low for him to hear what they were saying. He thought they must be playing sex games, doctor, something like that, but now that he was looking closely he could see they were all boys. They probably had their pants unzipped, looking at each others' dicks, comparing size and color; maybe somebody was jacking off. As he watched, one of the boys looked up, his head jerking around. He had the startled look of a child caught playing an innocent game that was nonetheless all about losing innocence.

The boy smiled, tentatively at first, then grinning as the others tore their eyes away from the inner circle. One of them started to bolt, squatted back down for an instant, and decided to bolt after all. There was a second or two of indecision, then they all took off, running in several directions, leaving behind something that had been at the center of their tight circle.

Burgess went to see what it was. He looked down into the ghost of their circle, as if looking into a kaleidoscope, and saw a design of little plastic baggies filled with grass and powder and rocks. In the shadows of the buildings he had to kneel and pick up the baggies to see that the grass was pickings from the new lawn, the powder was cornstarch, maybe baby powder, the rocks light-colored pebbles. Beside them were scraps of paper with amounts of money written on them.

He closed his eyes. When he opened them he thought he could see his whole life in that ghostly circle, a tight, claustrophobic life with few choices: deal drugs or be poor. And whatever the choice, live with fear and die young, younger than the people who lived outside this world of danger and violence. The choice he'd made, he hadn't expected to live to be thirty. But he had, and now he wanted to keep on living, he'd developed a taste for it, it seemed, but if he was going to keep on living, then he was going to have to run, run for his life.

He walked back between the buildings out into the yard, passing from the shadows into the bright sun, which was burning away the overcast, taking the edge off the cold. The door to Sherree's apartment yawned wide, inviting him. He went cautiously at first, thinking there still might be cops around, detectives wearing street clothes, watching and waiting, but the warmth of the sun made him brave and he tossed caution into the clear blue sky and went to the open door.

Dexter sat on the couch in the front room, his head thrown back, his leather duds covering him like an overgrown husk, too big for the shrunken body inside them. Burgess thought he was asleep but the moment his foot touched the threshold, Dexter's head snapped upright and his glassy eyes shone on Burgess, perhaps not seeing him clearly as he stood against the rectangle of bright sunlight. Burgess could see that Dexter had been crying, wet streaks running in shiny lines off the sides of his face.

"Dexter," he said, to let Dexter know who he was, to let Dexter know he was sorry, trying to say everything in a word because all other words eluded him.

Dexter stared at him, he thought without recognition still. But then he blurted, "What you still doin round here, man?"

The alarm in Dexter's voice raised the hair on the back of Burgess' head, but he went on in, noticing the splintered door, the cushions of a chair on the floor, a few things strewn around, the drawers to a table left open. He moved the chair and sat away from the door. If he didn't look at the door, if he didn't know a search was the cause of the disarray, then he might find it hard to believe anything out of the ordinary had happened in this apartment, for he could see no signs of violence and death from where he sat. All he could see were the scuffs of a lot of foot traffic into the hallway. But he could smell death, or he imagined he could, a prickly sensation up his nostrils. He held his breath, not wanting to let it in. Dexter moved and his leather clothes creaked, and Burgess breathed and smelled the leather.

"What you doin sittin around here like this, Dexter?"

"I'm sittin here with that door wide open 'cause I'm waitin for em," Dexter said. "They'll be back, you know they will. An I don' want em come huntin me down again, 'cause it was me they was after, not Sherree." His head fell back on the couch and he screwed up his eyes, but the tears escaped anyway, running back into his hair. "They can come get me now," he said, his voice tight, tear-choked.

"Case of mistaken identity, Dexter."

Dexter lifted his head and two tears dropped off his cheekbones, landing with little thuds on the front of his jacket. "I know that. It was you they was after but they don' know that yet. They fucked up when they killed Sherree, so they got to come back. An when they do, Burgess, I'm gon do it again."

"Do what?"

"You know, tell em. The same way. I did about the hat." And while he was admitting his weakness, he wanted to tell Burgess he'd lied about Burgess' mother and the Cadillac, but he couldn't bring himself to do it. He'd lied to Sherree about the Cadillac too, and he could hear that sharp tongue of hers clearly inside his head, lashing out, saying one of the last things she'd ever said to him: "That Burgess think he the fuckin pope and so do you."

He said, rather defiantly, "I'm gon do what I got to do and say what I got to say 'cause I'm more afraid of them than I am of you."

Burgess felt the weight of those words. He didn't care what Dexter told the police; he didn't expect Dexter would ever have to tell them anything, but if he did, Burgess wouldn't blame him for it. Dexter had never tried to be anything other than what he was. He didn't talk big and let the fear screw into his insides like a worm—long, endless, screwing in. It was laughable, afraid as he was, keeping his control by making other people afraid. And here was Dexter, admitting he was afraid too. Burgess said, "I didn' know you was afraid of me, Dexter."

Dexter lifted one hand weakly, no more energy than that to protest. "I'm afraid of them," he said.

Yeah, me too, Burgess wanted to say, but even now he couldn't let Dexter see how spineless he was. "It's okay," he said stupidly. "It don' matter what you tell em." But he knew if Dexter ever talked, it wouldn't matter if he forgave him, Dexter would never forgive himself. Or, consider this, something worse: Dexter might not believe he would ever forgive him, he might only become more afraid, figuring Burgess would use it against him one day. Even if Burgess didn't, he might hang the fear over himself, a deadly game of waiting for retaliation that would eventually turn his fear into hate.

Dexter seemed to have a small burst of energy. He looked at Burgess with a wild glint in his eye. "But we did it, didn' we, Burgess? We turn the Convent round." And then his energy flagged. "But I guess they always be a Ferdie lookin to prove hisself, ain they, Burgess?"

Burgess wanted to laugh. Ferdie, as if Ferdie was to blame. Dexter was blind in his loyalty. He refused to see it was Burgess' own weakness, his inability not to run, his inability not to accept the inevitable. He couldn't stand and fight and wait for it. He was a coward, but Dexter would never see that. He felt great affection for Dexter at that moment as well as a ridiculous desire to make Dexter promise he would stay in the Convent, that he would do the standing and fighting and waiting. But Dexter was waiting in his own way already, and admitting he was weak.

Burgess stood up. "I'll be leavin soon, Dexter. I guess this is good-bye." He walked over and put his hand out.

Dexter took Burgess' hand, then he pulled himself up and threw his arms around Burgess. He said, "You get as far 'way from this place as you can get. Don' never come back."

"I won't," Burgess said, Dexter's leather jacket cold under his hands.

He walked out into the sunshine, into a day too bright and too perfect, hostile in its perfection. He wished for the gloom, the overcast, the better for running and hiding.

It was as if his dreams were coming true, the bad dreams, the dreams of being pursued. Standing there in the Convent yard, he had a moment of panic, and he could feel those hands clutching him from behind. And for a moment he had that wish that it was all over with, a wish for relief from the fear, a death wish.

And in the next moment he felt a sudden urge to run, to find a safe place, for it not to be over with yet, not to get caught, to keep death as far away as he could. He wanted to do what he'd gotten used to doing when he needed to feel safe, what had become his habit. He wanted to force his feet to walk slowly and deliberately out of the Convent, and then go as fast as he could to Thea's house.

That's what he wanted to do, but what he needed to do, while everything was still quiet in the Convent, was talk to Janine.

27

She was still sleeping, her body curled protectively around Sherree's little girl. Burgess put his hand on her shoulder, lightly at first then with a bit more pressure, as if to hold her down. He was afraid he would startle her and she would jump or cry out and Lucilla would wake too. But only her eyes opened, wide and alert, and she got up, hardly moving the bed at all, and followed him into the living room.

They sat close together on the red plush sofa and he talked to her, his voice low and urgent with the effort of keeping it down. He told her about the fire at the apartment house, and even though she had liked the idea of moving there before, she showed no emotion now. He told her she could take Lucilla and go stay with his mother for a while, but she didn't agree or disagree. He told her he couldn't depend on Dexter not to give him away, but she didn't panic and tell him he had to hide the way she once had, grabbing his arm, her eyes dark circles of fear.

"There's no tellin what gon happen now," Burgess said. "The best thing prob'ly is for me to go 'way for a while." He waited for some indication from her that this was the right thing for him to do, but there was none. He went on, telling her he didn't know where yet, but when he got there she and Lucilla could come too. "Maybe," he said, "we jus give up on this town, start someplace new altogether, the four of us." He put his hand over her womb.

Janine heard him out with a sinking heart. They weren't the exact words, but they were close enough. It was as she had imagined all those times before: it was what had happened to her mother, coming true for her too. There would be the phone calls and the road stories, and then one day there would be nothing and she would never know what had happened to him, and she would

155

be living out her mother's life all over again and putting the seeds for it to happen again and again in her own child and Sherree's child too. The idea of being alone could make her feel sick, but the idea of passing this sickness on was unbearable.

Janine put her eyes on Burgess, steady and determined. "I got two children to think about now, Burgess," she said, "and I can't be thinkin 'bout where you are and if you really gon send for us. I can't be waitin like that. Waitin poisons a woman, sure as if you fed it to her 'fore you left."

He tried to persuade her and she tried to let herself be persuaded. She tried to imagine a life someplace else; she tried to imagine another city, Detroit, Chicago, New York. But she couldn't imagine another city: she could make herself see the ladies in their fringed dresses drinking pink drinks out of little straws, but she couldn't imagine herself being one of them. All she could imagine was being alone.

She watched him walk through the door and she thought her insides were going to just sink out of her body and try to go with him. She told herself she was going to have to get used to being lonely, no Burgess, no Sherree, only these children she was going to have to be there for, and she promised herself right then that they were never going to think that being alone made you weak. She was going to reach deep down inside her and find that power she knew she had, but first she was going to have herself a good cry, one last good cry, and she was going to think of it as washing all the weakness out of her so that she would never have to reach so deep for that power again. It would just float to the top on her tears.

There must be a limit to how many shocks a man could take in a day. Janine had let him down; he couldn't believe she wouldn't go with him. He thought all women wanted to get out of the Convent, any way they could. But she was saying it was her home and she was going to stay, even after he said they could all leave together, he wouldn't make her wait. She told him, "Burgess, I don't want to end up someplace alone, someplace I don't know, where I don't know no one at all. Not with two little kids."

She doesn't have much faith, he was thinking as he walked to Thea's house. Walking those blocks in the brisk air, he still had Janine's voice running around in his head: "I'm not gon make it harder than it already is, draggin two kids God only knows where; I'm not gon spend my life runnin."

And at the very thought of running, his back crawled and he quickened his pace, his resolve to run strengthened more by what was ahead of him, the unknown, a future abruptly cut short, than by anything that might be behind him.

Thea opened the door and Burgess realized his hands were sweating inside his jacket pockets. He didn't know what to expect—dislike, disappointment, disgust, distrust. He was holding his breath. He only knew what he most dreaded to see on her face after he saw it wasn't there: fear. He let himself breathe; she was not afraid of him.

She held the door for him and he walked into the large foyer. This house had become so familiar to him that he had begun to enter it without really seeing it anymore, the way you would enter your own house, knowing so well what it looked like that you no longer noticed it. The way his mother must have been entering it for years and years now.

And thinking that made him remember something he'd said to his mother long ago. They were arguing, he couldn't remember about what exactly, but it would have been about where he'd been or who he'd been with or what he'd been doing, before she found out the answers to all those questions. She had told him, "You better watch out what kind of life you live, watch out how you end up." And he'd said to her, with all the haughtiness and condescension an angry and arrogant sixteen-year-old can spew without thought and without regard, "Look how you ended up, what kind of life you live. I don' know how you do what you do, go work in that white bitch's house every day." And for a moment he could feel the anger, he remembered it so well.

But today as he entered the house, he looked at it differently, without that exact sense of familiarity, more of a first-time look but without any rush to take it all in at once as he'd tried to do when he was a boy coming here for the first time, amazed at how big it was, amazed by all the things in it, amazed because he'd had no idea before of anything like it. He looked at it today slowly and deliberately, no rush, no amazement, yet with a certain bewilderment that he had come to take it so for granted, that he, like his mother, had come to work here, but under different circumstances, better circumstances, for it had not felt like a comedown in life to him; it had felt full of possibilities. He looked now with an eye to what he had accomplished, a professional eye. It was a last-time look, a long look that searched for more than what could be seen within these walls. And he began to see that what his mother had said had nothing to do with where you ended up physically, but with possibilities, and in this last look he saw all the possibilities fade.

Thea was waiting for him, standing there patiently while he took it all in. He was going to have to tell her he was leaving, but he didn't think he could do it right now, right here.

He asked her where Bobby was. The question seemed to distress her. She pushed her hand through hair she hadn't bothered to comb, messing it up more. There were dark circles under her eyes. She said, "There was a fire at the apartment house."

"I know. I went by there this morning."

"Oh." She hesitated before she said, "The other tenants got out, but someone was in the apartment."

"Who?" Burgess demanded, not knowing what he expected but steeling himself for yet another shock.

"Bobby thinks it's some homeless man who'd used the place before."

Burgess relaxed.

"I think Bobby's over there now," Thea added, and took a step toward the door as if to let him out.

"I come to talk to you," he told her.

"Oh," she said again, surprised, then, "Let's go in the back," and he was relieved because he'd thought at first she wanted him to go.

She led him through the foyer, past the living room, past Mr. Robert working in the library. Mr. Robert looked up, but Burgess only nodded to him; he would have to speak with him later. She led him through the hallway, and as they went past the kitchen the sound of the vacuum cleaner got louder. He glimpsed his mother tugging the machine, her back to them. Thea hesitated just past the door as if she thought he would want to step in and say hello. But he went on ahead, out the back door to the porch.

He stopped there for a moment. Before him materialized the two of them, children, squatting down to throw the baseball cards against the wall. Thea was funny, the way she sat, one foot under her, the other knee bent, her arms hugging her leg, her chin resting on her knee. She would rock back and forth, and the more excited she got, the harder she rocked. She rocked a lot when he threw a card too hard and knocked it away from the wall. When he looked at her, she would try not to smile.

Innocent games. Forbidden games. He felt a hot spot of rage in his chest. There was no time for old anger now.

He opened the screen door, touching Thea's back between her shoulder blades so she would precede him. Roux came bounding out of nowhere, jumping on her, jumping on him, not heeding in the least her command to get down. He hung back to watch her try to control the dog, just about her height when it stood up on its hind legs. Her harsh commands did nothing to settle it down. She pushed it away so she could walk, and when she got over to the gazebo, she sat and petted the animal, talking softly until it was content to sit on the floor next to her.

Burgess sat across from her, leaning toward her, his forearms on his thighs, his hands clasped.

She knew nothing of Sherree's death, had heard nothing of any kind of killing in the Convent: she'd been up most of the night at the apartment house. So he told her about the cops going into Sherree's with their search warrant, looking for guns or drugs, any excuse, but really looking for Dexter, mistaking Dexter for him, but not even getting Dexter, getting Sherree instead.

"They didn' find nothin," he said, "'cept Sherree's little girl under the bed." She stared at him, her eyes sunk deep inside circles of fatigue. "Even if you heard 'bout it, they's so many killins in the project, you might not of thought nothin 'bout it."

"It's outrageous," she said. "People will be outraged." Her voice wasn't tired; it was sharp in the dry windless air. All around the gazebo it was quiet and still, as if the very trees, all the foliage and the life it held, had been paralyzed by the sun shooting its rays through the cloudless perfect sky.

"Which people?" he asked.

"All people," she said impatiently, then thought, this is no time to talk around things. She said, "White people too."

"I be surprised if even black people be outraged very long."

"Why wouldn't they be?"

"They outraged so much, they get tired bein outraged."

"You mean they're tired of being outraged at white people."

"I mean they tired bein outraged at the way they got to live, with the dopers breakin in they houses, the killins goin on outside they houses, and they ain nothin they can do 'bout none of it. They ain safe, they kids ain safe . . . yeah, and at white people too."

She put her hand on top of the dog's head, scratching it distractedly. When she stopped, Roux whimpered and tried getting her attention by nuzzling her leg. Finally the dog lay down on the gazebo floor with a sigh. Thea started to speak but stopped. Burgess could see she was having trouble saying something to him and he was pretty sure he knew what, but he wasn't going to help her. When she spoke, it came out in a rush. "Aren't you responsible, at least for some of that, maybe a lot of that?"

He smiled. "I'm the good guy," he said. "I sell the dope so I can fix up the houses and run the other pushers out the project."

"But that's what I mean." She was angry. "You sell drugs to the same people you say you're trying to help. That makes no sense."

He remained calm. "I don' sell dope to them people. I been keepin the dope out the Convent—tryin to, leastways. You want to hear the way it is: they ain no one could do that but the richest dope dealer 'round."

She opened her eyes wide. "That makes even less sense," she said and added, "I think."

"Ain no way none of it could make sense to someone like you. Ain no way to explain it 'cept that just the way it be."

"Someone like me? Let me see if I get it: you sell dope to get rid of dope. Is that it?" She was baiting him. He refused to take it, but he could feel his own anger building.

When she spoke again, she didn't sound quite so hostile. "What did you mean when you told your mother you wanted to see if you could get away with it?" His brows came together. Thea prodded him: "She asked you why you were worried about doing good."

He was thinking he owed her no explanation, but he also knew he wanted her to understand. He leaned closer toward her, spreading his hands, then clasping them again. He said, "I mean I got away all these years doin bad and I never thought I'd get away with it. I thought if I didn't get caught it was 'cause I was dead. I was all ready to die too. I always said I'd as soon die as let them bastards get me." His heart was pounding hard, ferociously hard. "Now it's like I lived too long. Now I'm afraid to die. So I been thinkin it's time I better leave." He stopped, but he could see that

160

her anger had dissipated as he talked, so he went on. "Trouble is, I don' really want to leave. Don' want to get caught, don' want to die, don' want to leave."

"Quit selling drugs," she said, her voice husky. "Then they can't catch you."

"Don' mean they can't kill you; don' mean they ain other people out there besides cops won' kill you. Don' mean jus 'cause you say you don' want to die no more you safe."

She frowned. "You always make me feel so naïve, Burgess, like I don't understand anything that goes on beyond this house."

"That 'cause we talkin 'bout another kind of reality altogether. Ain no way you can understand black reality, ain possible. You white; you safe."

Her mouth, her whole face tightened. Her eyes, no longer tired and sunken, blazed at him. "When I'm in this house alone, I'm not safe; I'm terrified." Her voice was thick with barely controlled anger. "When Bobby leaves my house in the middle of the night, he's not safe; he's attacked. My parents weren't safe in their grocery store; they're dead." The dog, lying at her feet, had lifted its head. She spoke again, her voice rising more. "Who's to say that the two black men who killed them didn't take their money to buy drugs?" She stood up. The dog stood too. When Burgess stood, it barked.

"I'm sorry," he said. "It weren't right for me to say that." Her mouth trembled. She sat down again as if her legs had suddenly gone too weak for her to stand anymore. The dog backed off and Burgess sat down too. Thea closed her eyes, rubbing at her eyelids with her fingers so she wouldn't cry. He put his hand out and touched her knee, lightly, so maybe she didn't feel it through the jeans she was wearing. "I guess," he said and touched her so he knew she could feel, so she would look at him. She opened her eyes, wiping under each of them, then putting her hands, balled into fists, down close to where his fingers were. "I guess I don' have no idea 'bout your reality neither." She nodded, accepting his apology.

He moved back, taking his hand off her. He wished she would say something, but he thought maybe she didn't trust herself yet to speak and not cry. "Funny, ain it," he said, "you bein scared in this house and it bein the only place I'm not."

She smiled a shaky smile, and then it crumbled and she cried, silently, no sobbing. He wanted to move next to her, to comfort her somehow, but the dog blocked his way. He sat forward and put his hand out again. This time he took one of hers and held it. She just let him hold it at first, then she tightened her fingers around his.

Inside the house Delzora turned off the vacuum cleaner. She unplugged it and wound the cord and moved a chair back into place. She straightened a corner of the rug that had been flipped back by the suction. She turned to plump up the cushions on the sofa and through the window she saw the two of them sitting outside in the gazebo. She watched as Thea turned Burgess' arm over and pushed back his sleeve, looking at the scar on his arm where he'd caught himself on the top of a chain link fence, running to get away from somebody, she had no doubt, though he'd never told her.

It was funny how those two had always liked each other, even as little kids. Delzora had seen how sad Thea was when she realized Burgess wouldn't be back to play anymore on Saturdays. She never brought any playmates with her; she'd seemed alone and isolated even then, before her parents got killed. Delzora had assumed the parents shipped her off to the aunt to get her out of the way, and that she came alone because Althea wouldn't have wanted kids playing in her house full of fine breakables. But that was no reason to send Burgess away. He and the girl never played in the house, always out on the porch, or out in the part of the yard that was all overgrown like a small forest. Maybe that was the problem: Althea didn't want them underfoot but she didn't want them out of sight either. Just think how that straitlaced old lady's imagination could have run wild.

Delzora heard Bobby come in calling out for Thea. He sounded impatient, agitated. He came to the door. "Where's Thea?" The strain he'd been under was all over his face.

"They outside," Delzora told him. He glanced through the window then hurried out.

Delzora looked out at the gazebo again, a crowded scene with the three of them and the dog there. She watched them commiserate, huddled together over the dog, who kept trying to lick their faces as they kept pushing her down. She watched a few moments longer before she plumped the sofa cushions and went into the kitchen to finish up lunch.

Bobby went out to the gazebo with a feeling that he was at the cracking point. He needed to talk to Thea, to tell her about this latest affront, one more bad thing that had happened, to say he didn't know if he could take anymore, and knowing too that he shouldn't say that—because once you did, you usually got tested.

Maybe it was a Catholic thing, this wanting to unload, to confess—that's what it really was, he wanted to confess because he felt guilty. He didn't know why he should feel guilty; these things were happening to him, yet he could feel the burden of guilt sitting heavily within his chest, crushing, unmovable. The apartment house had burned down with a man inside, and he felt responsible. He'd gone home to get the insurance papers and discovered that sometime during the past week, while his mother had been in the hospital and he'd stayed at Thea's, the house had been broken into, everything dumped out in the middle of the floors for the thieves to sift through, leaving him with an ungodly mess from which to discover what was missing. His mother's jewelry was gone and so was the gun Lyle had given him. He had caught himself thinking that neither Lyle nor Millie ever needed to know, his friend now joining his mother as one who must be deceived. But he had lost heart completely when he realized his father's hunting gun, the Model 12, the old reliable Winchester, was also gone. That's when the guilt had come down with its weight like eternity: somehow he'd let his father down again.

He had come to Thea's to be soothed, perhaps reassured, at least to be heard, and instead here he was listening to Burgess Monroe talking about living on borrowed time, how it was because of him that a woman was gunned down in the project last night, how he wanted to live long enough to see his baby born. All the gravest matters of life and death, and riding over him a guilt that made Bobby's look small and sorry. And both Burgess and Thea looking at him as if there were something he could do about any of it.

He sat back in the gazebo, drawing his hand down over his face, feeling tired to his bones. All he could think of was his father saying, "When in doubt, go fishing," and he closed his eyes and got a whiff of salt air, felt the sun beating down on him, the lethargic swing of his swivel chair as he reached for a beer, and he opened his eyes because a thought had come to him with that whiff of salt,

163

a way that he might finally be able to move this guilt, get out from under it.

He said to Burgess, "My man, let's go fishing." It wasn't what they were expecting—two pairs of eyebrows arched in concert. "It's not meant as a solution, just some space where you can gather your thoughts, figure out what to do. Nothing like a little lethargy to put things in their proper perspective."

Burgess thought on it only a few seconds before he agreed, and Bobby spent the afternoon getting gear together, going to the bait shop and the grocery store, getting plenty of beer and food, all the things he and his father used to like to take on fishing trips. He made a ritual of it, gathering all the necessities, stacking the rods, oiling the reels, checking the line, reorganizing the tackle box, packing the ice chests. He performed the ritual slowly and thoroughly, not the way he was used to doing it, throwing things together at the last minute, usually forgetting something, but in the deliberate way he'd seen his father do it countless times, so carefully, with such attention to neatness and compactness that it would get Bobby aggravated, especially since his father never did anything else with an eye to such detail. Like his will.

Bobby had gone fishing only once after his father died, and that's when he'd been so overcome with guilt he'd never gone again. He'd even thought about selling the boat since he wasn't using it and he needed the money. But he couldn't bring himself to do it. It wouldn't have lessened his guilt; it would have seemed like another offense against his father, another way of disappointing him.

So the ritual was a way of getting rid of the guilt, a way to restore his sense of well-being, a way to be at peace finally with his father.

Only one thing remained to do and he would be ready. Late that afternoon Bobby made another trip to the ill-fated apartment house to get the most important element for the ritual, the element needed for the final cleansing act. He filled a plain brown paper bag with ashes from the burned house, symbolic ashes from the place his father had once seen as a sort of salvation, to scatter over the blue water of the Gulf at daybreak. It was a ritual Bobby thought even his father, lapsed Catholic though he'd been, would appreciate.

Bobby and Burgess left at four o'clock the following morning.

Bobby, full of purpose, was wide awake and energetic. As he drove, he tried to get Burgess to indulge in some repartee, but Burgess was still groggy from a long and difficult night with Janine. He had told her again why he thought it was best that he leave, and she told him again why it was best that she didn't. They had the same conversation over and over, using different words, coming at it from different angles, until Burgess, frustrated and angry, stormed out, telling her he'd be back for his belongings in a day or two.

The car sped down the deserted highway in the dark, the clumpy low marshland brush like apparitions of danger, lurking strangers behind every bush in Burgess' peripheral vision, and all at once the drive took on that feeling of stealing away in the night, moving under cover of darkness, off and running before sunup. It made him tired, more tired than he already was, too tired to think. He hunkered down on the car seat, taking his eyes off the road, focusing instead on the softly lit dashboard, Bobby's monologue droning just beyond comprehension. After a while he closed his eyes, and then he couldn't hear Bobby anymore, only Janine saying, "I'm not gon spend my life runnin." And he knew that Janine saw more clearly than he did that if he wasn't running from place to place, then he was running in place, no good way to spend a life. Always trying to stave off the inevitable.

He sat up straight. Bobby was telling a long fish story from his childhood about his father baiting Bobby's hook with the boiled eggs they'd brought for lunch. "He promised me I'd catch a chicken-fish. But when he tried to put a whole egg on the hook . . ."

Burgess cut into Bobby's punchline. "I can't go fishin," he said.

"What?"

"I can't go fishin. I gotta go back."

"Why?" Bobby asked. "What's wrong?"

"Nothin's wrong. I just figured somethin out." Burgess looked directly at Bobby and said it again. "I gotta go back."

"But we're halfway there. More than halfway."

Burgess said, "What I'm tryin to tell you, man, I don't need to go fishin anymore, I need to go back."

Bobby turned back, annoyed with Burgess for spoiling his chance to scatter the ashes right at daybreak, but he decided he would take Burgess to the Convent and go on out to the Gulf without him. Without Burgess, though, it somehow wouldn't be the same, although Bobby wasn't sure why. Was it because he needed a witness to his act, that without a witness the act wouldn't be as meaningful, that it wouldn't be legitimate, that it would have no memorable substance, something like the sound of one hand clapping?

When he dropped Burgess off at the Convent, he had a strong feeling that it was the last time he would see the man, that Burgess thought so too, but neither of them said good-bye as if it were. There was only a brief moment of awkwardness after they shook hands, a moment of lingering and nothing more to say.

Bobby drove along Convent Street in the direction of the Interstate, his full intention to carry through his plan. He took the bag of ashes from the back seat and put it on the floor up front. He kept glancing at the bag and, maybe because of the change in plan, the delay, all the driving, he wasn't so sure anymore that scattering a bag full of ashes and pieces of charred wood from a house that for his father had become a source of aggravation, even humiliation, rather than salvation, and, worse, a place that had become a crematory for another man, was going to do a thing for his guilt. And all that business about lethargy putting things in proper perspective. What a lot of crap. Lethargy was a way of putting things off, and guilt couldn't be put off, couldn't be tossed to the wind, swallowed by blue water. What it could do, though, was confine his father forever to a place of unhappy thoughts, so that Bobby tried not to think about him, a place his father wouldn't have wanted to be any more than he had wanted to be in that tomb.

At the edge of the Convent, behind a convenience store, Bobby spotted a dumpster. He pulled the car to the curb and sat there with the engine idling. After a few moments he picked up the bag of ashes and got out of the car. He walked over to the dumpster and threw the bag into it. When he turned away to go back to the car, though he'd had no such expectations—maybe that was the trick to it—he felt much better.

He drove to Thea's, slipped quietly into the house, then into her bed. Here the ritual was not about a preoccupation with the past. It was about making a future.

28

The shooting of Sherree divided the city in a way that only the very astute or the very cynical could have foreseen.

Blacks were outraged and they stayed outraged for a long time—Burgess had been wrong about that. They wanted indictments against all the policemen involved and they wanted them fired from the police department.

The chief of police defended his officers' actions. He said they went into Sherree Morganza's that night with search and arrest warrants based on information and observation. The residents of the Convent told the media how the cops got their information. They told how they were rousted from their apartments, how they were lined up and marched like POWs. They told of racial slurs, rubber saps, and plastic bags. They cried that their civil rights had been violated, and this time the media jumped on it.

The black mayor of the city saw his political standing begin to crumble: because half of New Orleans' population was black, his reelection was in jeopardy. Someone was going to be sacrificed and he didn't intend to be that person. Within days, the white chief of police had handed in his resignation. Once this convenient scapegoat was dispatched, official interest in the case rapidly waned. The investigation dragged on for months, and during that time the names of the officers involved were not made public nor were the men fired. The mayor said that he couldn't dismiss a police officer summarily; each had a right to his hearing. The status of the officers was not disclosed during the investigation. Meanwhile, a federal probe into civil rights violations began.

And so the city became divided. The outrage in the black community was such that the whites became more afraid. They feared race riots; they called for more police protection. The blacks feared more police brutality, more murders; they called for protection against the police.

The atmosphere in the Hindermann household was thick with unrelieved tension. It crowded the house, making it seem smaller, leaving nowhere to go to escape. It clung to the Hindermanns themselves, tenacious, moving with them from room to room, spoiling the mood in each carefully created sanctuary of muted colors and soft, unfocused lighting.

It showed on Sandy's face, in her tired, puffy eyes, the downward turn of her mouth, two vertical lines between her brows that she smoothed away with the tip of a finger now and again but that returned the moment she forgot them. It showed in a blemish on her cheek, a twist of unruly hair, in the way her clothes were wrinkled, uncomfortable on her body swathed in all that tension.

It was showing on the children too. They were crankier than usual, harder to handle. One of their babysitters had quit, although Sandy didn't think that had anything to do with the children. The woman had quit without notice, simply failed to show up the day after the incident in the project.

It was a struggle, but she got the children to bed and went down to where Lyle was sitting in his big armchair in front of the TV set. He'd been sitting there all evening, unmoving, unresponsive, his head bent down, looking at the screen from under the jut of his eyebrows and the deeply imprinted scowl on his forehead.

Sandy blew at the lock of unruly hair as she let herself fall onto the sofa. She was worn out and it was only eight o'clock. "What's on?" she asked Lyle but he didn't answer. She raised her voice. "Lyle, I said, what's on?"

He turned toward her. "What?" But he didn't wait for her to repeat the question. "I don't know, wasn't really paying attention."

"You've been staring at the TV for over two hours," she said and she could hear the shrill edging into her voice. He'd been staring at the TV ever since the evening news, as if his fate would be revealed to him there. But there was no point in getting irritated with him; it would only make matters worse. Her nerves were already stretched to snapping and the ordeal was far from being over.

This was the worst, the waiting. And the wondering. What was going to happen to Lyle, to her, their family?

Very few of their friends knew of Lyle's involvement in the Convent killing, and Sandy wondered what the ones who did know were thinking. She got the impression that Bobby wished Lyle hadn't told him. Thea said all the right things; it was what she didn't say that Sandy wondered about. She dreaded the time that Lyle's name would be released, when everyone would know.

She had lost him again. He'd turned to the TV screen, drawn back into its low drone, a way to escape. He was so far removed from her now. She looked at his profile and remembered how he'd been ten years ago, even five years ago. He'd been ambitious, he'd been sociable, a social figure too, belonging to the best men's club, two of the oldest Carnival organizations, the yacht club, the country club. And then something happened that changed Lyle: their neighbor across the street and her young daughter were held at sawed-off-shotgun point. The daughter had been out front playing and went inside when it started getting dark, but she didn't close the front door behind her. A man followed her inside and grabbed her by the hair. Dragging her into the kitchen, he pushed her mother away from the stove with his gun. He made them lie face down on the floor, shoving the gun into the backs of their necks, then loading their possessions into their car, forcing the woman to drive him into the Convent, threatening to kill them both if they so much as turned around and looked at him.

It had done something to Lyle, that such a thing could happen right across the street from him, that next time it could be his wife and child, that next time they might be left dead on the floor and the killer drive himself into the Convent.

That had been the beginning of Lyle's imagination turning morbid. That had been when he'd started driving around with the neighborhood patrol until he decided that wasn't doing enough and became a reserve policeman. That was when he stopped being a social figure, no time left for clubs and Carnival organizations, and became a loner. That was when she had lost him.

"Lyle," she said, and she thought she might cry she felt so lonely, "come sit over here with me, sweetheart."

He turned, scowling at her, and she thought he was going to bite her head off, the way he'd been doing lately, if she said even the simplest thing. But he got up from the arm chair and moved next to her on the sofa. She looked hard into his eyes. She wanted to say to him, "Come back, come back," to say it without any words, to say it with her eyes, to make him come back with the force of her will. She held him like that until she became exhausted looking at his tired, worried eyes. She put her head on his shoulder and he slid down on the arm of the sofa, half sitting, half lying, her head on his chest now, the strong steady beat of his heart in her ear, drowning out the drone from the TV. He put his arm around her, and he pushed back the lock of unruly hair, smoothing it into the rest of her hair, smoothing it over and over around her ear, his fingers following the curve of her skull beneath the soft thick hair. Her nerve-wired body began to relax as she lay heavily on him. Her eyes closed. There was such comfort in the way they were lying together, in the way they fit, such familiarity about this particular position. But for several moments Sandy was at a loss; she couldn't remember why it was so familiar to her, and then it came rushing over her like the warm humid breeze coming off the lake and through the windows of Lyle's father's Cadillac when they used to go park out at the Point until it was time to go home. Sandy would lie up against Lyle just like this, he half sitting, half reclining, his back against the door, his fingers in her hair.

She laughed, her body rising slightly then sinking into him again.

"Hm?" It was a low rumble against her ear.

She said, "I was just thinking about how we used to park at the Point. We used to lie together like this in the front seat of your daddy's car." He laughed too, a short one-syllable grunt, and she could remember bouncing just like that against him, especially when Bobby and Thea were with them, Bobby cracking jokes, hardly ever shutting up because Thea wouldn't let him do much except kiss her right before it was time for them to start heading home.

She went on, continuing her thoughts out loud. "And then you would rev up the Caddy and peel out and go as fast as you could down Breakwater Drive with Bobby hanging out of the window yelling, 'Hi ho silver, away!'"

His fingers slowed as they curved around her ear, and she wondered if he was remembering the way he used to slow the Cadillac at the curve in Breakwater because sometimes on the other side of the curve, next to the picnic pavilion, police cars would park and wait. Better not to think about police tonight.

She tipped her head up slightly. "You should have seen the Cadillac I saw at Thea's the other day," and she described it to him and described Dexter, the black-leather-clad chauffeur holding the door for Delzora. "Thea says Delzora's son sends it for her every day but he never uses it himself. He drives a beat-up old pickup truck. Isn't that crazy?"

His fingers stopped. She tipped her head up farther, to try to see his face. He pushed her shoulders and she sat up.

"What are you saying?" he demanded, his hands still on her, holding her shoulders as if to break her arms off, that policeman's look on his face, "Delzora's son owns that Cadillac?"

Sandy was confused by the sudden change in him, his alertness, by the way he'd put that question to her, as if she'd said something wrong, accusing her. She tensed defensively. "That's what Thea said," she told him, accusing Thea.

He got up. He said no more. He explained nothing. He punched the button on the TV and turned it off. He left the room and before she realized what he was doing, he left the house.

"What the hell?" Sandy said out loud, poised on the edge of the sofa. She started to get up but couldn't see the point. She sat back with a long sigh of exasperation and helplessness and sorrow. She was too angry to cry, too sad to be very angry. It was no good; he was gone, not just for now, for tonight, but gone from her for good. There was no going back, no matter what happened, no matter if everything turned out all right. Because no matter what happened, no matter how you looked at it, this time Lyle had gone too far.

Sandy could not sit still any longer. She got up and wandered about the house, going from room to room, looking at all the details, all the things she had spent so much time thinking about and picking out and putting all together. The house was the one thing in her life that remained unchanged, and she loved it, never tiring of looking at it and being in it. She walked around, trying to recapture her feeling of calm again, seeking comfort from the house. She went outside through the French doors in the dining room into the chill of the night. She walked to the edge of the swimming pool and listened to the water gurgling out of the stone frog's mouth into the three-tiered lily pad fountain set into the foliage at the other end of the pool. She loved hearing the sound of the water and looking at the variety of plant life, the drama of the hidden lights around the black pool. She loved it and never got tired of it because it contained her life, the life she had been so pleased with, but the life that was changed forever now. She stared into the black water, watching her reflection undulate on its calm but ceaselessly moving surface. The restlessness of her reflection began to unnerve her. She wanted it to be still, as if then life would be able to go on the same as always, but it continued to fold upon itself, break up, tear away at the edges until she turned from the pool, unable to look at it any more.

She looked up. Through the glass doors she looked into the house, its beauty and serenity belying the ugliness and anxiety that existed there, obscured by the false image of quality and richness. She felt betrayed by the deception and by the separation she was beginning to sense, as if those doors had closed and she was to be left outside forever, cursed to gaze longingly at what she wanted but could not have.

29

When Dexter woke up it was dark. He was disoriented for a few moments because when he'd gone to sleep the sun had been streaming in through the bedroom window, making a bright warm patch of light over his legs. The warmth had helped lull him to sleep. He had no idea how long he'd been out or if it was still the same day on which he'd gone to sleep. He twisted around to look at the clock. He'd been asleep for more than seven hours, the only sleep he'd had in two days.

He stretched out his arm to Sherree's side of the bed. Even though she was gone, he could not yet bring himself to lie there, to take up the whole bed. He lay where he always lay, close to the edge of the bed, because Sherree had not liked to be touched while she was sleeping. To sleep in his arms, she had said, made her feel trapped.

Dexter moved his hand up and down on the sheet, rubbing the place where she had slept. Things she'd said kept playing in his mind, things that had mostly annoyed him when she was alive, and now, unaccountably, made him feel the stunning size of his loss. She was gone; she would never lie next to him again. Before this he had been in a state of disbelief: now he believed it with a nausea at the pit of his stomach that burned upward, a rising bile full of helplessness and anger.

He swung his legs over the side of the bed and sat there, his head in his hands, the heels of his palms kneading the skin on his forehead. The bile retreated and he got up, finding his clothes where he'd laid them out on the floor next to the bed, and he began to dress in the dark. The leather creaked and groaned and seemed to protest its use. The sound of the big silver zipper on the jacket was more like a rip than a closing.

When Dexter finished dressing he left the room and walked through the dark hallway, past the bathroom and into the kitchen, where he finally turned on a light. He washed his face and rinsed his mouth at the kitchen sink. He still couldn't bear to go into the bathroom though some of the neighborhood women had come and cleaned it up for him. He had even peed into an old coffee can. He hadn't gone back there during the day and he never turned on any lights in that part of the apartment because he couldn't stand to see the bullet holes in the walls or the splintered door-jambs. He had only ventured into the bedroom—after two days—when he realized he would never be able to get any sleep on the old uncomfortable sofa in the living room.

Dexter removed the chair he'd stuck under the doorknob to keep the broken front door shut, and left the apartment. He didn't care if anyone came into the place while he was gone, though he knew no one would unless it was the police. As for coming back, he didn't plan to until past daybreak, when he could see if anyone was in there with a gun turned on him.

He got into the Cadillac and drove over to the Solar Club. He thought he'd have a couple of drinks there then get some of the guys to go downtown with him to the strip joint where Sherree used to work. Dexter could not contain his grief any longer: he needed to share it, to spread it around at places where Sherree had been known.

He parked the Cadillac right outside the front door of the Solar Club. It was an illegal space, too close to a fire hydrant, but he didn't care, he wouldn't be there long.

There weren't many people on the street. The temperature was dropping again, the air so cold and still it was as if everything was frozen in place. The bare skin under his jacket tightened with goose bumps. He hurried into the close, fetid warmth of the Solar Club. The air in here was blue with smoke, dense with the sound of a blues band playing in a corner of the big room.

The usual large Friday night crowd was there. He began to move through the crush of bodies, his own body warming from the friction of getting past elbows and shoulders, bellies and back-sides. Someone called out his name and everyone realized he was there. He became the center of the crush. Over the music he heard several voices saying, "Drinks on me, Dexter." There were back claps and embraces and sounds of sympathy: waves of brotherly love carried him toward the bar. He'd done right to get himself out; his burden already seemed lighter.

He was floating on the warmth and the voices and the music, his body buoyed, his head in the smoke, his feet hardly touching the floor. All around the room colored Christmas-tree lights winked off and on and their colors thickened the atmosphere. He felt a rush of heat up his neck and he was looking forward to some ice-cold beer sliding down his throat. The heat reached his jaw-bone and exploded in his head with a loud *whoosh* that seemed to turn the club into a vacuum. The band stopped playing and there was a brief moment of almost dead silence before the crowd surged, a panic of elbows in ribs and feet on feet, pushing and shoving and trying to get out of the room. Dexter found his progress toward the bar reversed. He was now being carried back to the front door. Above the yells and groans and hoarse cries he could hear the crackling and spitting and wind of fire. He tried to run and would have landed on the floor had there been any room to fall. He fell up against the person in front of him, whose head jerked back and caught Dexter in the mouth. The sweetly bitter taste of blood covered his tongue.

He lurched and stumbled, and when he caught his feet up on the threshold of the door he saw that the Cadillac was in flames, singeing the outstretched limbs of an oak tree, fouling the air with a gasoline smell. There was another explosion, flames leaping higher, and the crowd on the sidewalk fell back to the outside walls of the Solar Club, pushing Dexter inside again. He began to struggle, pulling at people, blindsiding them, thrusting them out of his way until he was on the street and as close to the Cadillac as he dared get. He stood there trying to figure out what to do, eying the fire hydrant, his whole body poised for action until he figured out there was nothing he could do, and that's when he noticed the fire-blackened gasoline can behind the front wheel of the car. He looked from one side to the other, as if he expected to see the face of the culprit leering out of the crowd at him. But Dexter knew that he, or they, would not be there. They would have run back into the bowels of the Convent already, back to their own ruined piece of turf after leaving not him, but Burgess, their message.

The flames shooting up from the car kindled all of Dexter's frustration, all of the helplessness and rage that had been suffocated by grief over the past days. A storm of fire broke out in him, leaping from his mouth. "Fuckin *nightmare!*" he shouted, his hands balled into fists, his arms rigid at his sides. He turned to the crowd behind him. "This is a fuckin *nightmare!*" he cried. "My life's a fuckin *nightmare!*"

He could hear voices all around him. They were voices of assent, the word *nightmare* rippling across the blur of faces in front of him. He could no longer pick out individuals; he could not put voices and faces together. He saw them all as one.

"*Nightmare!*" he shouted again and he heard its echo coming from the mass before him. He shouted again and again, waiting to hear his shout repeated, until his voice and theirs rose into a chant of "*Nightmare, nightmare.*"

He pushed around them, moving perilously close to the burning car, the flames reaching out to take him but repelled by his leather suit. The chant continued and followed him as he walked down Convent Street toward the river. He kicked at cans and bottles that littered his way, but there was not enough satisfaction in their careening off to the side. He picked them up and began to throw them, and the crowd followed his lead. Glass shattered on the sidewalk and the street; cans landed on front porches and bounced off car windows.

It still was not enough. Dexter began to pick up stones and pieces of brick. He stuffed his pockets with them until the leather was stretched with hard points of rock and metal. When the leather would not stretch to take more he picked up the bottles he saw until his hands were full too. The crowd stopped and stuffed their pockets as he did. They did this all the way to St. Charles Avenue, where he and the faceless mass behind him stopped traffic as they crossed.

Across St. Charles their chanting vandalized the atmosphere of quiet, it swelled under the canopy of oaks. Hedges protecting manicured lawns were broken under their feet, and branches were stripped of their leaves by so many passing bodies.

Dexter threw the first stone. The sound of breaking glass instantly turned into a scream, the unnatural, high-pitched whoop-whooping of a burglar alarm. The crowd abruptly stopped its chanting as it moved, a frenzied, roiling mass emptying its pockets into the windows of the giant, once-formidable houses now screaming in dissonant pitches and asynchronous rhythms from their sharp-edged wounds.

Sound filled the inside of Dexter's head as helium fills a balloon. It seemed to lift him off the ground and whisk him along, for he could no longer feel his feet hitting the concrete sidewalk. His head pounded each time his feet hit the ground, but that they were his feet could not penetrate the cocoon of noise around him, the constant blast against his eardrums, eradicating everything else, all feeling, all understanding, so that he could not distinguish the shrieks of the alarms from the wail of police sirens; he did not notice the crowd splintering off behind him. Someone grabbed at him but he slid through the grasp. He was unstoppable in his weightlessness, impregnable in his cocoon. He was carried along until recognition stopped him and his feet were on the brick walkway in front of those fancy glass doors he watched Burgess' mother go in and come out of every day, and with the recognition came the idea that Burgess wasn't watching out for what was going wrong in his own backyard because he was messing around with those white people too much.

Dexter's pockets were empty. He cut across the lawn and squatted down to remove one of the bricks from the zigzagged border in front of the azalea bushes. He stood and hurled the brick at the leaded glass. The lead stopped it from going all the way through and it thudded on the wood floor of the porch. He stopped and picked up another. He threw the bricks until all the tiny glass panes were broken and the lead was dented and pitted and wrecked out of shape. He threw a brick through each of the long uncovered windows. He was aiming for a gas lamp when a voice over a bullhorn broke through his anger and he turned to see a line of guns pointed at him.

30

Mr. Robert finished nailing plywood across the front of Thea's house and left for the day. With its plywood patches the house was graceless, awkwardly large. Shutters hung at odd angles to the boarded windows; Mr. Robert had removed some of them altogether. A few rusty mailboxes tacked to the side of the door and the house could have passed for a deserted tenement: danger, no trespassing.

Thea paid Mr. Robert for the week and watched the old carpenter walk up Convent Street toward St. Charles. Despair and a gray, wintry sky covered the neighborhood. The big houses were boarded up, their lawns were trampled and muddy. The street was littered under the canopy of oaks. It was dark and dank and dirty. In less than a quarter of an hour the landscape had been dreadfully altered. Thea went back inside reluctantly, the gloom here more depressing than the ugliness outside, with no light coming in through the long windows or being cut into cheery patterns by the leaded glass doors. The glass could be replaced, new doors milled, but what, she wondered, could replace her feeling of violation, of the unfairness of it all. She could understand Burgess' friend's rage but she could not understand why he had picked on her house and personally attacked it; her.

She went down the hallway, stopping when she reached the door to the library. It was nearly finished; Mr. Robert had started varnishing the wood. She looked at its beauty coldly. The pleasure she had felt viewing it only yesterday seemed to have gone through the broken windows last night. It was the same with the rest of the house: the comfort she had begun to feel as its owner was gone, replaced with the old ambivalence, though the ambivalence was grounded not in whether she could make the house hers instead of

Aunt Althea's, but in whether she wanted the house at all if it could be ruined for her so quickly, so easily. These big grand houses, they became so all-consuming, so all-important. They demanded constant attention and more money than anyone ought to spend on more space than anyone needed. And yet the city would be a lesser place without them, and Thea happened to be one of the people with the time and money to spend to keep one. Perhaps, she thought, one needed to be born to it, groomed for it, like Sandy. For Sandy it was a birthright; she had no ambivalence; for her it was not a frivolous way to spend time.

Thea went to the back of the house where Zora was ironing, her Saturday chore. She had told Zora she didn't have to come anymore on Saturdays, but Zora had said she preferred to. For Thea, moving back to New Orleans had meant adding too many contradictions to her life, and for the moment, all of them were summed up in this woman who stood at the ironing board, ironing the sheets Thea slept on at night, as if anyone needed to sleep on ironed sheets, though of course, crawling in between them after a long day was a sensation of unmatched luxury and comfort.

The doorbell rang and Zora, through habit, put the iron upright to go answer it. Thea waved her back saying she would get it. She went to the front and turned on the hall light, but it only accentuated the gloom in the side rooms. She switched on the chandelier. Whoever was at the door began to pound on the plywood covering it. There was such a flimsy sound to the wood, such an urgency by the pounder, that Thea felt a stab of fear in her stomach. She did not like that she had to open the door to someone she could not see, though of course, if she could see, she could be seen.

"Who is it?" she called, turning her head to the side so her ear was up close to the plywood.

"Lyle."

Thea jerked back, startled, he sounded so close to her, nothing but half an inch of plywood between them. She opened the door. "Bobby's not here, Lyle. He's gone to check on his mother." She remained in the doorway, not inviting him in.

"That's okay," Lyle said, "I'll catch him later." He moved toward her, coming in anyway, so that she had to either stand there and block his way or let him in. She let him in.

The fear was still there: no relief that it was a familiar face, one wearing its usual scowl, his eyes like old dull varnish staring at her from underneath it. So why was she still afraid, as if she were opening the door to someone who might harm her, yet deliberately standing aside, letting him in? She closed the door after him, shutting them both inside.

"I see you had a rough time of it last night," he said, his eyes darting off to the side to the violation that had been done to the house. Thea nodded. "It's a damn shame," he said, "the way we all have to live boarded up in our houses one way or another." This was not social chitchat for Lyle. He said it angrily, but in his flickering eyes the anger was betrayed by fear. This was not the old Lyle talking, the one who made her stomach clench with apprehension because she didn't take his advice when he told her to get a security system, yet her stomach was clenched. She took a small, involuntary step backward. He closed the distance between them with a small step of his own. Now he looked at her so intensely that she had to force herself not to move away from him again. "I think you may be in some danger," he said to her. "That's why I'm here—I'm afraid for you." And indeed, Thea could see he was afraid, so afraid he was frightening. Just what Zora had said that day about Jared. Lyle was so afraid that his fear was reaching out to her, infecting her.

She couldn't help it; she stepped back again. "Why, Lyle?" she asked him, trying to speak levelly, not let her voice give away her fear.

"It's Burgess Monroe," he said, his voice lowered. "Is he here?" His eyes flicked away again.

"No."

"Monroe's the one who's been running all the drugs through the Convent."

"I think you've got that wrong, Lyle."

"No I don't. It was the Cadillac, all along I knew it was the Cadillac, and when Sandy said you told her Monroe owned it, I went straight down to the precinct. But I don't think they're going to move on it." He laughed nervously. "They've got enough problems down there right now, all that civil rights violations crap. They said they'll send a car around as often as they can."

"I see," said Thea; she saw that they meant to keep their distance from Lyle.

"It's not good enough. The one who did this to your house"—

he nodded in the direction of the boarded-up windows—"he works for Monroe."

"I know that."

"Did you know that he did this to your house, to all these houses, because the Cadillac was set on fire last night by some hooligans from the project? They yell civil rights violations, then they do something like this." He regarded her with that stony policeman look of his. The old Lyle was back. "Do you know how to reach Monroe?"

"No. He won't be coming here anymore. He told me to start paying the carpenter myself."

His eyes darted, this time to the back of the house. "Is his mother here?"

Thea seemed to have no control over herself. Her eyes darted as his did, in Zora's direction. "No," she said, and thought there was no way he would believe her.

But he was nodding, taking her at her word. "I want you to have this," he said, his composure fully restored. He put his hand in his jacket and produced one of his small, oily-looking guns. "I'm not so sure he won't be back."

The sight of the gun pushed Thea backward another step. "I don't want it, Lyle."

"I know you don't," he said, his voice softer now, stroking her. "None of us does." Talking to her as if she were a child. "I want you to be able to protect yourself if you need to."

"Why would Burgess . . ." she began, but her voice caught on his name.

"Thea, you've gotten yourself too involved with them"—she was a bad child now—"and the sad thing is they sometimes turn on those of us who have been kindest to them."

She blurted, in horror, "I haven't been *kind* to him."

"I know you don't think you have," he said in his avuncular tone.

She nearly staggered with fury. "The one who did this," she gestured wildly at the boarded doors, "maybe he saw *you* here."

He wasn't hearing her anger directed at him, her accusation. He shook his head. "He doesn't know me," he assured her, and he stepped closer. "Here," he said, holding the gun so she could see. "This is how you remove the safety." He clicked the safety off. "Then you just aim and shoot." He smiled.

Thea backed away from him. She was up against the lower part of the stairway, the banister and wood spindles behind her. She forced herself to be calm. "I don't want it, Lyle. I don't want any guns in this house."

"I know, Thea. I know it's because of your parents, but it's an unrealistic view now." His voice was as oily as the gun. He closed in on her; he was right on her, taking her hand, trying to put the gun in it. "Here, I want you to hold it, feel it." Thea tried to jerk her hand away but he wouldn't let go, his fingers holding her wrist.

"Look," he said. "The safety's back on." He clicked it on. "See?"

She closed her hand into a fist so he couldn't put the gun in it. "Back off, Lyle."

"Oh come on, Thea," he was smiling down at her, "it won't hurt you. Watch. The safety's off." He held it in front of her eyes, clicking it. "Now it's back on." He pointed the gun at the ceiling and showed her that the trigger would not pull back. "See? There's nothing to be afraid of."

But Thea's heart was pounding. "It's easy, Lyle," she said, and he smiled and nodded. "It's too easy. Your solution's too easy." His smile started to disintegrate. She opened her hand, his fingers still wrapped around her wrist, and held it out for the gun. "But it makes you feel you aren't helpless," she said, "is that it?" and his falling smile lifted. He nodded again and put the gun in her hand.

He let her wrist go. "Feel the weight of it," he said and moved away from her, off to the side. "Now, hold steady with the other hand and aim."

She brought her other hand up and held the gun with both hands. "It makes you think you have the power to do something," she said, "but it only makes you more afraid." She aimed the barrel right between his eyes.

"Not at me," he said sharply and tried to duck out of the way.

Thea followed the point between his eyes. "Everything keeps on going the way it is," she said beading hard down the barrel to the bridge of his nose, "There's no end to the madness."

"Stop it, Thea," he commanded and moved toward her.

She clicked the safety off. He stopped. "See? The safety's off, Lyle." He stood dead still in front of her. "Now get out of my house."

He swung a hand toward her and tried to smile, the corner of his mouth shaking. "Thea . . ."

"Out, Lyle," she said, and when he did not move immediately, she yelled, "Out!" He hesitated only a fraction of a second before he walked quickly to the door, fumbling at it, turning back to look at her, jumping when she yelled, "Out!" at him again and continued yelling, "Out, out, out!" Until he was gone, the door slamming behind him, his footsteps pounding on the porch.

Thea did not lower the gun right away. She wished she could see him going across the porch and down the steps so she could be sure he had left, that he wasn't creeping back, standing right on the other side of the flimsy plywood, waiting to surprise her.

Finally, she let the gun down. She rushed to the door and double-bolted it.

31

Burgess returned to the Convent, to hiding, to coded whistles, to bodyguards. He began wearing his black felt hat and mirrored aviator sunglasses again. And one more time, black hats became the fashion statement to make in the Convent.

The police raids stopped because of the ongoing investigation into civil rights violations, and once again the police avoided the Convent as much as they could, answering calls slowly and reluctantly, as they had before the cop killing. But the media remained curious as the front part of the Convent appeared to be a prosperous, tight-knit community while guns and drug wars ruled in the back. The line between the two areas, a street known as Purgatory Alley, was as closely patrolled by the drug dealers as the border between two hostile countries. The residents who were considered safe enough to interview and who agreed to talk continued to deny the Bishop's existence, though they also continued to say that if he did exist, then it must be the Second Coming.

Burgess saw what he had to do and kept the money coming into the Convent. It was becoming more and more difficult given his cloistered existence. He kept to the confines of the apartment as much as he could. Janine became his eyes, his ears, his legs, as if he were a blind man. And Janine saw what she had to do to keep the programs running and make them self-sufficient. Burgess tried to get Dexter to continue the contracting work, but Dexter appeared to be a lost cause, broken, unable to do much other than sit out in the Convent yard with the rest of the broken men, watching their neighbors and talking big.

Whenever Burgess had to venture out to conduct business, he chose from a variety of cars so that he would not become identified with any particular vehicle. One evening, a cold clear night in January, Burgess and one of the two men who went everywhere with him left the apartment through the back. They waited at the top of the stairs until the second man pulled up in a car in the back alleyway.

The car carrying Burgess and his two bodyguards traveled the length of the alley, shells and gravel crunching under the tires, and turned right on one of the Convent streets. As it turned, a car coming from the opposite direction accelerated suddenly. It sped by Burgess' car, and there was a burst of automatic-weapon fire. The car swerved, the tinted windows were shattered, and the guard in the back fell screaming on his side across the seat. He'd taken a hit in the neck. After that the guards never drove anywhere without Mac-10s across their laps, ready. It didn't do any good if the guns were under the seat.

A few weeks later, Burgess and one of the men again waited at the top of the stairs for the car to come down the alley. Leaving this way had become their habit. None of them was thinking that perhaps it wasn't good to fall into such habits.

It was twilight, another cold night, and a soft drizzle was just beginning, the kind of rain that would keep up for hours, steady and relentless.

Burgess and his man ran in the rain to the car, their collars turned up, their feet splashing in muddy puddles. They put their guns across their laps, and the driver pulled slowly down the alley, turning into the bordering street. Several yards ahead a small boy, running hard to get out of the rain, dashed across the pavement.

"Fuckin little Herbie Reginald," grinned one of the guards. "Look at 'im scoot."

This time the ambush came from the rear. The car, headlights dark, moved up on them fast, and as it accelerated, it skidded on the slick wet street. It fishtailed, then the driver gave it more gas. Tires squealed. On the sidewalk the boy slowed down, turning to see what all the commotion was.

"The fuck out the *way*, Herbie," the guard muttered irritably even as he clambered at his weapon.

Then the car was upon them, swerving alongside. Muzzle flashes licked at one another from both vehicles. For perhaps five seconds the night roared. There was a lot of sloppy trigger work, marks were missed, a fender was pitted with a line of bullet holes, and one bullet strayed off target to find Herbie Reginald as he stared open-mouthed at what was taking place before him.

Janine's legs ached. She put Lucilla to bed and when she stood she thought she could feel the veins popping out behind her knees and around her ankles. She would have looked down to see but there was no seeing past her huge belly. She couldn't wait to submerge herself in a warm bath.

She climbed into the tub awkwardly and lowered herself slowly, so big and heavy and tired it was as if she'd been carrying a fragile mountain around with her all day. Her arms felt heavy as she lifted them to wash her hair. Burgess came into the bathroom and watched her slow, tired movements. He knelt down on the floor next to the bathtub and took the shampoo bottle from her. He washed her hair and put some of the lather on a big sponge and washed her back. He came up around her neck and down her front, over her swollen breasts, her large stomach, her legs, her feet, washing and stroking away the tiredness. When he finished, she leaned back, her eyes closed, to soak there awhile in the fragrant bubbles of the shampoo. Burgess pushed himself up on the rim of the tub and left the tiny, humid, too-warm room.

He went into the bedroom and sat on the side of the bed, his elbows on his knees, his head in his hands. Ever since the death of Herbie Reginald he'd been overcome by bad feelings. A lot of it was grief and guilt, but there was something else too. He couldn't seem to stand being with himself any longer, not alone, not with the thoughts he had, trapped inside his own head. He couldn't have told anyone exactly what he was thinking that made him feel this way. He didn't know what to call it or what to do to make it go away. He couldn't even sleep to escape it, waking many times during the night, his body in a cold sweat, his head aching. If he was still running, it was no longer from anyone, nor out of fear of being caught. He was strangely unafraid, as if the fear had left him and spread like an infectious disease throughout the Convent, as if he could only be free of it once he had given it all away, spread it around, thick and palpable and feeding on itself. No, if he was running, it was from something deep inside himself, some seething turmoil that had nothing to do with the hard choices still to be made—leave or stay; kill or be killed. Yet it was about choice, choices that had already been made, a long time ago when it had been so easy and didn't require so much thinking. He still couldn't think about it. But he could feel it: self-loathing that ate away at him, demanding satiation—or something, he didn't know what.

Slowly he became aware that the smell of Janine's shampoo was being replaced by the odor of garbage left too long. It was a smell strong enough to move him out of this place of misery and carry him into the kitchen to bundle up the rot and take it outside.

The guard met him at the back door, his gun coming up, his hand reaching out for the bag.

"I'll do it," Burgess told him. The man started to protest. "You can see better from up here," Burgess said.

The guard held the gun with both hands and scanned the area as Burgess went down the stairs to the long row of galvanized cans flanking the alley. He opened one after another only to find them full. After the first few he began banging and clattering their lids back on to keep their ripeness out of the air, breaking the silent night with a growing fury until finally he was able to push the contents of one down enough to stuff in his own pungent bag. He slammed the lid over it.

Once the noise stopped, he heard the guard, halfway down the stairs, frantically, hoarsely calling his name, but Burgess didn't look back. A car was turning into the alley. The guard started calling again, louder now. Burgess, blinded by the headlights, took a step backward toward the stairway. As he did, the car stopped behind the building next door, then pulled into one of the driveways to turn around. It rolled slowly back toward the entrance to the alley. Burgess stepped forward to get a better look at it, and they opened up, firing straight through the back window, glass exploding in a rain of white light. Then tires were spinning on the gravel and the car shot out into the street. They were gone before the guard could get all the way down the stairs to where Burgess had collapsed next to the row of garbage cans, his blood pooling between them, running along the edges of their round bottoms.

There were many such murders in the housing projects these days. Burgess' death became just another one, his way out of the world as unheralded as his way in.

32

Delzora walked along Convent Street, her body shifting heavily from one foot to the other. It was early in the morning, still pleasant before the sky turned hard and white in the heat of the day. She left the sidewalk and went into the Convent Street Housing Project, her feet in their Chinese canvas shoes kicking up little puffs of dust as she cut across the dry dirt yard toward the vegetable garden. She was on her way to work at Thea's house, but for the past several months her routine most days included this early morning stop at the garden. She found her place in between the rows and took from her bag a small mat. She laid it down on the ground to cushion her knees as she knelt and began her weeding. Her fingers pulled deftly at the weeds that pushed their way up around the newly sprouted tomato plants, the tiny green eggplants, the summer squash. She made small piles of them along the row, moving her mat just ahead of them as she went.

She wouldn't try to do too much this morning. One of the old women in the project had taken sick and Delzora wanted to look in on her before she went to work. There was not much to be done other than try to make her comfortable; the woman would die soon.

She had surely come full circle to be here again, even if she still refused to live here, come to keep this vegetable garden alive, to keep vigil over the sick and dying. And to keep watch over the children when Janine needed her. One thing she and Janine saw eye-to-eye on, and that was watching those two young ones as much as they could themselves. Delzora still wondered if everything might have been different had she been able to watch Burgess more herself. She wondered if everything might have been different had Althea Dumondville allowed her to bring him with her to work on Saturdays, or might have been different had she never brought him.

These days when she found herself wondering about such things, it would always lead to thinking about the child that Thea and Bobby were going to have soon now, a child she would be spending more hours a day with than she would her own grandson. She would try not to let the thought in, but always it would slip by before she could catch it—the kind of life their child would have only a few blocks away from her grandson growing up here, in the Convent, in this place she had tried to escape.

She rocked back, putting her weight on her heels. Her hands, covered with dirt, rested on the front of her flowered shift. She looked all around her, at the familiar red-brick buildings, their green trim bubbling and peeling, screens that needed mending, the yard nearly all dirt again. A lot had happened to get her back here, yet the sad thing was, nothing much seemed to have changed. The Convent looked the way she always remembered it, as if Burgess had never existed. The city still beat on much as it always had, the rich and the poor, the black and the white, the old and the young, the fear and the hate and the drugs, and the kids who were going to go bad no matter what.

Nothing had changed but everything had changed. It had changed during one small pause, like a skipped beat in a piece of music, a brief time when things had been different, when people had been tied together with a common thread of hope instead of drifting off by themselves in despair.

Delzora didn't believe in despair, but it sometimes crept on her slyly, trying to attach itself to her through her memories: visions of Burgess, a headstrong young boy running across this very yard; or Burgess and Thea out in the gazebo, the girl looking at his scar; or Burgess giving her the greens from this very garden, his wet shirt against his dark skin, the feelings between mother and son angry, unforgiving.

She looked up at the sky turning brighter and harder, and pushed the despair away. Everything changes but nothing changes. There was nothing to do but keep on doing what had to be done. Delzora moved her mat along the row, pulling at the weeds again and thinking, It's a shame what we all do to each other, a terrible, terrible shame.

$\mathcal{V}$OICES OF THE $\mathcal{S}$OUTH